Secrets *of* My Temple

Secrets *of* My Temple

N.V. Love

Cover design by N.V. Love
Book design by Maureen Cutajar

ISBN: 978-0-9971975-1-8

This book is dedicated to my husband Alex.
Thank you for showing me what true love feels like.

Acknowledgements

MY LIFE EXPERIENCES prompted me to start this book, but my imagination helped me to finish it. So many people played a part in this project however none of this would be possible without my Heavenly Father. Your love and guidance helped me to find my voice.

I would like to thank my husband Alex. Without your constant support this book would have remained an unfinished project on my computer. Thank you for believing in me when I didn't have the courage to believe in myself.

A special thanks to Melissa and Randy. Your feedback was greatly appreciated.

Finally I would like to thank my editor. Your guidance throughout this process proved to be invaluable.

Chapter 1

EVEN WITH JUSTIN inside of me I still feel empty. I look up to the ceiling beyond the plaster and drywall and feel like I'm being watched by an unknown audience. I must be an idiot to lay here and endure this shit, but then again Justin's having a good time so at least one of us is getting something out of this. Maybe I'm being too hard on myself. I'm not an idiot in all respects; when it comes to school and work I'm ahead of the game but when it comes to sex to say I'm unskilled is putting it nicely. Of course it doesn't help my first experience came at the hands of my horny cousin who decided at nineteen a five-year-old was exactly what he needed to get his rocks off. But that was a long time ago; I should be over it by now yet no matter how hard I try it seems like every time I'm about to have sex, images of what he did to me creep into my mind. I've felt awkward in the bedroom all my life and it hasn't helped any of my relationships. Finding a boyfriend has never been hard; maintaining the relationship is where the real work comes in.

My current boyfriend Justin is the first guy I've dated that seems to tolerate my lack of skills in the bedroom however I'm sure that probably has something to do with our new lifestyle. It may sound crazy but I think I really love Justin and after all my failed relationships I'm willing to do anything to make this work. That's why I'm lying here under him like a doormat waiting for him to cum. Sex with Justin is so damn monotonous that I know exactly how many strokes it takes for him to have an orgasm. When Justin reaches stroke fifty-six he will find his release and grunt like an animal before rolling off of me.

Normally I'm patient however today we have a lot to do. We're moving to Chicago and there are still things that need to be packed.

"Justin, you have to hurry up, my family will be here any minute."

"Just give me a little longer Layla, I'm almost done."

I want to get on with packing. I desperately need to leave the cramped confines of this apartment—everything from the kitchen to the tiny bathroom is outdated and falling apart. When I first found my apartment on New York Avenue in Washington D.C., I had big plans. I got hooked on HGTV and thought there was no project too big for me to take on but I quickly learned how wrong I was. The thrill of finishing school and living on my own was short-lived. I don't know what happened but somehow all of the hope inside of me seemed to seep out little by little.

I thought when I moved out on my own my family would give me more space but the opposite occurred. Everyone became more involved in my life. It also didn't help that mine and Justin's mother became the best of friends. I can't make a move in this city without someone documenting my every step. I need for things to be different in Chicago. The sooner I get on the plane, the sooner I can really start to live my life however Justin's need for a quickie is seriously delaying my plans.

It's the same thing over and over again; he creeps up behind me and slides his hands between my thighs, letting me know he's ready. My body doesn't respond to his touch so he always makes sure we have plenty of lubricants in the house. Like an obedient dog I strip out of my clothes, assume the position and let him lather me up so he can enter me without it being too painful.

This is not how I envisioned sex. Growing up I became addicted to romance novels and the thought of finding my Prince Charming—the one man I could spend the rest of my life with—was alluring. I thought we would meet and my experience with him would be magical. Now I wish I could go back and burn every romance novel I ever read—that shit is not real.

I'm twenty-four years old and I still don't see what all the talk is about. After all of these years I've concluded not everyone is made to enjoy sex. Granted there was one night where I felt the magic but I can assure you William was no Prince Charming. I'm so ashamed of how the events of that night unfolded, I rarely allow myself to reminisce. I still think my past is the reason I don't enjoy sex but William left me contemplating new ideas. To this day he is the only man that ever made my body come alive.

I still can't wrap my head around the circumstances under which we met. For Justin I've tried some unusual things; to date meeting William and Angela has been the most unusual of them all. I'm starting to make peace with the realization I will most likely never be able to fulfill Justin's needs sexually. I'm in love with a man I can't satisfy which is why I'm usually open to trying new things for him. If my mother only knew what I let Justin talk me into she would probably splash me with holy water and pray for the devil to leave my soul. As far as I'm concerned, the devil ruined me when I was five so nothing I do really matters anymore.

Most of the time having sex makes me feel dirty. Every touch, taste and smell seems to bring up an old memory from my childhood, yet with William every touch, taste and smell only left my body wanting more. Justin has never had that effect on me but I still love him. He has the most beautiful bronze skin, a toned body and a smile that would make any woman weak in the knees, but that's not why I love him. He challenges me and forces me out of my box. If it wasn't for him I wouldn't have a social life. I would probably still live at home with my parents.

"Justin, are you almost done?"

"Goddammit, Layla! Why do you always have to ruin the moment?"

Oops, I didn't realize he was having a moment. His stroke count must be off today.

"Justin," I repeated "my family will be here any minute and we still need to finish packing."

I don't want to argue, not on a day when we need to work together. I'm praying things will be better once we get to Chicago. Maybe a change in scenery will help us both. I need to go someplace where I don't have so many memories.

Justin and I were friends in undergrad and officially became a couple during grad school. We've had our rough patches but he's never bailed on me and he's the first guy I ever dated that didn't pressure me into having sex, at least in the beginning.

He thrusts his hips two more times before he grunts like an animal and rolls off of me—typical.

"I'm done, are you happy now?!" he says panting, trying to catch his breath.

"There's no need to yell at me, I just want to make sure we get to the airport on time."

"We have four hours before we have to leave, that's plenty of time to wrap things up." Exasperated, he gets up and starts to get dressed.

"I know but we also still have a lot of things to pack," I say, trying to find the rest of my clothes.

"You're a beautiful woman but you can be annoying as hell at times."

He always says that, but I don't let it bother me anymore. Now that I think about it, nothing Justin does really bothers me anymore. I just look at the bright side; he thinks I'm beautiful. I'm sure we wouldn't be together if I wasn't. I hope this little session will hold him over for the rest of the day, but with his appetite for sex, you never know.

I blame Justin's sexual appetite for a lot of shit but the worst to date was his request we become swingers. I still remember the night when he first hit me with the question. We had been studying for finals and took a break to relax and watch TV.

"Layla, have you ever heard of swinging?"

"Swinging? What's that?" I asked, taking a sip of my merlot. My first thought was some new line dance. I received the shock of my life when he explained swinging was a lifestyle some couples participate in to swap partners during sex. As soon as he told me I spat my merlot out all over his beige couch. I had never heard of anything like that before! The entire concept still baffles me; I don't understand why people do it and I don't think I ever will. I certainly wasn't interested in hearing more, however Justin proceeded to give me a whole history lesson on the swinger culture and argued that it was a totally natural thing to do. Natural my ass! I should have known from the look in his eyes and how passionately he spoke about it that trouble was coming. Our discussion really got heated when he told me he wanted to try this "swinging lifestyle" with me.

I can only imagine the look of horror that must have been on my face when he asked. I wanted my relationship with Justin to work so much I would do just about anything for him, but becoming a swinger was pushing the limit.

"Just so I'm clear," I asked, "you want me to have sex with other men while you sleep with other women?"

"Layla, be serious" he told me, "I know you could never sleep with anyone else, that's one of the things I love about you. What I'm saying is that maybe we can find a single female or couple to have some fun with. You never know; maybe if you see another woman you can learn some new techniques and maybe even learn how to enjoy yourself."

I knew then this had nothing to do with me learning anything. This was strictly about his needs.

"I know our love life isn't perfect," I told him, trying to remain calm, "but are things really that bad between us that you would want to try something like swinging?" Justin's raised eyebrows said it all.

"Layla, I know you are trying and I really love that about you, but I would just like to experience this with you; I think maybe it could add to our relationship and spice things up a little. Baby, we need to switch it up and add some excitement to our love life."

I knew Justin wanting to become a swinger was the direct result of me being terrible in bed. Due to my flashbacks I made him wait a long time to have sex and after such a long wait he didn't feel I was worth it, yet no matter how bad our sex life is I couldn't see how swinging would be the answer to our problems in the bedroom.

"I have to think about this Justin" I told him, "there is so much to be concerned about. Have you even thought about diseases and the type of people who engage in this? Surely no one with any morals or values would ever consider such a lifestyle. I mean this goes against everything I was taught to believe in. It's bad enough we're having sex without being married... doesn't this feel wrong to you?"

Justin just looked at me and I could see the frustration on his face.

"How much time do you need?"

"I don't know; can we discuss it in a few weeks? I need to digest this whole thing; besides, we need to focus on finding jobs after graduation, not getting involved in the swinger lifestyle."

Truthfully I had no intentions of thinking about anything, I just needed to buy myself some time. I was hoping the whole thing would just blow over.

"A few weeks?!" Justin repeated, raising his voice at me, "Layla, there is a couple I would like for you to meet this evening. You don't have to do anything; we are just meeting for drinks to see if we are compatible."

After he told me that everything went down-hill and fast. I couldn't believe he had the audacity to contact someone about the lifestyle without talking to me first. I demanded he cancel but he insisted he couldn't on such short notice. Apparently William and Angela were only available that particular night and Justin had already confirmed everything. He pleaded with me to do this one little thing for him, which was actually one big thing. I remember part of me wanted to please him but the other part of me wanted to tell him hell no, find someone else to fulfill your fucking fantasies. Deep in my heart I knew I would be crushed if he had ever left me and ended up with someone else, so as always, I gave into him. Besides, it was just meeting two people for drinks I rationalized; how bad could that be?

"You promise we don't have to do anything?" He quickly promised we were only meeting for drinks. In the end I reluctantly agreed. As soon as I did Justin's face lit up brighter than a kid in a candy store for the first time.

"Layla, I will always love you for this."

I believed him but I prayed I wasn't agreeing to something that would later come back to haunt me.

Chapter 2

THAT NIGHT I was so nervous I didn't know what to wear. I was heading out to meet a couple that was into some kinky shit during sex. Just the thought of it is still incomprehensible to me. I mean, what kind of people would even engage in such activities? I've heard of people doing some wild things but this was on a whole new level. One thing for sure, I knew this was a clear indication my relationship with Justin was in real trouble. I tried not to think that way but how else could I have felt at the time? I knew Justin found me attractive and I've always been thankful to have the ability to turn him on, but how could I satisfy him when his touch made me feel dirty? He said I have the body of a goddess; it's just a shame this goddess doesn't know what to do with it.

My deep chocolate complexion and bright smile got me a lot of looks in high school but I didn't truly blossom until after my freshman year in college. I'm short in stature but thanks to my mother's genes I have a figure most women work out daily to maintain.

That evening I agreed to meet the couple, it took hours getting dressed. What the hell did one wear when meeting swingers;

was business casual even appropriate? After a long debate I finally settled on a simple black dress, high heels and I placed my hair in a loose bun. I went light on the makeup and didn't choose any accessories. I thought maybe if I looked plain the other couple wouldn't be interested and want to call the whole thing off.

We were scheduled to meet the couple at a restaurant close to the Verizon Center in downtown Washington, D.C. I'm not sure what I was expecting but I surely did receive the unexpected that night. When we entered the restaurant the lobby was packed with people. The dim lights added to a cozy atmosphere. Dark wood accents gave the restaurant a very masculine feel as servers bustled around with trays in their hand. There was a crowd around the bar and almost every table looked occupied. That's when it first occurred to me that I didn't know what the couple looked like. It's not like you could go around asking people "excuse me, are you a swinger?"

When I asked Justin he casually mentioned they all exchanged pictures on some website. I was furious. I couldn't believe he would share our private pictures with strangers.

I was so upset about the pictures I started working up the nerve to walk out the door when a woman approached us. At the sight of her I could not move. When she called out Justin's name and they embraced each other as if they were long lost friends, I still couldn't move. I looked over to Justin and I'm pretty sure my face said it all.

The woman was white. It had never occurred to me Justin would want to sleep with a white woman, not that I could fault him; she was beautiful. She reminded me of Catherine Zeta-Jones with her long dark hair and dark eyes but no matter how pretty she was, it still couldn't erase my state of shock. Most days Justin acted like he could barely tolerate white people and now he wanted to sleep with one? I felt like I knew nothing about the man standing next to me—it was as if I was with a stranger.

When the woman introduced herself to me she grabbed me in a tight embrace as if we were bosom buddies. She said something about me being beautiful and her being happy we could make it but I barely heard a word she said. All I could do was focus on the fact that she was white and Justin wanted to have sex with her.

Angela said William had arranged for a private dining room; I didn't even know this restaurant had private rooms. Following Angela down the hall I remember surveying the areas for quick exits. I didn't want to meet William. Not that it would have made this situation any better, but I would at least have preferred to deal with a black couple. I don't know why the hell Justin thought I would be interested in watching a strange white couple do kinky shit in the bedroom.

We followed Angela to the table and everything around me ceased to exist when I first laid eyes on William. I've never thought much about the brown hair blue-eyed type but anyone with sight would have to acknowledge the man was gorgeous, no that's too pretty of a word, but handsome is not a sufficient description either. He had a rugged yet refined look about him. He was tall, maybe 6'2" or 6'3" but I was never good at estimating someone's height. One thing for sure, it was clear both William and Angela were older than me and Justin. Angela looked to be in her mid-thirties but with William's demeanor and pristine appearance, I would guess he was in his late thirties or early forties. When he saw me he flashed a smile and I saw his perfect white teeth—blindingly white. Where the hell did Justin meet them, I wondered? They looked like perfectly normal people.

To this day I don't know how I got through dinner with my stomach constantly in knots. It also didn't help that I felt like William was scrutinizing every part of my body. I was fully clothed yet I felt completely naked under his stare. I felt his blue eyes penetrating me to the depth of my very soul. I was quiet through dinner; between Angela and Justin's flirting and William's intense demeanor I didn't have much to say. One thing I did find odd was William's ability to dodge any personal questions. The whole point of us meeting was to get better acquainted yet aside from his name I didn't learn anything about him at all.

Of course Justin and Angela were very chatty with each other—the two seemed to hit it off perfectly. I wondered how William felt about that, especially since the two of us barely spoke. From his expression he looked like he could care less about the chemistry shared between the two. When dessert arrived the conversation changed from mindless chatter and light flirting to a more serious topic; the reason why we were all there in the first place. Everyone quietened down while the waiter placed cheesecake with strawberry toppings in front of us. As soon as he left the room Angela announced it was time to go over some of their rules for swinging. *Rules* I thought to myself, Justin and I didn't discuss any rules. Then again, it wasn't necessary since we were only meeting for dinner.

As the conversation continued it became clear to me they were under the impression things were going to go beyond dinner that night. I remember secretly wondering how they would feel once Justin told them this was only a "meet and greet."

The list of rules shared by Angela and William wasn't very long. To me things like using protection and respecting your partners' wishes should have been standard but I guess they felt it necessary to state for the record. I occasionally glanced at William while Angela was speaking, trying to understand the man in front of me. He was by all standards handsome. I know enough women to know he could basically get any woman he wanted, so why then would he resort to this type of lifestyle? Was it the thrill of picking up strangers for one night? I'll never know the answers to my questions but that didn't stop me from pondering. I was so absorbed in trying to figure William out I didn't realize Angela had asked me a question.

"I'm sorry, what was your question again?" I tried my best to look interested; I didn't want anyone to know that I was thinking about William.

"I was asking what you were into."

What am I into? I'm not into the swinger lifestyle, that's for sure. I was at a complete loss for words so I just shrugged my shoulders. That's when Angela informed me she was bi-playful. Being new to the whole swinger lingo I asked what bi-playful meant. As soon as I asked the question, William looked at me like I had grown a second head. Angela giggled and said she was interested in being with both men and women. I nearly choked when she said that.

Personally I thought it sounded like a fancy way of saying closet lesbian but what do I know? Justin used that opportunity to jump into the conversation and announce that I wasn't comfortable with that yet. I nearly choked to death at his comment. Yet?! I knew men fantasized about seeing two women together but it almost felt like Justin was trying to turn me into a goddamn lesbian! I immediately spoke up,

"I'm not bi-playful," I said sternly, looking over at Justin like he was crazy but he paid no attention to me.

"Sure, no problem Layla, I just thought I would ask," Angela said winking at me.

William remained quiet although I did catch him watching me a few times and once or twice we made eye contact before I looked away.

Feeling uneasy about the conversation I tuned Justin and Angela out to take in my surroundings. The private dining room was much nicer than the tables on the main restaurant floor. There was a rustic charm to the place that I appreciated. The dim lights and candles made the ambiance very intimate. The wall mounted fireplace added warmth to the room but looking at William made my insides heat up more than the fire.

Turning my attention back to Angela and Justin I found they were going over a list of likes and dislikes during sex. Justin brought up some things he never even mentioned to me before. That conversation should have taken place between the two of us in the privacy of our home. Instead he was sharing his preferences with a complete stranger. Maybe if he had told me some of the things he liked up front our sex life could have been better. I felt myself getting angry and had to remember to keep my cool, but I made a mental note to take the issue up with him as soon as we got home.

The second we finished dessert the waiter came out to collect our dishes. He offered us all coffee but everyone declined. When the waiter brought out the check William took it and paid the entire bill. Justin didn't comment but I whispered "thank you for dinner" and he acknowledged me with a quick nod. He looked like he was more anxious than me to get the hell out of the restaurant and I couldn't have been more pleased. *What next?* I thought to myself. *When was Justin going to let these people know we were ready to go?* I was eyeing Justin when William finally spoke.

"Would you all like to accompany us to our room?"

Whoa! What?! Where did that come from? I thought he wasn't interested; I prayed they didn't act crazy when Justin thanked them for dinner and let them know the evening had come to an end. I had hoped he would let them down easy especially since William picked up the tab for dinner. I wanted to go home right away and forget about the night.

"Our driver is waiting out front and if you two are interested you can join us," he continued.

I turned to Justin who was saying yes without even asking me. I thought I must have misunderstood him. I don't know what the hell he was thinking. I had no intentions of going anywhere with two complete strangers. I looked over at Justin, practically willing him to look at me, but he refused to turn his head. He was too busy flirting with Angela. William looked me over and from his expression I could tell he picked up on my hesitancy to join them.

"Layla, I only want you to join us if you are comfortable," he said, and I immediately felt a shiver run down my spine. The sound of my name leaving his lips was the sexiest thing I had ever heard.

"Oh, she's fine," said Justin, as if he had the authority to speak on my behalf. William didn't even look at Justin. He kept staring into my eyes waiting for me to respond. We went from avoiding eye contact with each other to a staring contest and I was losing. Justin leaned over to me and whispered in my ear,

"Baby, don't worry, nothing is going to happen tonight, they just want to get to know us a little better that's all, I swear. Trust me."

Should I trust him? My heart said yes but my head was screaming: girl, don't be a fool!

"Layla, I don't ask for much. You will say yes if you love me and want our relationship to work."

I always hated it when Justin used my love for him to manipulate me. I knew what he was doing but I could also see how important that night was to him. I thought if I agreed Justin wouldn't have any qualms about finally asking me to marry him. After all, he did promise nothing would happen and so far, aside from enjoying a good meal, nothing inappropriate had occurred.

"Yes, we would like to join you," I answered. I guess my response was good enough for William because as soon as the words left my mouth he stood up from the table and extended his hand to me. I didn't want to accept but I felt drawn to him and before I knew it we were hand in hand. My hand felt so small in his yet strangely enough, for the first time that night, I felt protected.

Chapter 3

OUTSIDE, THE COOL air felt calming. William's driver held the door open for us as we all piled into his Lincoln to go to yet another private room. When we arrived at the hotel the only word that came to mind was grand. It wasn't part of a hotel chain I recognized. It was very plush with old world accents inside. I felt so awkward walking through the lobby. If the hotel staff only knew what William and Angela had planned for that evening they probably would've put them out.

We took the elevator to the top floor and I immediately noticed theirs was the only room on the entire floor. The first thought that entered into my mind was to wonder if anyone would hear me if I screamed out for help.

When we entered the suite I was in awe; someone had spent a lot of time setting a romantic scene. Candles were strategically placed throughout the room, giving off the scent of warm vanilla. By the bar there was an assortment of desserts and drinks waiting for us. The suite had a sunken living room and a beautiful view overlooking downtown D.C. I don't think I'd ever been in a hotel room that large before. Normally I would have loved to look around more but I wanted to stay as close to the exit as possible.

There was a lot of thought put into setting up the room. *What if we hadn't come*, I thought to myself. As if William could read my mind he leaned over and whispered "just in case." Oh. My. God. The sound of his voice and the close proximity to which he stood had my body all shook up. I had to remind myself to stay focused on getting out of there as soon as possible. To my far right I noticed Justin pouring Angela a drink. The bastard didn't even bother to offer me anything. After Angela took a sip she sauntered over to me linking our arms together.

"Layla, would you like to change into something more comfortable?" she asked.

Change? I never imagined a woman asking me that question. I knew then I should have never let Justin talk me into joining them.

"No, I'm comfortable in my dress," I quickly replied.

Angela said she was going to change into something more comfortable, leaving the three of us in the room together. Justin was not happy with my standoffish attitude and pulled me into a corner, practically begging me to loosen up. I caught a glimpse of William watching us and although I couldn't be sure, he looked pissed when he saw the way Justin was pulling on me.

Before our conversation could go any further, Angela re-entered the room wearing black lace lingerie. As soon as she walked in I knew I had lost all of Justin's attention for the rest of the evening. Even I could see she was beautiful. I could never wear something so revealing. I admired her confidence. I felt so out of place. I turned to look away and spotted William watching me. I crossed my arms over my chest trying to cover myself even though I was fully clothed. If I didn't know better I swear he could see right through me.

Angela suggested we play some adult game to break the ice. Justin usually hates any type of board game but of course that night he was all in. He offered to help Angela set up in the adjoining bedroom, leaving William and I alone. I decided then and there it was time to go. I was going to give Justin five more minutes before I went back there and dragged him out, demanding he take me home.

Left alone with William I felt very self-conscious. He offered me a glass of wine which I gladly accepted in hopes it would help me to relax a little. He stood close by and watched me drink the entire glass.

When I was on my second glass he said, "Layla, don't take this the wrong way, but if we do this I don't want you to be drunk. I want you to want me as I want you."

Do this? I thought to myself. My body may feel differently but I had zero intentions of doing anything. In reality Justin's five minutes were up but for some reason I wasn't ready to leave William's presence just yet. I was hoping the wine would help to calm my nerves but it did little to sooth all of my nervous energy. While I was nervous and edgy, William seemed to be completely at ease. He strolled across the room and started fiddling with the stereo. I was stunned when he put on one of my favorite jazz artists. I kept looking up at the clock behind the sofa table, praying Justin would come out on his own instead of having me barge back there to get him. I had no such luck.

William noticed my pre-occupation with the clock, "you keep looking at the time," he told me, "do you have some place you'd rather be?" At a loss, I just shook my head no and continued to look at the door Justin was behind.

"No matter how hard you stare at that door I doubt he's coming out right now."

That caught my attention.

"What do you think they are doing back there?" A broad smile crossed Williams face and I knew not to ask any-more questions.

"Tell me Layla, have you ever done this before?"

"Why do you ask?" I wasn't prepared to discuss my lack of experience in the swinging lifestyle. I should have just admitted that was my first time even meeting a couple who participated in the lifestyle but I wasn't sure how William would respond to that bit of news and I didn't want to find out on my own. Although he seemed very calm and reserved at that moment, something about his presence gave me the impression there was another side to him; a side I may not like.

"You seem very unsure of yourself and I can't figure out if it's me or your lack of experience that has you so tense and nervous."

I don't know why his observation got under my skin but something in his tone ignited a defensive spark within me.

"It's not my lack of experience that's the issue. No offense, but you're not my type."

"What, you like women now?" he asked with an obnoxious smirk on his face.

"No, I like men," I said while trying to put distance between us. He had moved closer towards me and I felt the need for space.

"Last time I checked I'm still a man so what is it? I can tell from your body language you find me attractive," he said continuing his slow pursuit.

Of course I found him attractive but he didn't have to point it out. I could tell he had a bit of an ego so I decided to let him know he just wasn't my type.

"This isn't about your looks... no offense or anything but I prefer black men." He laughed. I didn't know I said anything funny.

"I take it you find my preference amusing?"

"No, I find it amusing I'm being discriminated against."

He'd probably never been rejected in his entire life. I thought my comment would help put his ego in check. "Like I said, I just have my personal preference."

"That may be the case but that still doesn't address the fact that you still find me attractive." Me finding William attractive was never the issue.

"Just because I find you attractive, it doesn't mean I'm willing to let you touch me." He immediately stopped coming towards me when I said that.

"It's clear to me you are uncomfortable being here. I will noti-fy my driver to take you and Justin back to your car, but before you leave I would like to offer you a word of advice."

I didn't expect his demeanor to change so abruptly. I thought we would have kept up with our banter a little more but I was mistaken.

"What advice could you possibly offer?"

"You are clearly a grown woman and as such you are old enough to speak up for yourself and know what you do and don't want to do. You shouldn't let your partner talk you into things you clearly aren't ready for. You've wasted everyone's time tonight and my time is very valuable."

All of my nervous energy vanished. I couldn't believe that freak was telling me I'd wasted his time. That's when I lashed out at him, letting him know his time was of no concern to me.

"Do you know who I am?" he asked threateningly.

"Only someone who is completely self-absorbed would ask such a question. What you should be asking me is if it matters and the answer to that is no," I yelled back.

"I think it's time for you to leave," he said slamming his drink down on the bar.

"I'm way ahead of you," I said in response and slammed my wine glass down on the nearest table and headed towards the room Angela and Justin had disappeared into. Unfortunately I was so upset I overlooked the plug to the lamp and tripped over the cord. I fell to the floor hitting my head against the door jamb and twisting my ankle in the process.

"Shit, Layla are you okay?" William scrambled to my side try-ing to help me up but I was in way too much pain to try and stand again. *Don't cry Layla; whatever you do, don't cry in front of this man* I kept chanting to myself. Both my head and ankle were killing me but I tried my best to hide my pain. I knew I was fighting a losing battle and when I could no longer hide the pain I felt my eyes swell with tears.

Without me having to say anything William scooped me up from the floor and carried me into the bedroom on the other side of the living room. The moment I was securely in his arms I forgot about all of the pain I was in. A new sensation stirred between my legs and I had to remind myself to refocus on getting Justin and getting the hell out of there and fast.

Chapter 4

WILLIAM KICKED THE room door open and laid me on the plush king size bed to tend to my head and ankle. He briefly disappeared into the bathroom before returning with a bottle of Tylenol and a first aid kit.

"Here, take these, it should help with the pain and prevent swelling," he said offering me the pills. I declined them, which sparked argument number two. Exasperated by my stubbornness he finally yelled, "Jesus Christ woman, I'm trying to help you! Would you please just take the fucking pills!"

Who the hell did he think he was? And what kind of person called Jesus' name and cursed in the same sentence, I wondered. I didn't feel like arguing anymore so I snatched the pills out of his hand and quickly took them down with the water he brought. Although he was still way too rude for my personal taste, I did appreciate his attentiveness. After ensuring I swallowed both pills he elevated my foot and made a makeshift ice pack. I thought he would have simply handed it to me but instead he sat there holding it over my ankle.

We sat in silence for a while; I didn't know what to say. I probably should have asked for Justin but he would have made matters worse. Knowing him he would have scolded me for my clumsiness in front of William which would've only added to my embarrassment. I wasn't sure how long Justin had been in the room with Angela but what was most disturbing was that I no longer cared. Sitting that close to William with his hands massaging my ankle was a turn on. I felt myself getting worked up so I pulled my leg away and told him I was better.

"It's a shame," he said looking at me.

"What's a shame?" I asked

"That you are not more open minded. If given the chance, I think you and I would have had a good time together."

At first I was lost for words but then I developed verbal diarrhea and told him how I had only learned of the swinging lifestyle earlier that day and what I truly thought of it.

Do all white people change color? If they do, I never noticed until William changed color right in front of me. He went from a cool tan complexion to beet red in seconds and I knew the evening was not going to end the way I expected.

His immediate anger scared the shit out of me but I still didn't move. He just held my gaze. There was only the glow of a side lamp in the room but I wished it was off so he couldn't see my facial expression.

"Why did you agree to come to the hotel with us?"

William didn't know it but that was the million-dollar question. Why the hell did I agree to continue on with the evening? I could have easily said no and although Justin would have been upset, we still would have gone home. All of it could have ended much sooner and I could only fault myself.

That's when I decided to be honest and tell him the truth, "I think I'm here because I was curious about you… I mean could you really see yourself being intimate with me—a stranger?"

He didn't say anything to me. He just continued to look at me for a few seconds before he pulled me towards him and planted a very soft kiss on my lips. His lips lingered on mine for a few moments before breaking contact. I think the kiss startled him more than me.

"I can imagine doing a lot of things with you... so many things in fact that we would no longer be strangers. Too bad I don't fit the scope of your personal preferences."

That one soft kiss left my body aroused. I was surprised to find I no longer cared about any of my preferences. I didn't give a damn about what Justin and Angela were doing. I didn't care that we were all in a hotel room for all the wrong reasons. I just cared about the way William made my body feel and I knew I wanted more. I was too scared to make the first move so I silently prayed he would be brave enough to kiss me again. Fortunately for me, he was.

He worked his magic and before I knew it I parted my lips allowing him full access. He slipped his tongue inside and we started to explore each other. Finally, after a few minutes he broke our kiss and I found myself panting, ready for more. I still don't know what the hell was wrong with me that night. I've never been that impulsive with any man—ever!

"You taste very sweet Layla."

That comment left me speechless.

"I wonder if you taste this sweet all over."

Before I could even think of what to say slowly he leaned in over me placing another soft kiss on my lips. He then placed his hand on my jaw running his fingers down my neck through the crest of my breast, past my navel, past the hem line of my dress, before sliding his hands up and stopping at what my momma always referred to as my shuga. He looked at me intently and whispered, "let's see how sweet you taste down here." His words alone made my insides quiver. In all the years I had been with Justin I had never felt so turned on before.

Not taking his eyes off me he moved his hand beneath my underwear and started to lightly stroke my folds. He rubbed his fingers around my clitoris then sunk his fingers inside of me. Oh shit, I couldn't believe how wet I was. He leaned in, giving me a more passionate kiss and I loved the way he tasted. When our kiss ended I tilted my head back, arching my back, moaning from the pleasure he was providing me.

He slowly removed his fingers leaving me hot and wanting more. My head felt so foggy I didn't know what to think until I noticed he was lowering his body stopping with his head between my thighs. Oh shit, I thought to myself. Is he really about to do this? I definitely wasn't prepared. Justin tried oral sex with me but it was as enjoyable as being kissed by a dog with bad breath. Maybe William would be better, I thought. I probably should have stopped him before anything else happened but I didn't want to. I don't remember ever feeling that aroused before. My body started craving something I didn't even know existed. He removed my panties, sliding them down my legs. He then spread me wider apart and his warm soft lips were caressing me. Good God that man had talent. I felt the sensation of his tongue licking me while he used his fingers to penetrate me. My body was going wild with pleasure. I had heard rumors about men like him and now I could definitely concur.

Faster and faster he licked and fingered me. My hips were thrusting wildly in a circular motion. For the first time I craved the real thing in me, not caring who it belonged to. My hips were moving so wildly he put one hand on my hip to try and steady me. I was breathing fiercely enjoying the pleasure I was receiving. His mouth felt soft and firm at the same time. He continued moving his fingers in and out of me, making my body shiver. He paraded his tongue up and down my opening before sticking it deep inside of me. Occasionally he would take slight pauses to place soft kisses between my thighs. I'd never experienced anything like it before. My body started to tremble and I felt like I was approaching euphoria when suddenly William stopped. My head was in such a daze I felt confused. When he backed away from me I was prepared for him to undress himself. I couldn't wait to see what he looked like naked. With anyone else I probably would have felt terrified but the thought of William inside me was actually a welcoming thought. I was ready for his entrance when I noticed a smirk on his face.

"Normally I would let you finish but there's no need since I don't fit the parameters of your personal preferences." He then licked his fingers and smiled as he left the room, leaving me drenched and horny as hell.

Until I met William I'd never experienced wanting someone and hating them at the same time. I would never deny I wanted him but if I were to ever come face to face with him again, I would happily scratch his eyes out. Thankfully the likelihood of Justin and I ever seeing he and Angela again is slim to none, especially with us moving to Chicago. I'm happy to put that night behind me but sometimes it's nice to think about what almost happened.

Chapter 5

"LAYLA, ARE YOU listening to me?"

Shit, every time I think about that night I space out. "I'm sorry Justin, what were you saying?"

"I said I think your sister just pulled up outside."

I glance out the window and see Cynthia making an attempt to parallel park her car. I love my baby sister but she can't park for shit. I would send Justin down to help her but the two of them are like oil and water. She doesn't like Justin and makes no qualms about letting me know it. Fortunately for me my parents love him and the rest of our family gets along great. Both of our mothers are excited about us one day getting married; everyone's just waiting for Justin to pop the question.

I hear Cynthia making her way up the stairs. I swear she doesn't believe in wearing quiet clothing. Something on her is always swishing, jingling or clashing.

"Justin, please be nice to Cynthia, don't forget she's here to help us move."

"Whatever; I don't have time to play nice with your bratty little sister. I've got to run some errands—I should be back in about two hours."

"Run errands! Justin, I need your help packing and loading up some of these boxes."

"Layla, I've got to take care of a few things before we leave."

Cynthia chooses that moment to enter the apartment, eyeing the both of us suspiciously. I do my best to not let her see Justin and I argue. She has a knack for taking a small disagreement and turning it into a war.

"What's going on?" she asks, with that knowing look in her eyes.

"None of your business," is Justin's response. I swear he starts their arguments half the time.

"I'm just trying to convince Justin we need his help loading the van." Cynthia looks over at me and smiles.

"Don't worry Layla; Marcus will be here soon and he said he will help load the van."

"You invited Marcus?"

"Correction, mom invited Marcus and from the looks of things you're definitely going to need his help."

Marcus is the last person whose help I need. If anything, he's the one person I can't wait to escape from.

"See Layla, I told you everything will work out. While I'm running my errands Marcus can load the last of the boxes in to the van, problem solved."

Justin looks quite happy with himself. Marcus and Justin never got along. When we started dating Marcus tried to take on the role of big brother and interrogated Justin on our first date. Ever since then, the two have barely uttered a word to each other, which is fine with me.

"Fine, go, but please don't take forever," I say with resignation. No sense in starting a fight now.

"I won't baby." Justin comes over and gives me a quick kiss on the lips before grabbing his jacket and heading out the door.

"I still don't know what you see in him."

"Please don't start with me Cynthia; I have a lot to do in a short period of time."

"I know—that's why I'm here. I still can't believe you're moving to Chicago."

"If we don't get going I won't be moving anywhere."

Knowing Marcus was on his way made me move into overdrive packing; the sooner I get this place packed up, the sooner I can be on my way to Chicago. I think this move is exactly what Justin and I both need. After graduation we decided to look for jobs out of state and both ended up landing jobs in Chicago. I accepted a position with Prescott Incorporated. It's a new marketing firm that recently took off and has quickly become one of the largest firms in the U.S. Justin got a job with Franklin, Feinburg and Nash; another agency only a few blocks away from my office. My company offers furnished corporate apartments so we only have to worry about packing our personal items, which has added up to a lot more than I originally anticipated.

Cynthia and I are diligently working together, wrapping all of my fragile keepsakes, when I hear a knock at the door. Knowing it's probably Marcus, Cynthia makes a bee line for the door in excitement. Just looking at him makes me want to hurl but I've been trained to put on a smile for the sake of my family since I was a child. To be honest it's so engrained in me I probably don't even know how to turn it off.

"Baby girl, how are you?" He always acts so ecstatic to see me.

"I'm fine Marcus," I say dryly. I notice Cynthia giving me a mean glare before she launches herself into Marcus' arms for another hug. They are always extra excited to see each other. I just don't get it.

"Where is Justin?" Marcus asked.

"He just needed to run a few errands. We're going to go ahead and get started loading the van, he should return shortly." I watch as Cynthia and Marcus exchange looks before grabbing boxes and heading downstairs.

It takes two hours but we finally get everything loaded onto the van. Part of my relocation package includes transporting my personal belongings from D.C. to Chicago. When the drivers arrive they do a double check before they start the long drive. I watch nervously at the clock; Justin still isn't back yet. While waiting for Justin, Cynthia leaves to go pick up my parents, leaving Marcus and I alone.

"So… you all ready for the big move Layla?"

"Yes. I think living in Chicago is going to be a great start for Justin and I."

Marcus clears his throat, "I actually wanted to talk to you about that."

"Talk to me about what?" Marcus is the last person I would ever discuss my relationship with.

"Layla, I know you are in love with Justin, and I'm sure he has some great qualities, but I just want you to be careful. You are such a beautiful, talented woman and I don't want to see you get hurt."

Of all the fucking nerve! He knows he can say shit like this to me because I'm too scared to confront him. Is he so delusional he forgot who the first man to ever hurt me was? I'm not having this conversation with him.

"Justin would never do anything to hurt me," I say, looking him square in the eye. He shakes his head and backs off.

"I just wanted to make sure you were okay."

"I'm fine thank you." As if on cue Justin comes walking up the stairs to the apartment. As soon as I see him I launch myself into his open arms. He knows I hate being alone with Marcus and places a protective arm around me while planting a kiss on my lips.

"Hey Marcus, when did you get here?" Justin casually asks.

"I got here about two hours ago, where have you been?"

"Out running some errands," the look on his face lets me know he's irritated about Marcus questioning his whereabouts. "Is there anything else left to pack?"

"No, we are all done here."

The tension in the room is almost unbearable. Justin keeps a firm hold on me; I wish he was always this protective. Outside I hear commotion. I can already hear my mom fussing. Justin releases me and laughs,

"I guess our families are here."

Everyone bursts through the door at once talking a mile a minute. Justin and I are tugged and pulled in every direction, receiving kisses and bids of well wishes. We barely escape to the airport in time to catch our flight.

The flight into Chicago O'Hare airport goes by fast. By eight o'clock that evening we are exploring our new home—a gorgeous two-bedroom apartment—set up for us by Prescott Inc. The living room is spacious with beautiful panoramic views of the city; the floor to ceiling windows gives off the illusion of living in a glass house. I am grateful to find the control panel for the electronic blinds; I'm not used to living in a space where anyone with binoculars can watch my every move. Entering the master bedroom I stop and smile. The color scheme is beige with deep chocolate accents. The large king size bed takes up most of the floor space but there is still room for night stands and a separate sitting area with a large picture window that overlooks the city. As I walk into the second bedroom I notice it is set up as an office, complete with a desk, chair, printer, computer and all the accessories and office supplies you can ask for. I look in the bathroom where everything is clean and neat with fresh towels and linens. I can really get used to this. Walking back to the kitchen I find cherry wood cabinets and sleek modern stainless steel appliances. Clearly no expense was spared when putting this home together. Even Justin is surprised by our new accommodations. He hasn't said much but I know he's happy. I think he is still a little pissed because he applied for a position with Prescott Inc. but was never called in to interview. When I told him they offered me a position it was a bitter-sweet moment. We didn't really get to celebrate my job offer until he received an offer from Franklin, Feinberg and Nash. The company Justin will be working for also has a stellar reputation but they are still number two in our industry.

The next morning Justin and I are both running in a mad dash to get to our offices on time. I had spent most of the night unpacking and was so tired from the day's events that I forgot to set the alarm clock. I race out of the building in hopes of having enough time to grab breakfast. As soon as I walk into the coffee shop I see everyone had the same idea I did but the line seems to be moving at a rapid pace so I should still make it into the office on time.

I'm able to get a cup of coffee and bagel with time to spare. Walking out the door I start to relax until something hard slams into me making me drop my bagel and coffee. I look up and all I can see is the back of a man dressed in a navy blue suit who keeps walking as if he didn't just cause me to lose my breakfast. I'm a reasonable person, I understand accidents happen, but the jackass didn't even stop.

Walking towards the rude stranger I yell out to him but he's on his phone and doesn't even bother to turn around. He's yelling at someone and doesn't give a second glance towards me. Angrily I snatch his phone out of his hand, "excuse me but you just bumped into me causing me to spill my breakfast!"

He whips around to face me and I feel all of the air escape my lungs. I do a double-take; it can't be I mutter to myself, backing away from him. I keep telling myself that it can't be him, but if memory serves me correctly I swear I'm looking at William. He's expressionless, making me doubt my eyes. I continue backing away until the front door is only a few feet away. I turn and quickly bolt out the door and head straight for my office, using my adrenaline rush to get me there.

When I reach the building I bypass the security guard at the front desk and take the elevator straight to the twentieth floor. Inside the elevator I do my best to regain my composure. This is crazy, I think to myself, I don't know why I'm acting as if he chased me to the office. I need to get myself together; I don't want to walk into the office on my first day looking disheveled. I look down at my feet and silently thank God I decided on sensible shoes. My apartment is only a few blocks away and I thought walking would be a good way for me to familiarize myself with the neighborhood. Summer is only a few weeks away and I want to enjoy spring as much as possible before the intense heat of the summer months take over.

Stepping off the elevator I head straight to the receptionist desk on my floor, (I was told I would have my own office but I don't know where anything is yet.) The receptionist is a petite brunette. She introduces herself as Amanda and leads the way to my new office.

"I'll let Ms. Sparks know that you're here," she says, stopping outside my office door.

"Thank you." Amanda seems like a nice girl but I notice something mischievous in her eyes. Shaking off the weird feeling I sit at my desk and look around. I can't believe I'm here. I never thought I would land a job like this fresh out of grad school. My office is small but functional. I'm grateful I have a large window since I'm not a fan of enclosed spaces.

"Layla, I'm so happy you're here."

I jump in my seat—I didn't expect Ms. Sparks to make it to my office so quickly. I need to get a grip but the possibility of William being here in Chicago has me on edge. I need to regain my composure, especially if I'm going to make a good impression on the company VP. We first met at a career seminar hosted by my school. We exchanged emails and I provided her with samples of my work. I didn't think much of it when she said she was impressed: I heard that from a lot of people but nothing ever materialized. When she called to schedule an interview I was both shocked and thrilled. Prescott Inc. is owned by Jonathan Prescott, but from what I've gathered so far, Georgina Sparks really runs the company.

I step out from around my desk to shake hands with her when I realize I still have the phone I snatched from William, or at the very

least a William lookalike, in my hand. I hadn't realized I held onto it.
If my eyes were not mistaken, and I truly saw William, he must think
I'm an idiot. Not knowing what to do I toss it in my desk drawer;
maybe I'll try dropping it off at the coffee shop during lunch. I still
can't believe William could possibly be here in Chicago but now is
not the time to dwell on any of that; I need to focus on making a
good impression. I really like Ms. Sparks, she knows her stuff and I
can tell she's no nonsense when it comes to business.

"Ms. Sparks, I'm thrilled to be here," I say, shaking her hand
and smiling brightly. She's dressed to impress in an Armani
Collezioni business suit. With her wavy blond hair pulled up in a
loose bun and her designer specs, she definitely looks the part of a
VP.

"Please call me Georgina." She releases my hand and follows
me to my desk. "Normally I would give you time to settle in but
I've called an emergency staff meeting to go over the Bradford
account since it's in danger of being terminated. You can leave
your stuff here; just grab a pencil and notepad so you can take
notes. After the meeting I'll have Amanda get you settled in and
I'll try to meet with you this afternoon so we can go over some
upcoming projects."

I was hoping to slip out and grab something to eat. I haven't
eaten since I left D.C. yesterday afternoon and thanks to my run
in at the coffee shop, it looks like I won't be able to eat until
lunch. I grab what I could find in preparation for the meeting and
follow Georgina into the conference room.

When we enter the conference room I am surprised by the di-
versity in the team. Georgina starts the meeting by introducing
me to everyone, before she hands out the agenda and wastes no
time in getting started. We are only a few minutes into our meeting when I hear commotion in the hallway. Amanda rushes into
the conference room all wide-eyed and bubbly.

"Ms. Sparks, Mr. Prescott is here."

Everyone in the room comes alive. The entire atmosphere has
changed; the women start fidgeting with their clothes while the

men do their best to look assertive. Mr. Prescott must be quite the man to evoke such a reaction.

Amanda steps aside allowing the infamous Mr. Prescott entrance. I look up and develop an overwhelming need to pass out.

"Jonathan!" Georgina says his name with great enthusiasm. I can tell from her body language she too is excited to see him. "I thought you were flying out of the country today."

"I changed my plans," he says surveying the room. When his eyes land on me I know this day is not going to end well. I am so fucking fired—I can feel it.

"I see we have a new member in our marketing team," he says, singling me out.

"Yes…Layla," Georgina says waving me over, "I would like for you to meet the President and CEO of Prescott Incorporated, Mr. Jonathan Prescott."

Chapter 6

FROM GEORGINA'S INTRODUCTION you would think she was announcing the arrival of the President of the United States. With great dread and a heavy heart I make my way over. There is no doubt about it, not only is William in Chicago but his real name is Jonathan Prescott. The realization alone makes me feel faint. With shaky knees I head over; I don't know what to say.

"Layla," he says my name and extends his hand with an obnoxious look on his face.

"Jonathan," I reply, feeling sick to my stomach.

"Please address me as Mr. Prescott."

Silence sweeps through the room—did he really just tell me to address him as Mr. Prescott? I start to shake from the rage growing within. First he lied about his name, then he makes me spill my breakfast and now he has embarrassed me in front of everyone on my first day on the job. It takes a lot of effort but eventually I reel in my temper and gain my composure.

"I'll remember that in the future," I say, plastering a fake smile on my face. There is no way in hell I'm going to run around this office referring to this bastard as Mr. Prescott. From here on out I'll just refer to him as Prescott; that should annoy the hell out of him. Even if it doesn't, I'll feel better knowing I've defied him.

Prescott takes the first seat available, which happens to be next to a woman by the name of Veronica. I'm not going to pass judgement on her yet but as soon as Georgina introduced me she was very standoffish towards me. Anyone can see how excited she is that Prescott took the seat next to her.

"Georgina, please proceed with the meeting, I want an update on the Bradford account."

I could be wrong but I doubt he cares about this account. He's up to something but I don't know what. With nervous energy taking over I return to my chair and Georgina moves forward with the meeting agenda.

She starts with what she calls a few "housekeeping items" before delving into the Bradford account. That's when Prescott interjects, taking over.

"Ms. Brown, I heard you submitted a proposal to Georgina on the account she is trying to save. Please share with myself and your colleagues how you developed your ideas and finalized your submission."

As soon as I accepted the position the office manager had sent me a packet on some new accounts the company is looking to both acquire and save. I had no clue I was going to be called out in front of everyone to discuss my proposal. He knows this is my first day, yet he wants to put me on the spot in front of all my new colleagues. So that's how he wants to play—no problem. I may not know what I'm doing in the bedroom but marketing is something I can do in my sleep. I take a deep breath and turn to address my new co-workers. I make sure my tone is crisp, professional and eloquent. I run through some of my original brainstorming concepts, results from surveys and research I conducted and then give them a breakdown on how I put the final proposal together. I can tell from everyone's faces they are thoroughly impressed. Most of my colleagues nod in approval, except for Veronica. I can tell by her expression she feels threatened by my presence. I'm not intimidated by her at all. Growing up I've become accustomed to conflict with women who are insecure. I have the face of an angel and a head for business and I'm not afraid to use either.

"Thank you for your summary, Ms. Brown. Before lunch I would like to meet with you in my office to go over some of the details on the numbers you ran and I also want a list of all the remaining vendors you need to hear from regarding materials."

"Sure thing, Prescott."

He immediately looks at me with a challenging stare. I raise my chin, letting him know I'm prepared for battle—there is no way in hell I'm calling him Mr. Prescott. To my surprise he lets it go and moves on—I've won round one.

During the meeting each person makes mini presentations on their ad concepts. I could be wrong but Prescott looks bored. I notice he doesn't ask anyone else to meet him in his office to go over numbers. I know our private meeting has nothing to do with running numbers for the account—my only concern is if he plans to fire me today. If he does I'm screwed. I would be left totally dependent upon Justin, which is the last thing our relationship needs.

Lunch comes quick, and while I'm dreading our private meeting, my stomach is thankful.

"Ms. Brown," the sound of my name leaving his lips makes my traitorous body quiver.

"Yes, Prescott."

"My office is on the 40th floor. Don't keep me waiting."

I need this job, I need this job, I need this job, I keep chanting to myself. I wish I never let the son of a bitch touch me but there's nothing I can do about the past now. Feeling defiant I stop in the cafeteria for a quick bite to eat before heading to his office; no sense in getting fired on an empty stomach.

Stepping off the elevator I notice Prescott's is the only office on the floor. He must truly enjoy solitude. I look around for the nearest exit in case I need to make a quick getaway. I know this meeting is not going to go well. I brace myself for the unexpected and prepare to knock on his door when his voice startles me.

"Come in, Layla."

How the hell does he know I'm here? The bastard's been watching me all this time, how else would he know it's me? I can't spot the camera but the hairs on the back of my neck stand at attention. The thought of being watched creeps me out. I open the door and take a deep breath before crossing the threshold.

Prescott is seated behind his desk with papers scattered around him, "what the fuck are you doing here?" he blurts out.

I didn't expect him to beat around the bush but I also didn't anticipate him going on the attack the second I entered his office.

"I work here."

"Not for long, you can't work here," he says simply, looking up from his papers.

I need this job; I can't let him fire me, not without having the chance to find another job first.

"I just relocated from D.C. for this job, if you fire me now I'll be left with nothing."

"You should have thought about that before you came to work for me. How did you find out I owned this company anyway?"

"I didn't know who you really were until you entered the conference room this morning. Until then I thought your name was William and that you lived in D.C. How was I supposed to know you lied about who you were?"

Prescott pushes off from his desk and starts to pace, "this is what I get for trying something new."

My ears perk up at his comment, "what's that supposed to mean?"

"There are rules to what I do so shit like this doesn't happen," he says, motioning between the two of us. "This is what I get for going outside my group."

"Going outside your group? So what did you and your girl-friend decide to do that night, experiment with black people?"

"Put your race card back in your wallet, this has nothing to do with skin color; I have a specific group of people I usually meet with. We have standards to make sure we are all in the same bracket so shit like this doesn't happen."

"Same bracket! What the fuck do I look like, orphan Annie?"

"I'm not trying to offend you."

"Really? Because everything that comes out of your mouth so far has been offensive!"

"At this point it really doesn't matter. I need you to get your shit and leave, you can't work here."

I was about to respond when we hear a knock at the door.

"Come in," he commands.

Georgina enters his office and I can tell she's a little nervous.

"Hi, I just wanted to stop in and see how things are going. I gave Mr. Bradford Layla's preliminary report and he loves her ideas, she may really be able to save this account."

Smart woman! She can tell Prescott's not happy with her decision to hire me; why else would she be laying it on so thick?

"And when did you send her proposal to James?" he asks leaning against the

corner of his desk.

"As soon as I received your approval to hire her."

Ha! That should be a point in my favor. He probably forgot he gave her the

thumbs-up to bring me on board. She's sharper than I initially expected; she knows something's up. I liked her before but now I've gained a new respect for her.

"Georgina, please excuse me and Ms. Brown for a few more minutes." He's definitely not happy.

"Sure thing," she gives me a little nod of encouragement before leaving his office.

"I don't know how you did it but you've already impressed Georgina, which is no easy task. I'll tell you what; I'll let you work here as long as you keep what happened in D.C. to yourself. If I even hear one whisper throughout the office about anything going on between the two of us, I'll fire you on the spot. Is that understood?"

I loathe this asshole but he has me over a barrel right now. If I lose this job I won't only be out of a paycheck, I'll be out of a place to live.

"You won't have to worry about anything coming out. I wouldn't want anyone in my group to know I once scraped the bottom of the barrel."

The look on Prescott's face is priceless as I leave his office— I'll give myself another point for winning round two!

Chapter 7

WHEN I GET home Justin is happier than ever. His day went a lot better than mine. As soon as I had discovered William was really Jonathan Prescott I couldn't wait to tell Justin. Now, after hearing about his day, for some reason I don't feel like filling him in. When he asks I just tell him my day was uneventful and leave the room to take a shower.

I'm standing in the shower letting the hot water run over me as I try to unwind. For some strange reason I feel the need to protect Prescott's identity, even though the bastard doesn't deserve it. Justin has often questioned me about that night but I have never told him what really happened. If he ever discovered William was truly Jonathan Prescott there's no telling how he would react, and I don't want to find out. By the time I am ready for bed I've made peace with my decision not to tell him; I just hope this doesn't come back to bite me in the ass. That night I toss and turn, replaying my day over and over in my head, until exhaustion takes over and I finally fall asleep.

The rest of my work week goes by in a flash. I spend the majority of my days in meetings. Thankfully my interaction with Prescott has been limited. We haven't had any more one-on-one meetings, which I am grateful for. The few times that I have seen him he remained polite yet distant. While I appreciate him keeping his distance, I still can't keep him off my mind. The image of him tasting me still makes my body shiver. Will I ever get over that night? I find myself thinking about Prescott during sex with Justin and it almost makes sex enjoyable.

Justin and I have settled into a routine of going to work, meeting some place for dinner and then coming home to do more work. Both of our jobs are very demanding. Not a second goes by without one of our phones ringing letting us know we've received some email that needs our immediate attention. This particular weekend my emails have been coming directly from Prescott himself. He's rarely in the office and when he is he barely utters two words to me, yet as soon as I log onto my computer there is always an email waiting from him with a laundry list of items to complete. He must have emailed me over a dozen times asking for numbers and requesting edits to my proposal. He's kept me so busy I haven't had time to hang out with Justin all weekend.

It's yet another Monday morning and I'm getting dressed. Summer is in full swing now and my hair is not happy. The humidity wreaks havoc on it but I do my best to pull it together. Justin comes into the bathroom dressed in one of his best suits.

"You look extra good today," I say, commenting on his attire.

"I've got an important meeting this afternoon. Oh, just to let you know a few of us are going out for drinks this evening so I'll be home a little late."

"That sounds like fun, can I join you?"

"You know I would love that but it's just going to be my colleagues and I don't want you to sit there being bored when we discuss work."

I know I shouldn't be jealous but I am. Outside of Justin and my family I really don't have any friends. It's always so easy for Justin to make friends wherever he goes. It's not that I'm not social; it's just that I always get so tied up with our relationship I never make time for friendships. I keep telling myself Justin is the only friend I need but at times I do wish I had at least one good girlfriend I could call on for advice.

"Well, you all have a good time. I'll probably end up working late anyway," I say, feeling a little disappointed.

"Cool. Well I'll see you when I get home tonight."

Justin pauses in the doorway and I give him a perplexed look. Is he waiting for something?

"Is everything okay?" I ask.

"Well, I've been thinking, now that we are all settled in, maybe it's time for us to meet some new couples in the lifestyle."

Oh God; not this shit again.

"Justin, we haven't even made regular friends since moving here and you're already ready to go out and meet more swingers?"

"You know I am so why are you even asking? Look, I have to get going but make sure you take the next few weekends off. I've got some prospects I want us to meet okay?"

My lips would not form the words to verbalize my agreement so I just nod my head as he walks out the door. Unbelievable! Here I thought he'd given the lifestyle a rest when really he's been scouting out new couples. When is this shit going to get out of his system?! In the few months since my experience with William, or should I say Prescott, I had refused to meet any more couples. Justin kept begging me to give it another try but so far I'd been successful at thwarting his efforts. Once we got the jobs in Chicago and had to focus on moving he gave all talks about swinging a rest but clearly he's ready to delve into the swinger scene in Chicago.

When I finally arrive to my office, Simone, the office manager is waiting for me and I get this uneasy feeling in the pit of my stomach.

"Mr. Prescott wants to see you right away."

Good grief, I just got in. He already dominated my entire weekend. Now he won't even let me have the opportunity to get settled before pouncing on me with more requests.

"Please let him know I'll be right up."

Simone gives me a little wink before leaving my office. At least she understands my pain. She has a no-nonsense personality like Georgina but I'm learning she also has a great sense of humor. By anyone's standards she would be considered pretty but most people don't notice her face. I'm not into women but Simone has an ass that makes both men and women turn their heads.

I grab my notes from the weekend and head to Prescott's office. Approaching his door I feel a nervous energy take over my body. This is the second time I will be meeting with him in his office; hopefully this meeting goes better than the first. His presence still unnerves me. I take a couple of deep breaths before knocking on his door.

"Come in," he says in that commanding tone that I find both sexy and irritating. He makes me wait a few seconds before looking up and acknowledging my presence.

"Ms. Brown, nice of you to finally join me," he says putting extra emphasis on the word finally.

What the hell is that supposed to mean? I arrive thirty minutes early but apparently that still isn't good enough for him. You would think after he kept me working all weekend he would appreciate the extra effort I put in on this campaign. Instead all I receive is his ungrateful attitude.

"You do realize I start work at nine o'clock," Prescott looks down at his watch and shrugs his shoulders.

"Close enough."

Okay its way too early for any type of confrontation. Although I would love to hit him back with a smart remark I decide to try another tactic.

"How can I be of assistance, Mr. Prescott?" I ask with a polite smile pasted on my face.

His face splits into a full blown smile and I can tell I've shocked him with my change in demeanor. That's right, I know how to play nice when I'm ready.

"Mr. Bradford would like to hear three of our top presentations today at two o'clock and your proposal has been selected as one of the top three."

"Really?" I know I have a stupid smile on my face but this is the best news I've received since moving here. I can't help but give myself a mental pat on the back. Being the new girl in the office is already stressful enough. Everyone has complimented me on my work but for Prescott to choose mine as one of the top three in the department is a big deal.

"Will you be ready to present this afternoon?"

"Absolutely," I say, not even attempting to hide my enthusiasm.

"Thank you. That will be all."

I give Prescott a small smile before turning to leave his office. Maybe we can come to some middle ground after all.

Chapter 8

IT'S BEEN A week since the Bradford presentation and I haven't heard a word on how things went. Today's Friday and I would prefer to not go into the weekend without any updates. Prescott's been away on business all week and is returning today. Rumor has it he'll be announcing the winner of the account.

I take extra time in selecting my attire this morning. I choose a black knee length skirt that complements my curves, a navy blue blouse with buttons running down the front and a large black belt. I put on my stiletto heels and make sure my hair is combed back into a trendy ponytail. I still go light with the makeup and select my favorite diamond studded earrings for effect. I look very much the part of the cute and sexy executive. Before leaving this morning Justin stopped to comment on how sexy I look. He's been bugging me all week about getting back into the lifestyle but I've been dodging the conversation. I keep telling him work has me extremely overwhelmed right now and as soon as things slow down we'll talk about it. I don't know how long I can keep him at bay but for right now it seems to be working.

As soon as I arrive at the office the rumor mill is buzzing; I pass some of my colleagues in the hall and overhear that Veronica may have landed the account. Veronica and I never hit it off and if she really did land the account I doubt her ego will let her make it through the door. She is constantly looking for ways to make me look bad and if she wins the contract I know she'll enjoy rubbing it in my face. I pass her in the hallway on the way to my office and notice a fake smile plastered on her face. Its official; I can't stand that woman. I feel like wiping that bullshit smirk off her face but I wouldn't give her the satisfaction of letting her know she's gotten to me.

Before I can make it into my office Carlos, the office flirt, greets me at the door. It's such a shame he acts like a total whore in the office. If it wasn't for his constant flirting I would definitely find him attractive. His family is from Puerto Rico and he has the smooth accent to match. All the ladies go crazy over him, which is understandable, but I still don't feel any sort of attraction to him.

"Hey Layla, have you heard?"

I step around Carlos and get settled in my office, "if you're referring to Veronica winning the contract; yes, I've heard."

I hate it when people approach me first thing in the morning; doesn't anyone have the common courtesy to let you settle in anymore?

I'm not shocked Veronica won, she's really good at what she does; I do wonder where this information came from though. Did Prescott call and let her know she landed the contract? I guess it shouldn't matter yet I'm still pissed. You would think there would be some professional courtesy but I guess that doesn't exist in this office. As soon as Carlos walks out of my office Georgina comes in. Every time I see her she's all perky and extremely upbeat.

"Good morning Layla, I just wanted to let you know we are having a staff meeting in five minutes."

"Okay. I'll be right in." Georgina gives me a big smile before leaving my office. I have a lot of respect for her; she practically runs this place and from what I hear still manages to have a social life.

As I'm walking down the hall to the conference room I overhear some of the girls in the office talking in hushed voices. I hear Prescott's name and immediately slow down. They're gossiping about some ex-girlfriend of his named Melony. Who the hell is Melony? Immediately I wonder if that's the same woman Justin and I met at the restaurant. I know I shouldn't be so damn nosy but I can't help it. I pretend to drop my notebook, taking my time in retrieving it so I can better hear their conversation. The brunette with the thinning hairline is speaking.

"Well, I heard Miss Melony went ballistic when Mr. Prescott told her he only wanted to be friends."

"Friends! I know she's pissed. She's been chasing that man for the past two years," replied the redhead with freckles.

"You know things between Melony and Mr. Prescott have never been the same since they took some trip out of town a few months ago. She's been working over-time to win him back ever since. Jason from security told me she even showed up half dressed to his condo with dinner but two minutes later she was getting off the elevator, pissed off, with the same dinner bag in her hand."

Damn! How does the brunette know so much about Prescott's personal life I wonder? These women must monitor his activities like hawks!

"Is he dating anyone else?" asks the redhead.

"Not that anyone can tell. All I know is that it's no longer official between them and Miss Melony is even further from getting that ring she so desperately wants from him."

I wonder if they broke up after meeting Justin and I? Hell, I don't even know if this is the same girl Justin and I met. Of course the woman I met went by the name of Angela, but if Prescott used a fake name it would stand to reason that Angela used one as well. Maybe seeing her with Justin really did get to him after all. Once again, I have questions but no way of getting any answers. Get a grip Layla, Prescott's personal life is none of your business. Besides, I need to focus on how I'm going to talk Justin out of joining the swinger scene in Chicago, not Prescott's dating life.

I enter the conference room and all of the executive staff is gathered around the large conference room table. As with any meeting that Prescott attends, Veronica makes sure she is seated towards the head of the table near his chair. When Prescott walks in I see her smile brightly; this woman is pathetic! Prescott approaches his seat and she actually pulls it out for him. She can't be serious. I'm all for the feminist agenda but now we're pulling out chairs for men? I wonder how little Miss Uppity would feel if she knew he had tasted me and loved it, I think to myself with a smile.

Clearing his voice Prescott calls for everyone's attention.

"I apologize for the late notice for this meeting but I received some great news that I want to share with everyone. As you all know we were in danger of losing the Bradford account, which is one of our biggest accounts to date. Thanks to all of your hard work over these last few weeks, not only have we saved the account, but we were able to renew the contract for the next two years."

This is exciting news but from the tone in his voice he might as well be reading aloud from a dictionary. Anyone can tell he is a man who is all about business but if you look past the expensive suit and power stare he doesn't look like he could give a rat's ass about the world of marketing. Everyone in the office must be accustomed to his lack of enthusiasm because they all burst into applause.

"All of you worked very hard but I must give a special thank you to our newest team member, Ms. Layla Brown."

Oh shit, me!

"Layla, Mr. Bradford chose to go with your proposal. He was thoroughly impressed with your ideas and looks forward to working with you. Your budget proposal and attention to detail really helped us save this account. I want you to know I genuinely appreciate all of the hard work you put in, especially since you were thrown into the mix at the last minute."

If I were white my cheeks would probably be bright red by now. His words were kind but they lacked sincerity. He's not fooling me. I know he didn't want me to be the one to save this account—now he can't justify firing me, which is exactly what he's wanted to do since I stepped foot into this office. Everyone around me is looking and waiting for me to say something. I am speechless. My colleagues start chanting "speech, speech, speech." Everyone except for Veronica of course.

"Um... wow, this is totally unexpected. I thank you for the opportunity to work here and I thank all of my new colleagues. You all have been very supportive and helpful in getting me started and up to speed on this project."

I don't really mean that shit. No one but Carlos even offered any real assistance but when you're in a meeting like this you never want to be viewed as the type of person who takes all of the credit, even if it's well deserved. Everyone applauds and when I look up I see Prescott's eyes are locked in on me. His stare is so intoxicating yet intimidating at the same time. I wish I knew what he was thinking.

He nods his head in what I assume is approval before continuing.

"I'm treating everyone to happy hour after work tonight. And as a very special bonus I'm flying everyone to Jamaica on Monday for a week-long vacation. Ms. Sparks thinks you all deserve a break," he says, in an impassive tone.

Does anything excite Prescott? Everyone in the office is excited by the news. People are hugging and high-fiving each another while he stands there with a very stoic expression on his face. Personally, I can't hide my smile. A week in Jamaica is exactly what I need after these intense few weeks.

"Please everyone calm down, and take your seats." Prescott is trying to regain order in the room but everyone is excited about our upcoming vacation. He whistles and everyone finally stops talking and gives him their undivided attention.

"Before anyone asks; no, this does not count as your personal vacation time, and yes, this is a company-sponsored trip. You are allowed to bring one guest free of charge. We are leaving Monday morning so please take the weekend to prepare. This trip is for you all to relax and enjoy yourselves so we will probably only have one or two short meetings within the week. Amanda and Simone will provide everyone with all of the details so please check your email; again thank you all for your hard work on this project."

We briefly make eye contact, holding each other's attention before being pulled into the mix with everyone in the room.

I gather my things and head to the door leaving all of the ruckus in the conference room behind. I've got a lot of details to wrap up before leaving for Jamaica. Justin and I always talked about going there after finals. I know it will be tough for him to take time off of work since he's just started but hopefully his company will be flexible. I'm so excited about the news I decide to give him a call on his cell. It only rings twice before the line is picked up.

"Hello?" I say, thrown off by the silence on the other end.

"Who's this?" A woman's voice says in response.

I immediately feel myself get defensive, "where is Justin?" I probably shouldn't be rude before getting details but my anger is swift. Just hearing another woman on the other end of his phone pisses me off.

"May I ask who's calling?"

She's asking me?! "This is his girlfriend, who are you?"

"Girlfriend? Are you sure you have the right number?"

What! Damn right I have the right number. "Excuse me but this cell phone belongs to my boyfriend Justin—where is he?"

"He stepped out to buy me lunch. He does that every day. It's funny; I've had lunch and sometimes dinner with Justin but he never once mentioned having a girlfriend."

Of all the fucking nerve! "Well now you know and you should also know we live together." That should shut her up!

"Well I guess he does need a place to live since he just moved here."

"What's that supposed to mean?"

"Exactly what it sounds like. If I were you I wouldn't count on him for his half of the rent much longer—have a nice day," she says hanging up his phone.

My body heat rises from all of the anger boiling up inside. I want answers and I want them fucking now! Is Justin really cheating on me? We haven't even been in Chicago that long; he couldn't possibly be cheating on me. I know we've been a little distant but it's only because we are both working long hours. Despite the hours, I've done my best to make time to have sex with him. There has to be some rational explanation for this.

Lost in thought, I don't hear Prescott enter my office. He takes one look at my face and closes the door behind him before walking over to my desk and handing me a tissue. I have a death grip on the phone but that doesn't stop him from prying it out of my hands.

"Another woman just answered his phone," I mumble in disbelief.

The look on Prescott's face is priceless. It's clear my tear-streaked face is making him uncomfortable. I never would have expected him to try to comfort me yet here he is in my office handing me tissue.

"It's not my place, but if you're still with that same guy Justin I met in D.C., it's time for you to get rid of him and move on."

"I don't want anyone else," I mumble but then I realize that's a lie. Part of me wants the man standing in front of me. The thought of me wanting Prescott scares me. I grab another tissue dabbing my eyes and move away from him—I need space. "Is there something that you needed?" I ask, trying to pull myself together.

He looks uncomfortable. "No. I just wanted to stop by and let you know Bradford would like for you to personally handle all of the details on his account."

I don't believe him for one second. That's not the reason he came into my office—clearly him catching me crying has thrown him off.

"I'll be sure to let Mr. Bradford know I'll be his primary source of contact. Was there anything else?"

He pauses then shakes his head no. I've scared him off.

"I'll let you get back to work."

Prescott moves towards the door and glances back at me as if he wants to say more but changes his mind. Instead he just gives me a slight nod and leaves my office.

I spend the remainder of the afternoon tying up loose ends. Part of me wants to try dialing Justin again but in the end I decide to wait and talk to him when I get home. Just about all of our relationship issues revolve around sex and there's nothing I can do about that over the phone so putting our talk off for when I get home is probably best.

"Hey, everything okay?"

Startled, I look up from the pile of papers on my desk; what the hell is it with everyone in this office not knocking? Carlos is standing in front of me with a huge grin on his face. I wonder how much pussy he gets with that smile of his? I still think he's sleazy but he has a certain charm about him that makes him tolerable.

"Hey Carlos, I didn't hear you come in. What's up?"

"Nothing, I just wanted to see if you wanted to walk down to Hancock's with the rest of us. We are getting ready to leave in a few minutes." Damn, I hadn't even realized so much time had already passed.

"Sure, I'll be down in five minutes, I just have a few things to wrap up."

"Cool, I'll see you downstairs." Carlos gives me a little wink before leaving my office.

Chapter 9

AS IT TURNS out, when Carlos asked if I wanted to walk to Hancock's with the rest of "us" he really meant himself. When the two of us arrive the place is packed. It seems like everyone in the city must come to Hancock's after work.

Prescott had his personal assistant Loraine reserve the entire VIP section for the group. Once we're seated Carlos gets the attention of a waitress to order us a round of drinks. As soon as she looks at him I can see she is mesmerized. Carlos must get so much pussy thrown at him I'm sure he finds it odd that I don't give in to his advances.

I scope out the room and conclude Hancock's is a very nice upscale bar. It has a panoramic view of downtown Chicago. The décor is very modern and sleek with a few vintage accents dispersed throughout. White leather sectionals can be found in secluded areas for more intimate seating. The bar is located in the middle of the lounge with just about every type of alcohol imaginable on display. Maybe when Justin and I finally have some down time I can bring him here for drinks after work. There are a lot of young professionals here and I know this is just the type of place he would love to hang out in.

"Here you go Layla, one lemon drop martini for the woman of the hour."

I politely accept my drink while continuing my scan of the room. I notice what looks to be a band setting up on the other end of the floor. I love live music. Maybe it will help me relax. I still feel overwhelmed by this afternoon's events. I'm happy my proposal has been accepted but as for Justin, I know I will have to deal with him as soon as I get home tonight. He has a lot of explaining to do.

Some of the women from the office spot Carlos and I sitting together and decide to join us. The women surround him like a swarm of bees. I feel uncomfortable watching this pitiful display of flirting. These women look desperate and I don't want to be seen with them. I refuse to spend my evening watching them shamelessly flirt. Before Carlos can object I excuse myself and search the room for another place to sit. I see one of my co-workers Simone in a corner and decide to head in her direction; she's always nice to me.

"Hi Simone, is anyone sitting here?" I know it shouldn't be a big deal but I've never been really good at making new friends. I feel nervous just asking to sit here which is ridiculous.

"Have a seat girl. Have you met Pamela and Stephanie?"

I smile at the other two ladies. We all shake hands and I try to make myself feel comfortable. I've seen Pamela once or twice around the office. She rarely makes eye contact. Her mousy brown hair, pale skin and fragile frame make her look vulnerable. Stephanie is the complete opposite. She has a beautiful face but a very masculine presence. Everything about her appearance screams lesbian.

"So does everyone from the office come here often?" I ask, trying to make small talk.

Stephanie rolls her eyes, "unfortunately, yes," she says in a dry tone.

"I t-take it you don't like it here?" Whoa, I need to watch myself, I just slurred my words.

"What's not to like, a bunch of fake-ass people from corporate America getting drunk and handing each other business cards like it's going out of style." I laugh at her blunt remark and immediately decide I like her.

"It's not that bad," Simone chimes in, "besides, I've met some really cool guys here."

"Oh please," says Stephanie, "the only thing you walk out with from here is a brand new one-night-stand!"

"To hell with you bitch! Sometimes I may keep them around for two nights, thank you very much!"

We all start to laugh hysterically. This is what I've been missing; time with the girls. The band is in high gear now and we are swaying to the music and enjoying our drinks. I notice Simone is actively scanning the room. I wonder what she's searching for.

"Now look at that shit!"

"What?" everyone asks at once.

"Look at how he's dancing with that woman. They need to get a fucking room!" I look over to where she's pointing and my heart sinks into the pit of my stomach. Justin is on the dance floor grinding up against some redheaded woman. I must be staring because I can feel Pamela, Stephanie and Simone's eyes all on me.

"You okay Layla?" asks Simone "you look like you just saw a ghost!"

"No, I haven't seen a ghost, just my boyfriend who looks like he's lost his damn mind."

"What?!" They all shout in unison.

"Excuse me, I'll be right back."

I get up and immediately approach Justin. My stomach feels sick and I know this is not going to end well. How could he do this to me? I wonder if this is the same woman I talked to earlier. If it is I would be happy to give her a piece of my mind especially since I already told her he has a girlfriend.

As soon as Justin spots me he stops dancing. I'm sure he can see I'm fucking furious! This is about to get ugly.

"Justin, what the hell is going on?! Who is this?" I say pointing at the redhead in disgust.

"What are you doing here?" he asks, clearly shocked. I'm sure he never imagined running into me at a bar.

"Never mind what I'm doing here, who the hell is she?"

"Layla, this is my co-worker Sylvia, Sylvia, this is Layla." Did he just try to introduce us as if him grinding up on her is no big deal? I've given Justin a lot of leeway in our relationship, but this time he's gone too far.

"We need to talk—in private" I demand.

I gesture for him to lead the way and we walk off the dance floor leaving Red behind. We walk over to the restrooms located in a quiet corridor away from the crowd.

"Justin, what the hell is going on? Is that the same woman you had answering your phone this afternoon?"

"Layla," he says cautiously, "there is no easy way to say this. I know you love me and please know I care about you deeply, but I feel like our relationship has run its course. I've tried but to be honest I don't love you anymore, not the way I used to." He lowers his head a little, looking up at me waiting for my reaction.

My vision becomes blurry from the water pooling in my eyes. My heart is racing and I feel like I can barely breathe. I have to keep reminding myself to breathe.

"Justin, I've given my all to you. I love you so much that I did things with you and for you I would have never done if I thought you would leave me. When we entered the lifestyle together, you told me if I did that one thing for you, you would never leave me. I did it and now you're still leaving?!" My voice comes out at a higher pitch as I work to keep my composure.

He sighs as if I'm draining him.

"I honestly thought swinging with you would help rev up our sex life, but truthfully, it didn't."

I feel an anger that I've never felt before rising in my body as I fight for self-control. Every bad thing any man has ever done to hurt me starts racing through my mind. Don't lose control here in front of everyone Layla, don't lose control, don't lose control. I keep repeating this in my mind over and over again as Justin continues to speak.

"Layla, we aren't sexually compatible and although you're a great person, if we stayed together I would have continued to cheat on you and we both deserve better than that. I think I have something special with Sylvia and I need to see it through."

"What? You two are in a relationship!?"

"Layla, it doesn't matter now, I'm trying to do the right thing by you, by giving you your freedom. Don't worry, I will have all my stuff moved out by the end of the weekend; Sylvia needs a roommate so we're going to move in together."

I shake my head involuntarily, "Justin, our parents think we are getting married. How could you do this to us?"

"Layla, sometimes people fall in love and sometimes they fall out of love. It turns out I fell out of love with you. You are beautiful but I need more. I need a woman who doesn't cringe every time I touch her."

"You know I've been working on that. You said yourself that I was getting better," I say with an desperate ache in my voice I wish I couldn't hear.

"What do you want me to say? I'm a man and I need more. I'm not your fucking cousin but I feel like I'm forever getting punished for his shit! That shit happened twenty years ago and you're still fucked up over it. I don't know if you will ever change and I can't wait around to find out. I don't have the patience to train you in bed any more so you're going to have to find someone who wants deal with all of your issues. What happened to you sucks, but you have to get over that shit if you want to keep a man, especially if you want to keep a man like me."

I stare at Justin, speechless. I know I had been chanting something about not losing control in my head but I forget the words. I slowly step back, slipping off my shoes. I subtly pick up each shoe and before he even knows what's coming I clock him on the head with my stiletto heels. Who knew my shoes would have more than one purpose? I continue to hit him over and over with both shoes in my hands, my arms flaying in the air. I hear a lot of commotion from behind me but pay no attention to anything except the task at hand; causing Justin as much pain as he has caused me. I want this bastard to look as fucked up as I feel. Maybe then the whole world will see what a piece of shit he is. Justin tries to cover his head but I still see blood running down his face. This gives me great pleasure as I continue to beat the shit out of him. I know only seconds have passed but I feel like everything is happening in slow motion. I hear people in the background calling my name and then I feel someone's arms around my waist as they pick me up mid-air. I'm actually glad I have more height. I use my feet to kick Justin square in his jaw.

"Layla, what the fuck are you doing?" Strong arms hold onto me, pulling me towards the rear exit. My body is wildly bucking, trying to break free of the stranger's grasp.

"Layla, what the fuck was that?!" The stranger holding me is still shouting but I'm still too pumped up to speak. All I know is that I'm in the arms of a very angry man.

My mystery man kicks open the back door. Finally outside he puts me down on the warm concrete floor and I notice that I'm barefoot, still holding my heels in my hands. He turns me around and I come face to face with Prescott. All I see is bright red skin, tousled brown hair and angry blue eyes.

"Layla, what the fuck was that!?" Prescott is hysterical and by all appearances he seems to be even angrier than I am, which I find astounding considering I still feel like ripping Justin's eyes out. Despite my adrenaline rush I find Prescott's anger very intimidating.

"I don't want to talk about it," I say, hoping he'll leave me alone.

"You don't want to talk about it? You should have thought about that before you decided to approach Justin and turn into the goddamn Hulk!"

I feel like a child being disciplined by an angry parent. His booming voice makes me pause and a moment of clarity seeps in.

"Listen," he says, lowering his voice slightly, "I don't know what the fuck is going on with you two, but whatever it is, it better be over. I don't want to even hear you hint about ever being with him again."

My moment of clarity is gone and anger once again takes over. Of course my relationship with Justin is over after tonight, but that doesn't give Prescott the right to order me around.

"You can't order me to end my relationship."

"Like hell I can't! I know you like to argue but don't you dare even think of fucking with me tonight Layla, I could fucking strangle your ass for making such a scene in there."

"You don't know what he said to me."

"I don't give a shit about what he said to you. Your behavior in there was unacceptable! You've not only embarrassed yourself but you've embarrassed the entire company as well. If you weren't such a good employee I would fucking fire your ass right now!"

"Go ahead and fire me, I don't give a shit!"

"Don't fucking tempt me Layla, because I just may do it!"

During our screaming match outside neither one of us notice the police pull up in their squad cars. Prescott's blue eyes grow even wider as the cops approach us. Oh shit! I've never been arrested before.

"Ms. Layla Brown?" one of the officers asks as he approaches us.

Prescott looks over at me, "don't fucking speak unless I tell you to" and leaves me standing alone as he walks off to speak with the officer.

I'm pacing back and forth wondering if I'm going to be arrested when I see Stephanie, Pamela, Georgina and Simone looking at me in disbelief. No doubt I will be the talk of the office now.

After a few minutes with the officer, Prescott walks back towards me and the cops leave the scene. Why are they leaving? I should be arrested for what I've done. At this point I don't care. I'm willing to accept full responsibility for my actions. I feel no remorse for hitting Justin. When Prescott reaches me he hunches down so we are both at eye level.

"You are to head straight home. I'm giving you a direct order to stay the fuck away from Justin or next time I will not stop them from hauling your ass to jail."

I know I should be thankful for whatever he did on my behalf but I'm pissed. Who the hell is he to tell me what to do? He doesn't know anything about me or Justin or what that son of a bitch has put me through. I will stay away from Justin but for my own personal reasons, not his. As much as I would love to avoid Justin there's one big problem; we still live together. I wonder what Prescott has to say about that.

"Although I have no intentions of ever speaking to Justin again it's going to be hard since we still live together," I say with a hint of sarcasm.

"I'll make sure he doesn't come home tonight. First thing in the morning I want you on the first flight out to Jamaica. While you're gone he should have plenty of time to move out."

"I won't be ready to fly out in the morning, I have a ton of things to do and arrangements to make." Who the hell does he think he is?

"Layla, I don't think you fucking heard me. I want your ass on the first flight out to Jamaica in the morning. This is not a negotiation, this is a direct order and if you even think of disobeying me I will personally call the cops back and have your ass arrested tonight."

"Who the hell do you think you are? Just because you're my boss that doesn't give you the right to order me around," I say yelling at the top of my lungs.

"Layla Brown, if you know what's good for you, you wouldn't dare try to disobey me tonight. Someone is going to escort you home and you will be on the first flight out in the morning, that's the end of this fucking conversation. Disobey my orders and I'll show you why every woman is this country calls me MR. PRESCOTT!"

Prescott walks away from me towards Georgina, leaving me standing in shock. His last comment sent chills through my body. I pace up and down the side-walk while Prescott and Georgina look to be in a very heated conversation, no doubt discussing me and my actions tonight.

Once my adrenaline dissipates the realization of what has happened finally hits me. How did I let Justin get me to the point where I self-destructed in a public place? I've never done anything like this before. When my parents hear about this they are going to flip out. My eyes swell up with water again and I silently start to cry. I turn my head—not wanting the others to see my face—as everything I was feeling earlier comes rushing in. At the sight of me crying, Stephanie, Pamela and Simone all crowd around me, and give me a group hug. No longer able to hold anything back I cry louder and louder as I release all of the pain and anguish from Justin's hurtful words out of my system. At some point Prescott must have summoned his driver; I hadn't noticed when the black Lincoln drove up to the curb. The ladies step aside as he lifts me up and puts me in the back seat of the car.

"Georgina, make sure she gets home safely and get her anything she needs."

"Of course, Jonathan."

I look up and I see all of the girls getting into the car and I realize none of them have left my side. The driver closes the door and I see Prescott give me one last look before heading back inside. I must look pathetic to him right now.

"How do you feel, Layla?" Pamela asks.

"Broken, my heart feels like it's literally broken," and I continue to cry all the way home.

Chapter 10

STEPHANIE AND PAMELA are holding each of my arms as we make our way into the building. It's weird, I wasn't hurt in the altercation but my entire body feels like I've been at war. Georgina is going through my purse in search of my keys and finally finds them as we get off the elevator. Before she can ask I mutter my apartment number. Once inside Stephanie and Pamela place me on the couch while Simone goes rummaging through my kitchen cabinets.

"What are you looking for?" I ask Simone.

"Liquor!"

"Layla doesn't need a drink right now, she needs rest," Pamela says in a disapproving tone.

"Are you fucking crazy?! She just watched her boyfriend get with another woman right in front of her eyes. If that doesn't warrant a good drink then I don't know what does!"

"Ex," I mutter.

"What's that?" asks Simone.

"He is officially my ex-boyfriend," I reply taking a deep breath.

Since I'm going to have to get used to referring to Justin as my ex, I mind as well start now.

Stephanie sits next to me and puts her arms around my shoulder.

"Layla, I know it's hard when a relationship ends but I say good riddance. You don't need a man like that in your life."

Georgina steps forward, bringing me a glass of water and two Tylenol.

"So what made you go all Madea on his ass anyway?" Georgina's question makes me laugh a little, even though I don't want to.

"Not only did I catch his ass cheating but he had the audacity to act as if I was the cause of his infidelity. He took that moment to tell me our relationship was over, along with some other hurtful things."

"What exactly did he say?" Georgina asks, chomping on some snacks. These women surely do know how to raid someone's cabinets.

I quickly recounted Justin's words to me about his cheating, my being horrible in bed, him no longer having the patience with me sexually and my needing to get over what happened to me as a child. As I told my story I saw fury in each of their faces. I know it's a good thing we left the club because if he was near any of these women right now, I'm pretty sure there would have been a round two.

"Well, all I know is that if I ever see that no-good motherfucker in the street, I would enjoy pushing his ass into traffic." Everyone erupts in laughter at Stephanie's candid remark and I realize how happy I am not to be alone tonight.

"What time is it?" asks Pamela, I look down at my watch, damn, I didn't realize so much time had passed.

"It's ten o'clock."

When Pamela hears the time I can't help but notice a panicked expression on her face.

"Layla, do you mind if I crash here tonight?" I wonder why she's so nervous about the time; it's not that late.

"Of course you can stay. I would love the company since Justin is obviously not coming home tonight."

"Hey, let's all crash and have a girl's sleepover!" Georgina is all smiles. I get the feeling she too is in need of some female camaraderie.

"Sleepover it is," I announce, heading towards my linen closet to take out some extra sheets, comforters and pillows. When I'm alone in the hallway I hear all of the girls laughing and sharing war stories about bad break-ups. This is what I've been missing, I think to myself. I never really hung around girls in college. Justin became my whole world. I let myself get so wrapped up in his world and trying to do things that pleased him I never took time out to do the things I like to do. I never made Justin do things that pleased me. If he didn't like something I liked, we just didn't do it. Maybe it's a good thing he's out of my life. I'm determined to make new friends and this time around I'm going to do things my way.

We all sit around in my living room drinking and discussing past relationships. I start thinking about my first time with Justin and I no longer feel like laughing. The realization that it's really over still hurts. Even after everything, it's still a hard pill to swallow. Justin is all I've really known and the thought of starting over is scary. I just always assumed he was the one, the one I would spend the rest of my life with. I guess the universe has different plans for me.

"Layla," Pamela calls my name and I look up at her teary-eyed feeling like a fool for crying over a man who clearly doesn't love me.

"Why are you so caught up on Justin? The man is clearly an ass."

"Believe me I know that now but that doesn't stop what he did from hurting. I thought we were going to get married. I thought he was my happily ever after."

"We've all thought that about some guy at one point in our lives but you'll get over it and before you know it you'll have some new dick," Georgina says with a smile.

"I seriously doubt that, I'm not very good in that department."
Georgina looks at me in disbelief.

"How could you be bad at sex?"

"Let's just say I had a bad introduction into the world of sex that has left me pretty fucked up."

"Did something happen to you?" Stephanie asks.

"Yes, but I'm sure you all don't want to hear about that. Besides, it was a long time ago and I prefer to forget about it."

"Who hurt you?" I just told everyone I don't want to talk about it but that doesn't stop Stephanie from asking more questions.

"Let's just say I occasionally have flashbacks that take me back to a bad time in my life."

"Probably a time when you slept with a guy who couldn't fuck," Georgina says laughing.

"You're probably right," Simone says. "Pretty boys usually aren't good in bed. I learned that lesson all through college."

"Would you all shut up!" Stephanie shouts, looking around the room at everyone. "Layla, what are your flashbacks about?"

I don't feel like going into my fucked up story but I know that's where this conversation is heading.

"I'm guessing this has something to do with him telling you to get over your childhood?" I don't answer Stephanie's question.

"Look, Layla, we are trying to help you but we can't if you don't tell us what's going on." I take a deep breath hoping I can get this out as quickly as possible.

"I was molested by one of my cousins when I was five and sometimes I have flashbacks during sex and I cry. You have no idea what it's like to be with a man and not be able to complete the act because you're in the midst of some breakdown."

"So you're crying because you were molested?"

"Georgina!" Everyone screams her name, appalled at how cold and callous she sounds.

"What?! Clearly Layla doesn't know what real pain is. Try being gang-raped by half of the fucking football team in high school and then tell me about sexual abuse!"

"You're not the only one who has been raped Georgina, so don't take that shit out on Layla," Stephanie says calmly.

I'm looking at Georgina and Stephanie in amazement, trying to digest their confessions. They are staring at each other, daring the other to say another word.

"Why are you two mad at each other? We really need to be mad at those fucked up men who did this, not each other!" Simone says, trying to be our voice of reason.

"Well, since we are all sharing, Pamela, do you have anything to bring to the table?" Georgina asks her question so casually we might as well be swapping recipes.

"I was molested by my uncle," Pamela quietly admits.

"Well I guess that leaves you Simone. Anything you wish to share?"

"Georgina, you can be a real bitch sometimes you know that!" Stephanie says, glaring at her. Something is up between those two, we may be off the clock but I still wouldn't call the VP of the company I work for a bitch. Then again most people wouldn't sit around having conversations like the one we are now having with co-workers.

"What?! We are obviously all fucked-up in one way or the other so let's go ahead and get the shit out in the open."

"No," Simone says solemnly, "I haven't been raped or molested. It was my mother who suffered and because she suffered I had to suffer as well—you happy?"

We all look around the room at each other in silence. We are like a group of sexual misfits.

"This is really fucked up," I say, and every woman nods her head in agreement. I knew the statistics on women being sexually abused were high but this is crazy. Here we are, five different women of different races from different backgrounds and four out of five of us have been wronged in one way or another. Georgina stands up with her hands on her waist.

"Where are you going?" I ask.

"To find something stronger to drink, we're clearly going to need it tonight!"

Georgina comes back with a bottle of Hennessey and shot glasses.
I didn't even know Justin kept so much alcohol in the house. We
all sit around on the living room floor in a circle taking shots and
exchanging stories about our hurtful pasts.

"Can I ask a personal question?"

Stephanie looks at me and laughs.

"More personal than everything we've already shared with
each other here tonight? Ask away."

"Do any of you have healthy relationships?" No one answers
but by the expression on everyone's face I pretty much gather the
answer is no. None of us are in healthy relationships. I knew it! I
will probably be alone and fucked up for life.

"Well, for those of you who didn't know, I'm a lesbian," Stephanie announces. To be honest the news doesn't surprise me since
she works overtime on dressing like a man. Stephanie is probably
the prettiest out of us all but it's hard to tell with the way she
dresses. She has a beautiful caramel complexion with long wavy
hair that comes past her shoulders. If I had hair like that I would
wear it out almost every day. Not Stephanie though. She wears
her hair in a tight bun every day and is always dressed in very
masculine attire that hides her very curvy and shapely figure. I'm
tempted to ask her if she has always been a lesbian but refrain.
Somehow I think in Stephanie's case her being a lesbian is more
of a choice than natural instinct, especially since I've never seen
her look twice at another woman.

I look over at Simone and I can't determine if the alcohol has
her fucked up or if she is in a dark mood. She opens her mouth to
speak but stops several times before finally saying what has been
plaguing her mind.

"Although I was never raped or molested, watching my mom
go through all of the changes was painful enough. I don't know who
my dad is, but apparently I look like him and she has reminded me
of that every day. Sometimes I think it would have been easier on us
both if she didn't have me but my family doesn't believe in abor-
tions. Growing up with her I felt like I was a weaker version of

her abuser and what she couldn't do to him, she did to me. Every time she thought about fighting back it was me who got the lashes, not him. I grew up in a household with no love and to tell you the truth I have no interest in finding love."

Simone's story brings tears to my eyes. I feel for her and somehow my issues with Justin don't seem that bad.

"Well, my therapist says being gang-raped is the reason why I'm very promiscuous. In other words, I like to fuck... come to think of it I like to fuck a lot," Georgina admits.

"I have problems being intimate with one person, how do you manage so many partners?" I ask, a little astonished.

"I like what I like. Maybe it's because of the rape, maybe not. It doesn't matter because I'm fine now."

"Don't you want to be in a healthy relationship?"

"I don't want a relationship of any kind. I like to fuck and when I'm done I like to be left alone. I'm not into all of that romantic shit. I don't have time for it in my life. I'm a self-made woman who learned to deal with my issues on my own," she says resolutely.

"Counseling didn't work?" I'm hoping she doesn't say no. I was deprived of counseling when my parents discovered my abuse and I've secretly always resented them for denying me help.

"Oh please. My parents stuck me in every counseling facility they could find on both the east and west coasts and you know what I found out?"

"What?" we all ask in unison.

"Some of those counselors are more fucked up than I am." Her admission shows there are some real scars there. Georgina plays tough but I can tell deep down she is lost and scared. Hell, we all are. I've been molested by my cousin, Georgina and Stephanie have been raped, Pamela was molested by her uncle and Simone is the product of rape. Dr. Phil could go into retirement dealing with the five of us.

I never imagined meeting one person I could discuss my past with let alone four different women. I know my situation is not unique. I look around the room, amazed by our stories. We're all silent; taking in everything that's been shared. Stephanie, Pamela and Georgina are all sprawled out on the floor. I opt to stretch out on the couch and Pamela is sitting in an arm chair with a cushion propping her head up. I would never have imagined that these beautiful capable women could have such dark pasts that mirror my own.

"I'm so sorry you didn't find help in therapy Georgina. Sometimes I've thought about talking to someone but I just don't see how it will help my sex life."

"I don't need your sympathy Layla. I don't even cry about what happened to me anymore. I would think getting over being molested is a hell of a lot easier than getting over rape. If I'm okay you should really toughen up and learn to deal with it as well."

"What!" I brace myself for my second altercation of the night. "Bitch, don't you tell me to fucking toughen up! You have no idea what it's like to have your family look at you as if what happened is your own fault. I was five and my innocence was stolen from me by a horny, disgusting teenager. Do you know what it's like to see your abuser every fucking Easter, Thanksgiving and Christmas?! Having everyone tiptoeing around the elephant in the room because one side of the family doesn't want to offend the other? Fuck you! I was robbed of my innocence the same as you. Being molested by someone who is supposed to love and protect you, finding out about sexual intimacy through a family member, is disgusting! What should be pleasurable is now full of pain for me and I don't know if I will ever have a normal fucking relationship again! I'm sorry you were raped, I'm sorry for everyone in this room, but don't compare me to you and tell me to toughen up! We can't all be a cold and callous bitch like you Georgina!" Now I understand why Stephanie didn't hesitate to call her a bitch.

"Everyone calm down," screams Stephanie.

"What is wrong with you two? We should be here comforting each other, not trying to size up whose story is worse than the other. We've all been abused in one way or the other. That's the bottom line, and as far as I'm concerned, that's all that matters."

I know what Stephanie is saying makes sense but I'm still pissed at Georgina. Georgina looks around at all of us and stands, heading back into the kitchen. I swear I hear her murmur something about us being a bunch of weak bitches on her way to the kitchen. Knowing what I know about her from tonight, she's probably looking for yet another bottle of liquor. After a few minutes pass by Pamela is the first to speak. "What's Georgina doing?" she asks.

The rise and fall of my chest starts to slow and I begin to calm down.

"I'll go check on her," I announce.

"I'll come with you, I don't need you two fighting in the kitchen!" Stephanie says as she joins me. At first I don't see her anywhere but then I catch a glimpse of her kneeling on the floor with a knife in her hand.

"Georgina, what the fuck are you doing?!" I shout. I rush over to her, grabbing the knife out of her hand and pull her into my arms. She holds me tightly crying into my shoulder.

"I'm so sorry, Layla, you're right, I am such a bitch! I hate myself. I hate the things I do and I hate the things I say but sometimes I don't know how to stop! I feel like it would be easier if everything was just over. I just want it all to be over!"

I hold Georgina in my arms rocking her back and forth trying to calm and sooth her pain. Pamela and Simone rush into the kitchen and join us all on the floor. They look at the knife on the floor and then at Georgina and are quickly able to sum up the situation. I don't let Georgina go; I just continue to rock her from side to side while she cries in my arms. Her soft sobs finally end with hiccups and I can tell she has no more tears to release. When I can tell her breathing has returned to its normal rhythm I release her from my arms, wiping the tears from her face.

"I know you are used to being strong but we are all here and we all understand your pain in one way or another. You don't have to be strong all the time. It's okay to let go."

"Layla, I'm so sorry about everything I said. Sometimes I'm just so angry I verbally assault people who don't deserve it."

"Girl, we've all been there."

"Who wants another round?" asks Simone.

We all look up and laugh. We have bonded on my kitchen floor and I know I will care for these women for the rest of my life.

Chapter 11

MY HEAD HURTS. The violent throbbing from my temple wakes me up. I've never suffered this much from a hangover. Suddenly I realize the vibration from my cell phone safely hidden under my pillow is the cause for my excess discomfort. I look around the living room and everyone is still passed out. Who the hell is calling me at this ungodly hour? I don't recognize the number but decide to answer it anyway.

"Hello."

"Layla, it's me, Jonathan." My mind is still a little fuzzy from all the drinks as I try to recollect a Jonathan from my memory.

Oh shit!

"Mr. Prescott?"

"Yes."

Hearing his voice reminds me of last night's events. Prescott is the last person I thought about talking to this morning. I feel both ashamed and embarrassed by my behavior but I know I better get this conversation over with. He probably has a lot to say but I'm hoping the words "you're fired" never leave his mouth.

All the girls are still asleep all over my living room floor so I head into my office closing the door, careful not to disturb them. I take a second to clear my throat before I start damage control.

"Mr. Prescott, I can't begin to apologize for my behavior last night. Please be assured I have never done anything like that nor will it ever happen again."

"No need. I'm not calling to discuss last night's events. I just want to make sure you're packed. The car to the airport should arrive in an hour; make sure you're packed and ready to go."

Normally no one would have to convince me to take a free vacation but I'm not convinced the timing is right. I have so much to straighten out here. Justin and I haven't even talked.

"Prescott, I heard what you said loud and clear last night but now is not the time for me to take a vacation. All of Justin's things are still here and we have some personal things we need to figure out before I leave."

"All of the details have already been arranged. Justin will enter the apartment with a security escort and remove his personal belongings while you are away."

It's only six o'clock and he's already coordinated moving arrangements for Justin? Doesn't he know anything about boundaries?

"Prescott, you can't just step into my personal life and start running things. I'm a grown woman and I can handle this situation on my own without your interference."

"Layla, I think you showed everyone what type of adult you are last night. I'm not going to debate this with you. If I have to pick you up and remove you from the apartment myself I will do it. When Justin comes to move out you are not to be there, end of discussion."

"You can't tell me what to do outside of company hours!" I yell back at him. I don't know how he does it but Prescott can get my blood boiling faster than anyone I know.

"Layla, don't fuck with me this morning! Your bullshit has already cost me enough money. Just do what you're told for once in your life."

Now that's funny! I usually do what I'm told but with Prescott I'm always ready for battle.

"Look, I'm sorry for the inconvenience last night's display caused you and the company but how exactly did I cost you money?"

"I agreed to put Justin up in a fully furnished apartment for one year if he agreed to not press charges against you."

"Why the hell did you agree to that?"

"I know you think you're tough but trust me when I say you wouldn't last five minutes in jail, especially in Chicago."

"So you spoke directly to Justin?" I never told Justin about William being Jonathan Prescott; I wonder how that conversation went.

"I had my legal team take care of it. I have no interest in talking to your ex."

"So that's it? Justin gets an apartment with his new girlfriend."

"Why don't you try focusing on the part where I've kept your ass out of jail?"

Of course he has a point, and yes I'm thankful to be waking up in my own home versus some disgusting county jail, however the thought of Justin and Red living rent free on Prescott's dime still ticks me off.

"Layla, you're wasting valuable time talking to me. Get your stuff packed and be ready by the time the car pulls up." Click.

I look at the phone in mock amusement. I don't think I will ever get used to Prescott's way of handling things. I slump down in my office chair feeling more confused than ever. When I head back into the living room Stephanie is awake.

"You okay, Layla?"

"I was just on the phone with Mr. Prescott."

"He called you directly?" she asks, looking a little surprised.

"Yeah, is that unusual?"

"For him it is… what did he say?"

"In order to keep Justin from pressing charges against me he agreed to put him up in a fully furnished apartment for a year."

"Are you serious?" she asks, waking everyone else up.

"What's going on?" Georgina asks, wiping the crust out of her eyes.

"Mr. Prescott just called Layla and told her he agreed to pay Justin's rent for a year in order to keep him from pressing charges."

"Are you serious?!"

"That's what he said."

"Wow. You've made quite the impression on Jonathan. To be honest I'm surprised he didn't fire you on the spot last night. Normally he doesn't put up with shit like this. Did he say anything else?"

"Shit!" I say, looking at the time, "I don't have much time before the car arrives to take me to the airport."

"He's sending a car?" Simone asks, sharing the same look of disbelief as Georgina. Apparently Prescott's behavior has thrown everyone off.

"Yes," I say, starting to feel a little frantic. There is no way I have enough time to get dressed and packed for a week's vacation in under forty-five minutes.

"Layla, you go get dressed," Georgina says, standing up to stretch. "I'll go pack your suitcase while you shower."

"You don't have to do that."

"Don't worry about it. Now go hurry up and shower; knowing Jonathan the driver will be here soon to take you to the airport."

When the black Lincoln arrives I hug everyone, thanking them for being there for me last night. They all wave me off but not before Georgina makes me promise to have a fling with a hot Jamaican. I can't even think about men right now. I just need time to relax and get back in touch with myself.

When I arrive at the airport I notice the driver passing all of the departure gates. "Um...driver what departure gate are you heading to?"

"We're heading to terminal H ma'am, that's where all of the privately owned planes take off."

Privately owned planes? I'm not going on some private plane. My ticket is for Air Jamaica.

"Driver, I don't think we are heading the right way. I need to make a call to find out about my flight."

"Just following orders ma'am, besides, we're here." He stops the car and I look out the window to see Prescott Inc. in gold bold letters on the exterior of a plane. Holy shit! Did Prescott arrange for me to fly to Jamaica on his private plane? I'm still looking out the window in amazement when the driver comes around to open the door for me. I get out of the car feeling dumbfounded. I wonder if I should call Prescott before boarding. The driver is already at the plane handing my bags to members of the crew as they store my luggage below in the cargo area. Hell, don't dwell on this Layla, I think to myself, you have enough shit to think about. Besides, the thought of going to Jamaica on a private plane brings a slow smile to my face. I did always want to travel in style and at least this way I don't have to sit next to a bunch of strangers in uncomfortable seats.

I walk towards the plane and climb the stairs, turning around once more to look at the view. Goodbye Chicago and hello Jamaica! Stepping inside I look around the cabin—it is absolutely gorgeous. There are 14 plush leather seats and a bar! Hallelujah! I plan to make great use of the bar. I choose a window seat, reveling in how comfortable it is. I close my eyes, lean my head back and finally start to relax after this morning's and last night's events.

"Are you comfortable?" I shoot up from my seat and see Prescott smiling at me.

"What are you doing here?" Damn him, I feel like I've just been caught stealing or something.

"I'm accompanying you to Jamaica."

"What?! Why? It's not necessary." Why am I in such a state of panic? It's his plane and he has every right to be here.

"None of the major airlines had seats available for today's flight so I moved my trip up by a day so we could fly out together.

It's not a big deal; I was planning to leave tomorrow but staying an extra day in Jamaica won't kill me."

"You changed your travel plans for me?"

"It's no big deal. Besides, I'll rest easier knowing you and Justin are not in the same country right now." Why do I feel like Prescott is always inadvertently saving me from some disaster?

"I'm sorry about all of this," I say, feeling guilty for all the trouble I've caused. I used to be so private but now I feel like my life is playing out on an open stage.

"Layla, we are going to Jamaica, I think I'll survive." Prescott's demeanor catches me off guard. After our conversation this morning I thought he would be upset with me but at the moment he seems very amicable. He must be up to something. I watch his movements closely as he removes some papers from his briefcase before storing it under his chair. Something's off—he's never this nice.

Eventually the captain comes out and the two disappear into the cockpit. Left alone in the cabin I let everything sink in. Here I am on this beautiful plane about to take off for Jamaica. Focus on the good Layla. I refuse to dwell on yesterday's events. I'm starting a whole new chapter in my life, a Justin-free chapter. I'm deep in thought when the sound of clanging bracelets disturbs me. I look up and notice a Hispanic woman in a skimpy flight attendant uniform enter the cabin. She saunters over to me.

"Hello," she says in a very thick accent.

With great hesitation I tell her hello. Is this woman going to accompany us to Jamaica? Not that it should matter but I was just getting accustomed to the idea of traveling alone with Prescott.

"I'm Marcia and I will be taking care of all your needs today." She says it in such a slutty way I have a feeling she's talking about more than just food and drinks. Who the hell is this woman?

"That's not necessary," I reply curtly.

"Oh come now sweetie, I can tell by the way you're sitting you are way too tense. Let me work my magic and help you relax. I'm one of Jonathan's favorites and I promise to make this plane ride unforgettable! Come, sit up; let me show you." Her accent is so thick I have to listen extra hard to make sure I'm understanding her correctly.

"Show me what?"

"I give great massages. Trust me." I don't trust her but I could definitely use a good shoulder rub right now. I know my body is extra tense and I figure if she works for Prescott she must be worth whatever he pays her.

"Okay. Just a brief shoulder rub," I say. Marcia looks happy and rubs her hands together in anticipation. She stoops down and releases a lever transforming the seat into a table top position. I lay flat on my stomach with my head resting on my arms as Marcia starts to rub my shoulders. This is way better than flying on one of the major airlines; I never imagined I would be getting a massage prior to take off. I must admit this woman's hands must have been sent from God. Her fingers are petite but she is definitely giving me a good deep tissue massage. I make a mental note to take advantage of some of the spa treatments at the resort. I close my eyes as Marcia continues to work her magic fingers all over my shoulders and upper back. I'm oblivious to everything around me, finding myself lost in her hands as she works out my knots. Her hands continue working on me and my body goes limp. Slowly I feel Marcia's hands travel lower and lower as she continues her massage. That's when I feel her hands slip underneath my blouse pulling it up slightly exposing the small of my back. At first this is not a big deal, until I start to feel soft kisses being placed on my lower back.

"What the hell do you think you're doing?" I ask as I abruptly sit up and eyeball her.

"Relax, I'm here to make you feel good."

"Relax! You just kissed me!"

"I know and you like it, I can tell from the way your body responded."

I quickly stand, putting distance between us.

"Have you lost your mind?"

Prescott and the pilot must have heard the commotion; they

both come storming out of the cockpit at the same time. Prescott's blue eyes grow wide as he looks back and forth between me and Marcia. He turns to Marcia and starts speaking to her in Spanish. The two go back and forth in conversation. God, she's lucky I don't know what the hell they're saying. I wish I paid more attention in Spanish class. I spent four years learning Spanish and I still can't get past saying my name.

Marcia and Prescott end their conversation. She briefly looks me over before turning to give him a quick hug and a kiss goodbye. I notice their lips connect and a surge of jealousy takes over. No secret what she was doing here.

Once Marcia is off the plane the captain asks us to take our seats in preparation for take-off. I watch as Prescott acknowledges the captain then takes a seat directly across the aisle from me, acting as if nothing happened.

"Aren't you going to ask me what happened?"

"No."

"Why not?" I ask feeling annoyed by his nonchalant attitude.

"Marcia already told me everything I need to know."

"What if she lied?"

"Marcia doesn't lie."

"So you're just going to take her word for everything?" Prescott takes a deep breath—he clearly doesn't want to have this conversation with me but I refuse to let him change the subject. He may disagree but I think he owes me an explanation.

"Is there something you would like to tell me, Layla?" There's a hint of amusement in his voice—the son of a bitch thinks what happened is funny. I wonder how much Marcia told him. I change my mind and shy away from rehashing the story. I'm a little embarrassed by the whole thing. I've never had a woman touch me like that before.

"No, I have nothing to add."

"Good, let's just relax and enjoy the flight."

The captain comes on over the loud speaker and announces it's our turn for take-off. It only takes a few minutes before we are at top speed propelling into the air.

Chapter 12

As soon as the captain comes on over the loud speaker and announces we are free to move around the cabin, Prescott removes his seat belt and turns towards me,

"We need to talk."

Here it comes. He probably waited to get me three thousand feet in the air so I wouldn't have anywhere to run.

"After what happened yesterday everyone would have expected me to fire you, which under any other circumstances I would have."

"Why haven't you fired me?" I know I saved the Bradford account but now that the contract is signed and the ink is dry, Prescott really doesn't need me.

"Several reasons, but the one that matters the most is that you are very talented and I wouldn't want you to end up working for one of my competitors. If it were to get out you saved us from losing Bradford, anyone within their right mind would hire you on the spot. That said, you are on probation; while we are in Jamaica I expect you to be perfect. I don't want you doing or saying anything that will draw attention to yourself. Do not talk about the incident with any of your co-workers, as far as everyone is concerned you were attacked and were trying to defend yourself. The staff has been instructed not to bring it up and if anyone says a word to you I want to know about it ASAP, are we clear?"

"Yes." He gives me his power stare, probably a tactic he uses in meetings—it works. I slump further into my seat and turn to face the window. There's nothing like getting an earful from your super sexy, yet super arrogant boss. I let my mind drift a little but then I think back to him saying there were several reasons I still have my job and start to wonder about the other reasons. I look over at him but he's focused on whatever's in front of him so I decide not to interrupt him.

We are little over an hour into the flight when I start to feel restless. The bar is calling my name but after all the drinking I did yesterday I should probably just grab a bottle of water. Then again it would be a shame to only drink water on my way to Jamaica, especially since I see my favorite flavor of Ciroc staring back at me. If Marcia were here I'm sure I could have convinced her to make me anything I want. I still can't believe Prescott planned on having his little playmate accompany him on this flight. I wonder if he's disappointed she's not here.

"So, does Marcia accompany you on all of your flights?" My question grabs his immediate attention. He looks up at me with an amused expression.

"Let's just say I forgot to cancel some of my previous travel arrangements."

Looking at Prescott the only word that comes to mind is FREAK. This man may be the biggest freak I've ever met.

"I guess you're a member of the mile high club," I say sarcastically.

"You have no idea."

We are once again sitting in silence. This is going to be a long flight. Finally after another thirty minutes Prescott pushes his papers to the side and stands to stretch. He moves towards the bar and fixes himself a drink and grabs a bar of chocolate. On his way back to his chair, he hands me a bottle of water.

"Make sure you don't get drunk this week."

I accept the water from him and feel a light tingle when our hands make contact.

"I want you to know that I do plan to keep to myself this week but that doesn't mean I need you to monitor my every move and I'm certainly not going to let you dictate my actions all week."

"Are you always this argumentative?"

"Are you always this bossy?"

"I'm not bossy, I just give directions," he says smiling. I was getting ready to say something but stopped when I noticed the way he was licking the melted chocolate off his fingers. Immediately my mind races back to the first night we met when he licked my juices off those same fingers. He turns towards me with a cocky grin on his face. He knows what he's doing and I hate him for it.

"So what did you ladies do last night?"

"We drank, we talked and then we drank some more before passing out."

"Sounds like a blast," he says dryly.

I know he's being condescending but I don't care.

"It was the best. I haven't had girl time in forever. If they weren't there for me last night I wouldn't have had anyone to turn to." Prescott leans his head to the side as if he's considering what I just said. "What's on your mind?" I finally ask. I feel like I've lost his attention.

"You just reminded me about a friend I need to contact. Every time I think about calling, something comes up and I forget. I know it's not a good excuse but sometimes it really does feel like all of my responsibilities get in the way."

Being with Prescott one-on-one almost reminds me of the first night we spent together minus the drama. Of course nothing could ever happen between us but I feel so indebted to him. Through all the craziness from the moment we met until now he has, in his own Prescott way, looked out for me.

Surprisingly we spend the remainder of the flight having casual conversation without any disagreements. After lunch the captain comes over the loud speaker and asks us to buckle up in preparation for landing. I return my seat to its upright position and readjust my seatbelt. I'm hopeful this vacation will be exactly what I need to get over Justin but with Prescott so close I don't see that being a challenge.

We have a smooth landing and check into our hotel without incident. After check-in we go our separate ways. Junior suites were booked for all of the staff. I have a king bed all to myself with a sitting room and my very own liquor dispenser. After his comment on the plane I'm surprised he hasn't had the hotel staff remove it from my room.

My suite is decorated in traditional island décor with dark wicker furniture and light pastel accents. Beyond the living room there is a spiral staircase that leads to a second level bedroom and spa bath. The ocean front view from my room is spectacular.

I noticed an enticing pool and several lounge areas on the way to my room. Since I have the afternoon to myself I plan to relax poolside until dinner. Being away and alone is all new to me. I've never gone away by myself before and I feel a little lost without companionship. I refuse to let my break-up with Justin turn me into a hermit. No matter how nervous I may feel, I'm going to learn to enjoy my own company.

My first step is to get out of these clothes. I open my suitcase and stare. Oh. My. God! One by one I pick up each item of my clothing and realize those bitches chose every scandalous skimpy outfit in my closet. I don't have one pair of shorts that cover my full bottom nor one top that doesn't show cleavage or my midsection. The ironic thing is that everything they chose for me was purchased by Justin. What the hell were they thinking? I admit Justin has great taste in clothes but I never felt secure enough to actually wear anything he bought me. This has Georgina's name written all over it. How the hell did she find this shit anyway? I keep it in a box in the back of my closet.

I sort through the clothes once more, trying to decide on the most decent outfit and select a summer dress. It shows a lot of my cleavage and is very short but it's the best I can do with limited options. I will definitely need to go shopping later. Words can't describe Georgina. She's convinced the way for me to get over Justin is by finding someone to take his place. Her way of thinking may work for her but I'm not the type of person who indulges in flings. I've always liked long-term steady relationships.

I pull my hair into a long ponytail and apply some fresh make-up before taking a second look in the mirror and heading down to the pool. The resort we are staying in is beautiful. Everywhere I look I see unobstructed views of the ocean. There are several bars, restaurants, pools and even a couple of dance clubs on the resort.

When I reach the pool I look for an umbrella to sit under. The sun is intense but brings much needed warmth to my body. During my scan for a seat I spot Prescott sitting by the bar. He looks like he's engrossed in conversation with a cute little Asian girl. A pang of jealousy instantly hits my chest. Seeing him talk to another woman shouldn't affect me; his love life is none of my concern. But seeing the two of them together not only makes me a little jealous, it also serves as a reminder that I'm here alone.

I grab a lounge chair under an umbrella and pull out a book. I'm happy I remembered to grab a few novels before leaving my apartment. With work I rarely have time to read for leisure so I'll definitely use this week to catch up.

I'm holding onto my book but I haven't cracked it open yet, my eyes keep finding their way to Prescott. I think he's spotted me. Even from a distance I can tell his entire body language has changed. He's staring now, which makes me feel uncomfortable. For whatever reason he doesn't look happy and neither does the little Asian girl. He doesn't stop looking my way until he's joined by a tall African American man. Now that's the type of man I should be into. From what I can tell he has a lean build, beautiful locks and a smile I can see from here but my eyes naturally drift back to Prescott with his beautiful blue eyes and freshly cut brown hair. What the hell is wrong with me? I know what the problem is; my experience with Prescott is the closest I've ever come to having an orgasm and now I'm hooked. If I'm ever going to get past that night I'm going to need to move on.

I force myself to open my book and focus on the words in front of me. As soon as I turn the first page I feel the presence of someone standing over me. I look up and swear Prescott's clone is looking down at me.

"Hello," the clone says smiling.

Caught off guard by the uncanny resemblance I almost forget to speak.

The sexy stranger takes a seat next to me. I try to focus on my book but I've lost my concentration. I secretly eye him while he dries off. He's not as muscular as Prescott but he's definitely in great shape.

"If you're going to keep eyeing me like that I think I should at least know your name."

Crap! I can't believe he caught me staring.

"I'm Layla," I say feeling embarrassed.

"Layla, I'm Paul," he says, extending his hand. Paul's hands feel smooth...nothing like Prescott's.

"Did you arrive today?"

"Yes, our plane just landed a few hours ago."

"Oh, are you here with someone?" he asks looking around.

"Yes, I mean no... not like that anyway, I'm on a company trip. What about you?"

"This is strictly a vacation for me."

Talking to Paul is easy. He has a carefree attitude I find infectious. Now that my sunglasses are off and I can inspect him further, he's definitely no Jonathan Prescott. He's easy on the eyes, yes, but he's missing that rugged yet refined look that makes Prescott alluring. I also notice Paul likes to talk about himself and if I'm not mistaken he's even referred to himself in the third person—I hate when people do that.

The sun is starting to set. I would point out the beautiful sunset to Paul but he looks like he's enjoying the sound of his own voice. With the loss of sunlight my book has become a lost cause. I slip it back in my bag; maybe I'll get the chance to read tomorrow.

"Earth to Layla…"

I whip my head around to face Paul. I guess he's decided to include me in on this portion of the conversation. "I'm sorry, what did you say?"

"I was asking you if you wanted to grab dinner. It looks like the buffet on the terrace is open."

At the mention of food my stomach eagerly responds. I can smell all of the exotic seasonings in the air. I really don't want to have dinner with Paul but my only alternative would be eating alone which seems much more pathetic. I look over at the bar where I last spotted Prescott and watch as he and the little Asian girl head to the buffet. Watching her on his arm is like watching a parasite latched to its host. She's staking her claim. I watch them both as she glares at any woman who dares to give Prescott a second look.

"Do you know him?"

No use in pretending I don't. "He's my boss," I say, watching as Prescott maneuvers through the tables.

"And the girl with him?"

"Your guess is as good as mine." I stand up and grab my beach bag; I've done enough staring for one day. "Are you ready to eat?" I ask, ready for dinner.

Chapter 13

ASIDE FROM THE fabulous food, dinner with Paul is uneventful. I spot Prescott and the Asian girl eating together. We make eye contact a couple of times but I quickly turn away when I catch the way he is looking at me. He looks upset but I don't know why.

After Paul and I eat he persuades me to take a walk on the beach under the premise we should walk off some of our food. I'm a little reluctant to join him at first but agree when I notice the full moon. There's nothing like watching a full moon over the ocean.

When we reach the beach the sand feels soothing under my feet but I'm not prepared for the cool night air.

"It's chillier that I thought it would be; I should have brought a light jacket."

"I'll warm you up," Paul says, pulling me in close and wrapping his arm around me. Having Paul's arm around me doesn't feel right. I don't want to lead him on so I quickly step out of his embrace,

"I think I'll head inside now."

"So soon? We've barely started our walk."

I lie and tell him I'm still cold.

"Stay here I'll run up and get you a jacket."

Before I can protest, Paul takes off running. Left alone on the beach I walk to a cluster of rocks and take a seat to wait for his return.

"I thought I told you to keep a low profile this week?"

Scared at the sound of a man's voice my heart starts to pump erratically. I turn around and watch, shocked, as Prescott emerges from the shadows.

"Shit! You scared me!" I say, bringing my hand to my chest to calm my racing heart. He looks upset. I look around to see if the Asian girl is still following him but it looks like he's alone.

"Sorry, I didn't mean to sneak up on you," he says, coming closer.

"It's okay...what are you doing out here?"

"Keeping an eye on you; I thought we agreed you wouldn't do anything to draw attention to yourself."

"What are you talking about? I haven't drawn attention to myself."

"What do you call that dress?" he says, gazing over my body.

"If you don't like what I'm wearing you're going to have to talk to Georgina, she's the one that packed for me."

"I should've known better than to send her home with you." He looks irritated with himself. "I'll have the staff send you up some new clothes."

"That won't be necessary." Why is he treating me like this? Has he not seen what some of the women are wearing around this place? Compared to the little Asian girl I spotted him with, I'm overdressed.

"Don't argue with me, I'm sending some clothes to your room and I expect you to wear them."

"I appreciate your concern, but like I said before, that won't be necessary. I already plan to go shopping tomorrow."

My girls meant well but I'm not going to spend a week walking around in clothes bought by Justin.

Unexpectedly Prescott sits next to me and drapes a jacket around me. Appreciative of the immediate warmth it provides, I slip my arms through the sleeves and notice this jacket couldn't possibly belong to him. His arms are way too bulky to even fit through the sleeves but it's still definitely a man's jacket. It's more appropriate for Paul's body type than his own. Paul should be back any minute now. Although I'm not interested in him, I still don't want him to come back to find me and Prescott sitting together.

"Thanks for the jacket but my friend should be returning any minute now."

"So you and Paul are friends now?"

"You know him?" Paul didn't give me the impression he knew who Prescott was.

"I've familiarized myself with him. I believe he's at the bar inside entertaining some of the ladies."

Of all the fucking nerve! I can't believe he left me out here alone.

Prescott and I sit in companionable silence. Lovers should be out here under the moonlit night, not me and Prescott. I wish my girls were here... I don't want to be alone tonight. I look over at Prescott and an annoying tingling sensation between my legs starts to grow. I can't deny my attraction to him. The moonlight accentuates his features, making him look that much more alluring, if that's possible.

"Don't look at me like that."

"Look at you like what?" I ask innocently, he can't possibly know what I'm thinking.

"Like you want me to fuck you," he says, brushing the sand off his pants, "you work for me and you're too young."

I hate him. I really do.

"I'm tired," I say, removing the jacket and handing it back to him. The cool night air immediately brings a chill to my body. "I'm going to bed."

"I didn't mean for it to come out that way."

"Whatever." I track through the sand heading back to my room. It's time for this day to end.

"Layla!"

Prescott calls out to me but I don't bother turning around.

Strong arms stop me, pulling me into the shadows under the bridge that leads back to the resort.

"I know you heard me call your name."

"I don't have the energy to fight with you, what do you want?"

I can see the hesitation in his eyes but his lips know exactly what they want. When our lips connect my body comes alive. I open for him and his tongue wastes no time in darting into my mouth, exploring and tasting me. I sense his urgency. I feel the need in him grow. His rock hard erection is pressed against me, backing me into a corner. In the secluded darkness Prescott proceeds to take a moonlit tour of my body. I feel his hands everywhere. I wrap my arms around him running my fingers through his silky brown hair. This is madness. Everything is happening so quickly I barely have time to think about what we're doing. He slides his hands up my dress and in one quick maneuver my panties are gone, lost in the sand. His rough thick fingers enter me, spreading my wetness. Is this really about to happen? Is he really going to take me right here, right now with my back against a rock under a bridge?

"Yes!" I scream out in pleasure when Prescott replaces his fingers with his long hard erection. I can't believe my body is ready for him. I hold onto him tightly with my legs wrapped around his waist as he moves me over his shaft. I start to moan out of pleasure but he covers my mouth—we hear footsteps approaching on the bridge above.

"Jonathan, are you down there?"

It must be the little Asian girl who sat next to him at the bar. Little does she know we're right under her. I want to call out to her and tell her he's busy but stay quiet. Prescott doesn't miss a beat. He continues to fuck me senseless. Replacing his hand with his lips we both moan into each other. I've never felt or done anything so animalistic before. I wrap my legs tighter around him holding on for dear life. The walls of my vagina are soaked. Sex with Prescott is exactly what my body's been craving. I start to shake and my legs start to tremble.

"You feel incredible," he whispers into my ear, "tonight you're mine."

He has claimed possession of my body for the night and I willingly give myself to him. My body is being pulled into a whole new world. With Prescott inside me I feel everything, taste everything, sense everything. My body has been awakened. My senses are alert. I shake and shiver as my body finally enjoys the orgasm he previously denied me. I'm still panting when I hear Prescott growl my name. He holds me tight as his own orgasm races through his body.

"Is someone down there?"

I can see the little Asian girl's head poking out from on top of the bridge but she can't see us, our bodies have melded with the shadows. Neither of us moves or makes a sound. We're both exhausted from our intense orgasms and collapse to the floor. Hidden in the shadows I doubt she'll find us.

I've never done anything like this. Now that the fog has cleared and I've regained my cognitive abilities looking at Prescott and I half dressed in the sand I realize how badly I've fucked up. I just had a quick fuck with my boss on a beach in Jamaica. What happens now?

"I think she's gone." Prescott is the first to speak.

I'm still at a loss for words. Our bodies are still connected and neither of us makes a move to unplug. I find peace in his arms but one of us needs to get up, we can't stay here like this forever, someone's bound to eventually find us. I decide to make the first move but Prescott's firm arms hold me still.

"We should talk."

Here it comes…

"This can't happen again."

Do I see regret in his eyes? I just stare at him. He's still inside me; I can feel his cock twitching to life while he tells me this can't happen again. I've never been rejected by a man while he's still inside me. I'm not going to let him make a fool out of me. I still have my pride.

"Jonathan, are you down here?"

Shit! The little Asian girl is persistent; it's only a matter of time before she spots us. Prescott swiftly pulls away from me and moves to cover me up, blocking me from anyone's view.

"There you are! Didn't you hear me calling you?"

"I was on a private call," he says, holding up his cell phone. I'm safely hidden behind him and she doesn't seem to suspect that he's not alone.

"I need to make one more call then I'll meet you in the lobby."

"I can wait."

"I need privacy," he says in that commanding tone that I find both sexy and annoying.

Finally taking the hint she retreats back to the resort.

"She's gone," he says, turning back around to face me.

I say nothing as I hurriedly work to fix my clothes. I feel stupid and cheap for allowing this to happen. Knowing him he's probably going to take her back to his room tonight and have his way with her as well. Why the hell did I allow myself to get fucked under a bridge? I don't bother looking for my underwear; maybe some kid will find it when making a sand castle and use it as a flag—a sign that Layla Anette Brown has been conquered.

As soon as I'm put back together I take off running towards the resort. Prescott calls out after me but I don't stop. I'm in no mood to listen to more of his "this was a mistake" speech.

Once I'm safely in my suite I turn on some music and take a shower. Under the warm spray of the water and the sultry voice of Luther, I lather myself up and wash away all traces of sex on the beach. I'm quietly humming the words to 'So Amazing' when my shower curtain is ripped open. Prescott's seductive blue eyes don't miss a thing as he performs a once-over of my body.

"What are you doing here?" I ask, trying to cover myself up.

"You ran away before I could finish what I had to say."

"I think I got the gist of what you were trying to say," I say, yanking the shower curtain closed.

"No, I don't think you did," he says ripping it back open. I watch as he undresses himself, dropping his clothes on the bathroom floor.

"I said we'll allow ourselves this one night together—last I checked, the night's not over."

Chapter 14

THE NEXT MORNING I awake to the feel of the sun beaming down on me. What time is it I wonder? I glance at the alarm clock, it's ten o'clock. Damn, I didn't mean to sleep this long. I turn over and to my dismay Prescott's gone. I must have been in a deep sleep; I didn't feel him move when he got out of bed.

I scan the suite to see if there are any remnants of him left but all traces of him are gone. I only have the soreness between my thighs as a reminder of what happened last night. I feel a twinge of sadness. Maybe it's a good thing he's gone. After last night I wouldn't even know what to say to him this morning. I lay quietly in the bed thinking about last night before it finally hits me. I had sex without a flashback! I sit straight up in the bed in a state of shock. After all of these years of crying, I finally had sex—and not just any sex, mind blowing pleasurable sex—with no hang-ups. I didn't even think about my past once when he was inside me. How the hell did Prescott have the ability to make me forget? I feel like I've just had a major break-through. All this time it wasn't my fault; Justin just didn't know what the hell he was doing! Prescott may not be here with me this morning but I still feel good. I'm ready to get my day started.

After last night I need to take a quick shower before grabbing breakfast. Let's see, what skanky outfit will I have to wear today? I still can't believe those bitches selected these clothes. What the hell were they thinking? I pull out my white bikini and cover up. I'll have breakfast and then lay out on the beach for a few hours before going for a swim this afternoon. I pack my beach bag with a few sleazy romance novels and my headphones. Once I have everything I need for the day I head out in search of the dining area for breakfast. That's when I notice a note on my door. I anxiously open it thinking it may be a note from Prescott but instead its room service letting me know my new clothes are ready. I guess we were so caught up last night that neither of us noticed anyone knocking on the door.

On my way to breakfast I see a couple in a heated argument. Damn, it's not even noon yet and the man is clearly drunk. I turn the corner to head into the main dining room and come face to face with Prescott. My heart-rate instantly speeds up, after last night he looks even better if that's even possible. I may have wanted him in my bed this morning but now seeing him I realize how awkward it would have made things if we woke up together. This way we can casually greet each other as if nothing happened last night.

"Good morning," he says casually. My mind is slow to work; I take a moment to look him over. His blue eyes seem brighter and his brown hair looks damp –probably from his morning shower.

"Good morning." What else can I say? This is even more awkward than I thought. Do I mention anything about last night or should I pretend like nothing happened? I wish he could give me a cue to go off of, but he has his poker face on and I can't get a reading.

"I needed to take care of a few things in my room this morning and I didn't want to disturb you. You were sleeping so peacefully."

He looks so damn proud of himself. He really doesn't owe me an explanation but I'm happy he shared.

"Did you already have breakfast?" I ask, trying to change the subject.

"No, I was waiting for you. When I saw the time I thought maybe I had already missed you."

Oh, he wants to have breakfast with me? This is unexpected.

"I'm starving, you ready to eat?" he asks.

"Lead the way," I say, trying to act casual. I feel like he's up to something but I'll play along for now.

Breakfast is served in the main dining area buffet style but Prescott, being who he is, has arranged for a private table and a personal waitress.

"So what are your plans for today?" he asks, looking genuinely interested.

"As soon as I'm finished eating I'm going to relax out on the beach with a book. Then this afternoon I'll probably go for a swim. What about you?"

"When we're finished I'm going to rent a jet-ski." I can almost see a trace of boyish excitement in his eyes at the prospect of riding a jet-ski. I feel like I'm seeing a whole new side of him.

"That sounds like fun." Is this the same man that fucked me senseless last night? He's acting as if the two of us sitting down to breakfast is the most natural thing to do. With every bite he takes I imagine his lips on my body. I need to stop this. Maybe this is a test. He probably just wants to see if I can act normal around him after everything that happened last night. No matter what the case may be, it feels good to sit down with Prescott and have a normal conversation. He seems so carefree here.

"If you're up for it, I would like for you to join me." He looks at me anxiously awaiting my response.

"I guess my book and headphones can wait." I feel like a school girl with a stupid grin on my face but I can't help it. After the promises we made last night I didn't expect to spend anymore one-on-one time together.

After breakfast Prescott and I head over to the jet-ski station. The instructor is a true-blooded Jamaican. His skin is dark and smooth with locks that go all the way down his back. I love his accent but I have to listen extra close to his instructions so I don't miss anything. His accent is so thick I can only make out every other word. Prescott must have sensed my hesitation; he leans down and whispers to me, "don't worry, this isn't my first time on a jet-ski." I immediately relax. I was starting to rethink heading out into the open water not knowing how to operate the jet-ski but with Prescott close I know I'll be okay.

"Alright now, yuh-redy ta get out deer and have some fun mon?" Prescott and I look at each other smiling, answering yes in unison; that's about the only thing I understood clearly.

"Do you want to ride with me first until you get the hang of it?"

Hmm... ride on the back of a jet-ski with Prescott? That sounds tantalizing. "Sure." He mounts first and I slide on behind him wrapping my arms around his midsection.

"You ready?" he yells over the engine. Before I can get my reply out we take off. Riding the jet-ski is such a rush. We bounce over the water heading into the open ocean leaving a trail of rippling water behind us. Prescott is having a great time driving. We ride up and down the coast-line making waves and laughing as the water sprays over us. I hold onto him tightly with my chest pressing into his back. We are a good distance from the shore line when he slows down and comes to a stop. I start to panic.

"Is everything okay? We're not out of gas or something are we?"

"No, everything is fine. I just want to make sure you are having a good time."

"I know you can't see my smile, but yes, I'm having a blast!" I say, feeling care-free.

"Is this better than your book?"

"Way better," I say laughing.

"Good... Hold me tight," he says in his deep voice. Hold me tight? Not hold on tight, hold ME tight. I pull my thighs closer to him and I squeeze him tight as the engine roars to life once again and we take off heading towards the shore.

I hold onto Prescott tightly with my head leaning against his back all the way to the jet-ski station. As soon as we dismount my body feels cool and I realize I miss the feel of his body pressed against mine. Maybe this wasn't a good idea. I just know I'm going to spend the remainder of the afternoon day-dreaming about him.

I watch his every move as he settles up with the instructor. His presence is commanding and every move he makes looks flawless. How does he do it? How does he always manage to look in control?

"Cum back anytime mon, I'll take care of yuh," the instructor says in his thick accent. Prescott must have left him a good tip; the instructor counts the money twice with a look of disbelief on his face.

"You made his day!" I say laughing lightly.

"He is pretty happy isn't he?" he says glancing back at the man and shaking his head.

"You like making people happy don't you?"

"I always find pleasure in pleasing people." I know he's referring to last night but I make no comment.

"What next?" he asks.

"Do you feel like swimming? The water is absolutely beautiful." Also, I need to cool off. It's hard being this close to Prescott. My mind keeps going back to last night and when it does I feel hot all over.

"Come," he takes my hand and we claim two chairs by the water. I take off my cover up and drape my towel over the chair. Turning around I see him looking at me, his eyes devouring my body.

"You are a beautiful woman." His voice is even and sincere. My heart skips a beat at his subtle compliment.

All I can do is smile. Why am I letting Prescott affect me this way? I need to stop.

"Do you mind rubbing some sun tan lotion on my back?"

"Sure," like I would actually have a problem rubbing my hands over his body again. He lies down on his stomach as I squeeze the lotion in my hand.

I smooth it over his back, taking note of all his beautiful muscles. His shoulders are very broad. He's in even better shape than Justin. He probably has a personal trainer. His back is smooth and free from hair unlike his legs and forearms. Thank god he doesn't have bushy hair all over him. I hate when a man comes to the beach looking like a goddamned wilder-beast. Sometimes I really want to tell them to shave that shit off.

"There, you're all done," I announce.

"Thank you."

Prescott stands stretching his arms. He then turns to me with those intense blue eyes. "Last one in buys the first round of drinks," he says playfully. He takes off running into the water, leaving me in his dust. When I finally catch up with him I'm panting like I just ran a marathon.

"Not fair, you didn't give me any notice," I say, still trying to catch my breath.

"All is fair in love and war."

"Is that what this is?" I ask with a smirk on my face.

"I have no clue what this is, but whatever it is, I'm enjoying myself."

"How much are you enjoying yourself?" I ask flirtatiously. Are we actually flirting with each other? I should stop this but I feel so drawn to him. Yesterday he was all about business but today he seems relaxed and playful. I didn't think he had a playful bone in his body. He pulls me closer and whispers in my ear, "so much that I'm tempted to send the staff somewhere else for the remainder of the week."

"Oh, you really are having a good time," I say jokingly. Part of me wishes the staff could be diverted somewhere else but I know it's not possible.

We both let silence take over and I start to think about what we are saying and the implications it will have on our professional relationship.

"Why aren't you in a committed relationship, or better yet, why aren't you married?" I ask. I just can't imagine Prescott having trouble finding a woman who's willing to marry him. With his serious demeanor he doesn't appear to be the type of guy with commitment phobia. I hate seeing men in their late thirties or early forties still acting like they're twenty something. Prescott carries himself like a grown man which is a nice change from some of Justin's childish ways. I can't imagine Prescott staying up all night with an Xbox remote in his hand.

He mulls over my question before answering.

"Let's just say my work is very intense and although I do want a family I would need a wife to be understanding about my schedule. Also, I don't think it's fair to leave one parent to raise a family while the other is busy at work."

"I know the competition in marketing can be a little cut-throat at times and that clients can sometimes be demanding but I can't imagine it would prevent you from having a family. I mean surely there are a lot of CEOs in marketing with families."

"It takes a lot to be number one in my industry."

That's an interesting choice of words. One would think we were in two totally different lines of business. I haven't worked for the company long but from what I can tell in the office, Georgina is really the one who runs the show at work. He's away on business a lot but no-one ever knows what he's working on. I've even over-heard a few people say that aside from the Bradford account he's never shown an interest in any of our clients. With Georgina running things he should have plenty of time for family life.

"I know the company is important to you but nothing can re-place family, besides no-one can remain number one forever."

"Being number two is not an option right now." He speaks with such finality I decide to change the subject. In addition to him being a freak, he's clearly also a workaholic. I wonder if he's always been this way.

"Are your parents as driven as you are?" I ask out of curiosity. I wonder where he got his work ethic from.

"My parents always believed in hard work but I grew up in your standard middle-American family. My mom was a school teacher and my dad had his own landscaping business."

"Do you have any siblings?"

"What is it with you and all of your questions today?"

"Just curious, that's all."

"Well, maybe I should give you the third degree."

"I think you know more than you need to know about me, now stop dodging my questions, do you have any siblings?"

"My mom had a lot of miscarriages before finally having me. She calls me her miracle baby," he says proudly.

"Sorry to hear that, were you ever lonely growing up?"

"Not really, my dad coached baseball so there were always kids coming and going in the house. Why are you smiling?"

"I'm just picturing you in a little league outfit." I'm sure he was a cute kid. "Your parents must be really proud of you."

"I provide them with a lifestyle they've only dreamed about."

I know I shouldn't but I'm picturing myself having a family with Prescott. Sometimes I'm not even sure I want kids. What if I have a daughter who goes through the same thing I went through? I would never forgive myself if I didn't protect her. Or worse yet, what if I make the mistake of marrying someone who is a child molester. When I think about my cousin and how much his wife loves him it scares me. I could one day fall in love with someone with a terrible past. I loved Justin and look how that turned out. It may be the cowardly way out but sometimes I think it's easier to just be alone. Maybe sex with no strings attached isn't such a bad idea. I look at Prescott and my mind starts to ponder what a purely sexual relationship with him would be like. Just thinking about sex with him turns the dull ache between my thighs into full blown burning desire. I need to stop thinking about sex but it's hard when we're in such close proximity. My mind should be on something else but it seems to always come back to sex. Just looking at the way his body moves so gracefully through the water makes me want him more. I wonder if he feels the same way.

"Can I ask you a personal question?" He hesitates before answering.

"As long as this is the last question of the day, what else do you want to know?"

"Being in the lifestyle, is sex always just sex to you?"

"What do you mean?"

"Do you care for any of the women you're with or do they all just blend together?"

"Care would be a strong word to use since I don't get to know everyone on a personal level. It's more so a matter of respecting the women I'm with. I like to please women and I like to see my woman receive pleasure."

"From other men and women?"

"If that's what she likes, yes."

"You never get jealous?"

"No. It's all about pleasure. It's not a competition or an excuse to be with lots of women. I enjoy pleasuring women. I know most people think swinging is wrong but I don't. I think it's natural."

"Have you always had such a strong appetite for sex?"

Prescott smiles at my question. "Yes Layla, I was one horny little teenager." He says it like he is proud of his admission and all I can do is shake my head at him. I don't know why this conversation is turning me on. It should send me running for the hills. I take a second look at Prescott and I think I see traces of desire in his eyes. It gets me to thinking thoughts I should not be exploring but I can't help it. I've never felt so drawn to a man before. Of course I wanted Justin but I would be lying if I ever said I desired him sexually.

Prescott is looking at me with those hungry blue eyes. Maybe I should run for the shore but even my traitorous feet refuse to leave his side.

"Are you ready to eat?" he asks. Time truly does fly when you're having fun. I feel like we just had breakfast yet it's already time for lunch.

I tell him yes but I'm not really hungry, not for food at least. I should get out of this water and put some distance between us.

"Go get dressed; I'll meet you in the dining room in thirty minutes."

Is that his way of asking me to join him for lunch? He's definitely grown accustomed to barking out orders. I decide to let his rudeness slide, no sense in starting an argument especially since I'm enjoying his company.

I notice Prescott hasn't moved.

"You're staying?"

"Yes." He pauses for a moment then adds, "I need to cool off. Now go," he commands.

I hate it when he does that but then a very naughty idea comes to mind. I know I shouldn't play with him but I can't resist. Pretending that something caught my attention in the water I rub my ass against his groin before swimming off. After I'm a few feet away from him I turn around but I don't see him. Shit! Where did he go? It doesn't take long for me to see the water rippling beneath, he's swimming towards me. He's coming for me; I feel like I'm being hunted by a great white shark! I quickly start swimming to the shore like my life depends on it. My adrenaline is pumping as excitement courses through my body. I reach the shore and run to grab my towel and beach bag. Prescott is right behind me walking directly towards me taking huge strides as he quickly advances. I half walk half run towards my room. I almost knock down an elderly couple who get in my way. I look back at him and he is still approaching me, shaking his head at my near accident. Those blue eyes of his look hungry and I'm his food.

I make it to the stairs and take them two at a time, still racing to my room. I reach my door and fumble for my room key but by then Prescott catches up to me, still dripping wet.

"What are you trying to do to me?" he asks.

"What are you talking about?" I answer innocently. "You asked me to get ready to eat so that's what I'm about to do." He leans into me inhaling and nuzzling his face into my neck.

"It took everything in me to not wake you up for sex this morning."

That's an admission I never expected to hear from him.

"I know we said last night would be the first and last time but if you don't get in that room right now I may break another promise and take you right here."

"You promise?"

"Layla, don't play games with me. Get in the room—now!"

"I will, but only if you join me."

Chapter 15

HE TAKES A step back, searching me with lust-filled eyes. Ever so slowly he leans in and teases my lips, urging me to open for him. His taste is intoxicating. With only the caress of his soft lips my body is already prepared for his entrance.

"Same rules apply Layla. When the staff comes in tomorrow, this will end. Can you handle that?"

"Yes," I say trying to keep my voice even. I don't give a shit about the staff. All I want is some good sex. I've gone without for so long I could care less about anything or anyone. Prescott takes my key from me and unlocks the door. He quickly surveys the hall making sure we are alone before entering my room. Although technically we have all afternoon and night, I am so anxious I want him right away. I hurriedly try to take off his shorts but he stops me.

"I want to savor this moment."

Damn, he sounds sexy! I slow down mimicking his pace. He takes his time kissing me softly and slowly first before slipping down to my neck placing soft little bites along my neckline. We break contact as we move upstairs to my bed. Holding my hand he takes the lead up the stairs. I follow feeling like this is my first time. When we reach the top of the stairs he pulls me in close. His hands are meticulous. My bathing suit practically falls off at his commanding touch. Even lifeless garments obey him. I reach around his waist sliding his swim trunks down and watch in amazement as his long strong muscle springs to life right before my eyes. Lifting me by my hips he carries me to the bed, resting me down gently on my back. He takes one long look at me and I know what's coming. He's hungry. I spread my legs apart in anticipation. The feel of his tongue nudging my folds open is all I need for my body to come undone. The feel of his lips on the lips between my thighs is almost too much for my body to take. For the first time in a long time I wish I could return the favor but after my incident with Justin I'm way too scared to ever try oral sex again.

Prescott takes his time with me. I know he couldn't possibly love me but my body can't tell the difference. This is totally different from last night. After a few more moments he raises his head back and our eyes lock as he captures my lips in a kiss. I taste my wetness on him as our mouths intertwine.

"Layla, you are so beautiful…sometimes I wish we met under different circumstances."

The sad truth is if we didn't meet the way we did we would not be here right now. If it weren't for me trying to please Justin I would have never given into any of this. I guess in some strange way I should be thankful things ended the way they did. I can die knowing what a true orgasm feels like.

Prescott's mouth works wonders over my body. More than anything I desperately want to feel him inside of me.

"I would love to feel your lips wrapped around me."

My body freezes. I can't. Doing that just holds too many memories for me and now is not the time for a flashback.

"It's okay, baby girl, just kiss it for me, I want to feel your soft lips wrapped around me." Marcus' words echo in my head and I shake my head trying to clear my mind.

"I can't," I finally say, a little embarrassed.

"What's wrong?"

"Just trust me when I say I can't."

He eyes me suspiciously for a few seconds but thankfully decides not to make an issue out of it. He leans down and kisses me once more before looking around the room for his shorts. He pulls out a condom. The condom in his hand reminds me that we didn't use one last night. At least this time he's prepared, I don't need any little Prescott's swimming around inside of me. He removes the condom from its foil wrapper and slides it over his shaft. He then slides two fingers inside me making sure my body is ready for him before replacing his fingers with his long hard erection. I lean my head back against the pillow trying to contain the moan that's about to escape my lips from the pleasure of feeling his strength move within me.

This is totally different from our first night together. The first time he was rough. This time I can tell he wants to savor the moment. This time he's taking his time with my body. His touch is gentle but his strength is still intoxicating. I feel his muscle inside me pulsating. I don't even have to squeeze my pelvis to feel every inch of him.

"Oh Layla, you feel so good," he says as he continues to move, only slightly picking up the pace. It feels wonderful being with Prescott this way but for some reason I can't relax the way I did the first time. I try to focus, not wanting to break my concentration, but every time he says my name it becomes harder and harder to focus on the pleasure he is giving me. Instead my mind floats back to a time I wish I could permanently erase; instead I think of Marcus.

"Oh Layla, my sweet baby girl, you are so beautiful, I love our time together, promise me you will only do this with me and no-one else."

With each stroke it's becoming harder and harder to focus on Prescott. I keep seeing myself as that little five-year-old girl under Marcus. What the hell is wrong with me? This is Prescott for heavens' sake, the first man to make me experience an orgasm. I try hard to focus on how good he feels but each time he calls my name I find it more and more difficult to not travel the dangerous path I feel my thoughts leading me down.

Without warning Prescott dips his head down and starts to suckle on my bottom lip, "you taste sweet."

"Oh Layla, my baby girl, you taste so sweet."

I need to get Marcus' words out of my head. Prescott keeps calling my name, telling me how sweet and beautiful I am and I can't take it.

"No! No! No!" I scream.

All movement stops. I quickly separate our bodies.

"Layla, what's wrong!?"

My tears don't delay their arrival. I feel so stupid and embarrassed at my reaction. "I'm sorry, I can't do this." I rip one of the sheets off the bed and wrap it around me as I head into the bathroom to hide.

Shit, shit, shit, Layla why do you do this? Fuck! He probably thinks I'm an idiot. I hear movement outside the bathroom door. He jiggles the door knob trying to enter but I've already locked it.

"Layla, what's wrong? Did I hurt you?"

I hear panic in his voice but I'm too embarrassed to speak.

"Layla, talk to me. Tell me what's going on."

I need to pull myself together but I can't stop crying. What the hell is wrong with me? I can't believe I'm having a breakdown and in front of Prescott of all people! He's never going to want me again after this. I'm an idiot for-ever thinking I could have a normal sex life without my past ruining the moment. The cold porcelain floor lends no comfort as I try to pull myself together.

"Prescott, I'm so sorry, please, this is not your fault, I thought I could do this but I can't. Please just go to your room, I'll be okay." I need to get him out of here. I can't face him, not when I'm like this.

"Layla, I'm not going anywhere!" I hear a trace of anger in voice. Oh no, now he's mad at me. Why did I get myself into this?

I hear him slide to the floor. He's sitting on the other side of the door.

"I'll leave if you want but first I want to know what's going on."

His request is reasonable but there's no way in hell I'm going to sit here and open up to him about my past. I do my best to pull myself together before cracking the door open but Prescott pushes it open all the way. The look of confusion on his face makes me feel even worse.

"Did I hurt you? Was I being too rough?" I know that look; he wants answers but I can't stand to look him in the eye—I feel foolish. I just remain seated on the floor in silence.

"Layla," he says my name in exasperation, "talk to me."

"I'm sorry, this is my fault," my voice is barely audible. I hate sounding like this. I feel like that little five-year-old girl all over again.

"Your fault? What did you do?"

"I shouldn't have started something I couldn't finish. You did nothing wrong; this is about me and my past."

"What happened in your past?"

Why the hell did I say that?! Now he's going to want to dig into my past. I can't let that happen. "Nothing. I just need some time to myself, I promise I will be okay."

"You raced off the bed screaming NO with your face covered in tears so don't sit here and give me some bullshit about it not being a big deal because it obviously is… now what the hell is going on? I want answers and I want them now!"

"Why are you taking that tone with me? I said I was sorry." I'm used to men being annoyed when I have a flash back but Prescott looks angry and he's not even trying to mask it.

"I'm sorry if I sound abrupt, I don't mean to but if I didn't do anything to hurt you then someone else did and I want to know who. Is it Justin, were you still thinking about him?"

I could take the easy way out and say yes but I don't want Prescott to walk out of this room thinking I'm still caught up on Justin. "No, this has nothing to do with him."

"Then what is this about?"

"Please just drop it. This may sound crazy but I really did enjoy being with you," I look down at my hands; I can't look into his eyes. Sometimes I feel like he can see right through me and there are parts of myself I don't want exposed.

"I enjoyed being with you as well but something changed, so spill it."

"You're not going to leave this alone are you?"

"We both know the answer to that question so why don't you save us both some-time and tell me what the hell is going on. Whatever it is I'll take care of it for you."

My head snaps up. He looks serious. Does he seriously think he can take care of everything?

"I know you are used to being in charge but there are some things that are out of even your control."

"Try me."

He wants the truth… fine, I'll give it to him. This is not the way I thought the evening would end but once he hears how much baggage I'm still carrying around I'm sure he'll make a bee-line for the door.

"When I was five I was molested by my cousin and twenty years later I still can't get the shit out of my head. Is that what you wanted to hear?"

"First, don't let anyone ever tell you there are no stupid questions because you just asked one, of course that's not what I wanted to hear. What's your cousin's name and where is he now?" His eyes held a steely determination.

"He lives with his family back in D.C. but I'm not giving you his name."

"I need a name and address." I look up at Prescott and once again he has that no-nonsense expression on his face.

"Are you serious?" I ask somewhat dazed.

"Of course I'm serious.'"

"Are you crazy?! I'm not giving you his personal information."

"Have you told anyone what he did to you?"

"Yes, my family knows."

"So, what, is he out of jail now or something?"

"Jail! Marcus never went to jail!" Shit, I said his name; hopefully he will forget that little detail.

"Well, what happened in court?"

"We never went to court." There he goes changing colors on me again. I don't know why he even bothers to tan, once he gets upset—which seems to be quite often —he takes on a whole new shade.

"Well, what did your family do about it?"

"There was a rift in the family for a little while, no-one spoke. But when Nana got tired of the family being broken apart everyone decided to come together."

"That's it?! Everyone just got back together like nothing happened?"

"Yes."

"Not that it matters, but how old was this cousin of yours at the time?"

"Nineteen."

"So let me get this shit straight. A nineteen-year-old boy sexually abuses his five-year-old cousin and no one did anything?"

"It's not as bad as it sounds."

"Jesus Christ, you sound as stupid as those girls who defended their brother on TV! Of course it's as bad as it sounds! Layla, you are 24-years-old and just ran out of a room crying and traumatized because of what your cousin did to you! How can you say it's not as bad as it sounds?!"

"I'm older now; I should be able to control my emotions and move past this, I can't live my life stuck in the past."

"You're absolutely right. You can't live your life stuck in the past. But if you never face your past it will always come back to haunt you."

"I'll deal with it in my own time, okay?"

"Not okay. You've been holding on to this shit for way too long. I think it's time to confront your cousin. I know the statute of limitation has expired but I'm sure my legal team can still find a way to make him pay."

"Would you please just stop! I'm not interested in retribution. My family means everything to me and if I go starting stuff it will only tear us apart again. I know you are trying to help and I appreciate your concern but you have to promise me that you will leave this alone. This is not your problem to fix." Prescott motions to speak but I cut him off, "please promise me that you will let me handle this in my own time. If I know you are trying to take action against him it will only stress me out and I don't need any more stress in my life right now. Please promise me that you will leave this alone." I'm practically begging but Prescott looks unmoved by my plea.

"The longer he remains free the more victims he will have." I look at him with a startled expression; the thought of other victims out there makes me feel guilty. I refuse to believe he continued molesting girls after he was exposed. I'm sure the shame and embarrassment from when I told made him stop.

"I doubt there is anyone else that he did this to."

"Are you fucking serious?! Men like that don't stop with just one victim. They keep going until they are stopped. They're sick!"

"Trust me, he wouldn't do this to anyone else. Now please, promise me you will leave this alone." I can't have Prescott digging around in my family's past, all it will do is cause pain among the family and I don't want to be responsible for hurting anyone. Nothing really happened the first time I told, so there is no sense in causing trouble now.

"I will leave it alone for the moment but that's all that I can promise."

We remain seated on the floor in silence. I glance over at him and I can tell he's still trying to reign in his anger.

"I'm so sorry about this afternoon," I say feeling guilty. "It's getting late and you haven't had lunch yet. Why don't you go ahead and eat."

"What are you going to do for lunch?"

"I would rather just rest up a little. Please don't feel like you need to stay with me, I'll be okay."

"I'm not leaving you alone."

"Prescott, I've been dealing with these issues all my life. You really don't need to stay, I promise I will be fine by dinner." Prescott responds by pulling me into his arms and placing a light kiss on my temple.

"I'm not leaving."

This is totally different for me. The men from my past would bolt out the door as fast as possible when I had an episode. I can't believe he wants to stay. No one has ever offered to stay before. The thought makes me smile a little. I look up at his face and can tell he is genuinely concerned about me.

"Thank you."

"For what?"

"Staying."

We sit holding each other a little longer before he takes my hand and leads me back to the bed. He puts his shorts back on and lies on top of the covers while I snuggle underneath. He cradles me in his arms and I start to feel warm and protected as I drift off to sleep.

Chapter 16

THE SUN IS just starting to set when I wake up in Prescott's arms. I take a few minutes to study his strong facial features. The more time I spend with him the more I want to know. In the short period of time we've known each other I've seen so many different sides of him. One minute he's a domineering ass and the next he can be so gentle and protective. Lying here in his arms I feel like no harm could ever come my way. It's strange but even after this afternoon's disaster, I still want him. It's hard to be this close to him without erotic thoughts creeping into my mind. I feel my body go from cold to hot in an instant.

I slide my arm out from under the cover and place it over his chest rubbing my fingers delicately over his mid-section enjoying the firmness of his muscles under my fingers. Prescott lets out a moan but still doesn't wake up. Feeling brave I slide my hand south until I'm covering his sex. Slowly I rub my hand back and forth over it until I feel it start to grow. Another moan escapes his lips but this time his eyes fly open. I lift my head and place a light kiss on his lips while I continue my caress. Our kiss deepens and he pulls me on top of him before stopping.

"Wait. Are you sure you want to do this?"

"Yes."

"Are you sure you're okay? I don't like seeing you hurt especially when there's nothing I can do to ease your pain."

"You can do something. Show me how beautiful being with the right person can be." He doesn't move.

"Believe me when I say I want you right now but..."

"No buts," I say cutting him off. "The first time we were together was perfect and I want to experience that again. I need this more than you know. I want our last time together to be memorable. Words can't express how happy I was this morning. I just want that feeling again."

"You are quite determined aren't you?"

"Yes."

"Okay but the minute I do anything that makes you feel uncomfortable, you have to promise to tell me right away."

"I promise." Prescott pulls me into his arms once again as we start to kiss and taste each other. Breaking our connection he pulls back and asks,

"The first time we were together I was a little rough with you; do you think that's the difference?"

Was that the difference? He was rough but I liked it. This afternoon he tried to be gentle but that made me have a flashback. Maybe I do like it a little rough.

"Only one way to find out," I say smiling. A devious grin crosses his face before he lifts me off the bed and places me standing facing the wall.

Kissing my earlobe he whispers, "I've wanted you all day." He kisses and nibbles various parts of my body until he reaches the moistness between my legs. My legs start to quiver as he slowly gives my body the most intimate kiss possible. His hands feel strong around my waist as he holds me still. I feel my body arriving to the point of no return as I shamelessly cum all over his face. My legs feel like they are about to shatter but Prescott still doesn't stop.

"Are you ready for me?" he finally asks.

"Yes." Holding me tight I feel every inch of him as he slides inside filling and stretching every part of me.

"Damn, you're wet."

He takes hold of my body like I'm nothing more than a paper weight. Quickly he starts thrusting himself, never pulling all the way out. His thrusts are fast and deep like last night and I feel my body quiver from all the sensations of having him deep within.

"God, you feel good."

My body throbs from the pleasure. He spares nothing as he lightly bites my neck while thrusting his hips forward.

"Layla, I can't hold on anymore." Pulling out he spills himself all over my ass. I can feel the warmth from his seed as it makes its way down my ass. This is the second time we've had un-protected sex. Still panting I remain facing the wall with my hands pressed against it for support while he holds me from behind trying to catch his breath. I turn to face Prescott, running my fingers through his fine hair.

"I need more."

"Grab whatever you need, we're going to my room," he orders. "I don't have any more condoms here with me and I don't want to take any more unnecessary risks."

I don't think twice. I make a quick dash into my closet, grabbing a few items and throwing them into my carry-on bag before meeting Prescott at the threshold of my room. He takes my hand and leads the way to the other side of the resort.

Quickly we walk in silence to his room. He hurriedly takes out his room key and pulls me in without looking back. As soon as I enter I'm in awe; Prescott's suite is ten times bigger than mine. I have a liquor dispenser in my room but he has a full bar. He could entertain twenty people comfortably in his room and there would still be plenty of space. His suite carries the same island theme but everything is upgraded.

"Make yourself comfortable, I'll be right back."

"Okay." I drop my bag by the door and walk further inside. I hope he doesn't take too long. My body has never experienced anything like this and I crave more. I'm not sure how sex would be with someone else but I trust Prescott and for whatever reason my body naturally responds to him—most of the time. When he comes back he looks a little conflicted. His jaw is tightly clenched and the lines in his forehead are even more prominent.

"What's wrong?" I ask, wrapping my arms around him.

"I feel like I'm taking advantage of you."

"You shouldn't. I asked for this, remember?"

"That may be true but I'm worried about how you're going to feel tomorrow."

"What's happening tomorrow?" I was hoping to finish what we started in my suite but it looks like we have to have a meeting of the minds before we can continue. I'm so aroused I'd probably give in to anything right now.

"Tomorrow the staff arrives."

"I'll be fine, I just want to have fun with you tonight."

Slowly I can feel his muscles relax under my touch.

"I love kissing you. Your lips are so full I feel like I lose myself in you."

I smile as he leans into me. I think he is going to kiss me but instead we stand forehead to forehead nuzzling each other. Looking at me one more time he smiles before lowering his lips to mine, kissing me with a new intensity, hunger and need. My lips part and I give him the freedom to slowly slide his tongue inside as our kiss deepens. Then I slowly slide my hands up through his hair. I love running my fingers through his silky brown hair. It's different from what I'm used to but nice. Slowly we move toward the couch where he lays me down.

"I love being buried between your thighs."

He immediately removes my shorts and a smile spreads across his face while he admires my body.

"Fuck this, let's use the bed."

In one swoop he picks me up and carries me upstairs. With

more care than necessary he lies me down on his oversized bed and spreads my legs apart. Using both hands he pulls down my lace pink panties then gives me one quick kiss before delving in between my thighs.

"You taste so sweet."

OH MY GOD this man's tongue should be insured and patented; it has to be worth a million plus. He uses his tongue to stroke me back and forth, licking me like I taste of his favorite dessert. Taking his time, he kisses my sex. Not just on the outside but he loves to bury his face in me. He licks me up and down, in and out and continues this rhythm until I can no longer take it. My hips start to move and buck, not to encourage him but because I feel my body starting to pulse. Oh shit! I cum and to my dismay I actually call out his name. Panting, I try to recapture my breath. I look down at him and he has a mischievous look on his face. What is he doing? He looks at me and says, "that was just the warm up."

What?! I am still panting from my first orgasm as he dives his head in again, repeating the same rhythm on my now very tender pussy.

"Good?" he finally asks after making my body shatter once again.

"Very good," I confirm.

He gives me a smile which is something he doesn't do often. Before this trip I don't think I'd ever seen Prescott smile this much. Part of me wants to believe I'm making him as happy as he makes me. Slowly he kisses me; first my cheek, then the tip of my nose, and finally he closes in on my lips. I can taste myself on him. Next he starts to run his hands down my breasts but I freeze.

"Stop; not there."

"What's wrong?"

I don't bother to respond. I just shake my head no. I know he wants to ask me a question but stops himself.

"Do you want me to stop?"

"No, I want to you to make me feel whole again."

When Prescott's inside me I no longer feel the emptiness I felt when I was with Justin.

Satisfied I'm okay, he continues down to my stomach and naval while his fingers caress my folds. Convinced I'm ready he walks over to his closet and pulls out a new box of condoms. I get a chance to admire his full physique and impressive erection. This man is too sexy for words. He's nothing like the guys from my past. In comparison, Prescott makes every guy I've ever dated look like a little boy. He moves towards me but I tell him to wait—I want to admire the grown man standing in front of me. His body has a perfect form but what really has me gaping is his long hard erection.

"And just what are you staring at Ms. Brown?"

"It's very pretty," I say smiling. He follows my eyes and lets out a little laugh when he sees where my eyes have landed.

"Did you just call my cannon pretty?"

"You refer to your penis as a cannon?"

"Do you know what a cannon is?"

"Enlighten me."

"It's a large piece of artillery used in war."

"And that's what you have between your legs?"

"Goddamn right!" he says with a boyish grin.

I shake my head in amusement. Prescott gives me a few more moments to ogle at his cannon before joining me on the bed. Since this is our last night together we decide to make a full evening of pleasuring each other. I feel my body shiver from the thrills of his large manhood stroking my insides. He starts slow so my body can adjust to his size before picking up the pace. I'm shocked when I realize we move with the same rhythm. Faster and faster he pushes deeper into me as if he were using every limb in his body to climb the top of a mountain. Mt Layla. That definitely has a nice ring to it.

In the midst of being pleasured I close my eyes and sordid thoughts start to creep in. I think it's because he's slowed down and is becoming more and more passionate. I don't want passion;

I want a fast fuck! With each new stroke I can feel myself losing this battle—my insides start to dry up. I can also feel the change in his body. He can sense he's losing me.

"Open your eyes and look at me."

I don't want to look at him. I just want to experience my last orgasm with him.

"Layla, I know what you want but if you don't want to lose this moment you're going to have to look at me."

All movement has stopped. I'm no longer wet for him. I feel like shit for ruining the moment.

"Look me in the eyes, I'm not who you think I am."

I still don't move.

"Open your eyes and look at me!" His demand sparks new life into my body.

Finally I open my eyes and come face to face with caring blue eyes: not what I expected. A single tear slides down my cheek and Prescott ever so gently wipes it away and holds me tighter.

I had thought our evening of sex was over but my body responds to his tenderness. The internal drought inside me ends and my juices start to flow. With our eyes still locked in place we slowly start to move, recapturing our rhythm. Once he's reassured my relapse has passed, he picks up his pace. Faster and faster I feel him while the juices from my body slide down his delicious shaft. It doesn't take long before my body leaps into convulsions and I cum, feeling nothing but pleasure. Not far behind me he also explodes panting, trying to recapture his breath. I lie beneath him basking in pleasure with a smile on my face.

Chapter 17

THE NEXT MORNING I wake up to a sleeping Prescott. He looks so peaceful when he's asleep. I stare for a few minutes, taking a moment to appreciate his handsome face and then reality sets in. I've had an affair with my boss and now it's over. Reflecting on the last two days I don't have any regrets. After my ordeal with Justin it feels good to know someone else found me desirable.

I grab my clothes and get dressed, careful not to wake him. He's sound asleep. I guess it's my turn to sneak out on him. I wince at the soreness between my thighs while I work to gather my stuff. Maybe it's a good thing the staff is coming. I glance at him, soaking in one more look before slipping out of his room and heading back to my suite on the other side of the resort.

I order room service for breakfast so I don't have to worry about running into Prescott. After breakfast I lay out by the pool in one of my scandalous bikinis. I know the clothes he ordered are still waiting for me at the front desk but today I feel like wearing something sexy. Normally I wouldn't feel this comfortable but today my confidence level is soaring high. I don't remember the last time I felt so good about myself. If nothing else, these last two days with Prescott have helped me to realize there is a life outside of Justin and beyond my past demons. With time I could learn to make love without letting my past destroy the moment.

I'm lying in the shade reading a book when I hear a scream from the distance. I quickly sit up. A smile immediately graces my face when I see my ladies heading my way. My ladies are here! Stephanie, Pamela, Georgina and Simone are all beaming with excitement and wave as soon as they see me. I head over towards them before Georgina stops me dead in my tracks.

"Look at you!" she says loudly. "You look like you have been thoroughly fucked!"

"Georgina!" I scream her name and look around praying no-one heard her, "I swear your mouth has no filter! Besides, who would I have slept with here in two days? Give me a little credit." If they only knew I've been getting it on with Mr. Prescott they would flip out.

"You can play shy all you want but you definitely look like you have been getting it on. You are glowing!"

"I don't have time for this shit. How are the rest of you do-ing?" I ask, turning to the other ladies.

"I'm so happy to be here and off of that damn flight!" During our girl chat on Friday Stephanie had admitted she hates to fly. I bet a ride in Prescott's private plane would change her mind but I know better than to bring that up.

"Where is the bar?" Georgina asks, "I'm ready to get my drink on!"

We all look at her and laugh. She is so animated about every-thing. I love seeing my new friends again and I'm so happy they are here! I've been waiting for their arrival all morning while be-ing extra careful to make sure I avoid Prescott at all costs. I will miss him tonight but I'm sure me and my girls can find some-thing to get into.

"There are five different bars here; which one do you all want to go to?" Pamela asks looking at the resort guide.

Georgina immediately yells poolside bar and makes her way over. I head over to where I had been sitting and grab my bags before following my ladies to the bar. When we arrive we are able to grab five chairs together.

"Rum punch please," I order.

"Sure thing, Ms. Brown."

"Damn Layla, the bartenders know you by name already?" Simone says with a mischievous smile.

I smile back but honestly I don't know how the bartender knows my name, especially given I've never seen him before. Maybe he just remembers seeing me around. The resort is spacious but after a few days it's easy to familiarize yourself with all the guests. I pull out my money to pay for my drink but the bartender holds up his hands and motions for me to come closer.

"All of your drinks have been paid for Ms. Brown. No need to tip either—we are on notice to take care of all your needs for the remainder of your stay."

There is only one person who would do such a thing. Is this his way of rewarding me for a good time? I hope he doesn't think he needs to buy my silence. I don't know whether I should feel cheap or thankful for his gesture.

"You okay?" I look over and catch Stephanie studying me—she's very observant.

"I'm fine."

"We were all really worried about you, Layla."

"Thanks Pamela. Actually, thank all of you for being there for me. Aside from the scandalous wardrobe you packed for me, I couldn't ask for better friends."

"Scandalous! Girl, you are in Jamaica—if you can't wear it here then you shouldn't even own it! Besides, you look sexy!"

I won't burst Georgina's bubble by telling her everything she packed for me was bought by Justin. I'm actually a little thankful for my scandalous wardrobe. Although I've avoided Prescott all day, I can't deny I had him in mind when picking this swimsuit. If he sees me in it I know it'll drive him crazy.

We are all talking over each other enjoying our rum punch when the bartender interrupts our conversation.

"Ms. Brown."

"Yes."

"They have requested your presence at the front desk."

"Why?"

"They didn't say," he says shrugging his shoulders apologetically.

I excuse myself from the girls and head to the front desk. Hmm... maybe my drinks are not taken care of after all. I take my time getting there; I don't know why but I feel knots forming in the pit of my stomach. As soon as I turn the corner I see Prescott waiting. Shit! Did he call me? I approach the desk trying to look casual. Maybe it's just a coincidence he's here.

"Hello Mr. Prescott," I say, trying to sound nonchalant. Why am I so nervous? After everything that has transpired between us you would think I would feel more comfortable around him but at the moment I don't.

"Do you know what I did this morning after I woke up in bed alone without so much as a goodbye?" I guess he plans to skip all pleasantries. I motion to speak but he stops me. "I had a meeting with some local business owners in a conference room on the resort."

Okay, where is he going with this? I don't remember him mentioning any meetings yesterday.

"We all took a five minute break to refresh our coffee when someone noticed an enticing woman half-dressed lying out by the pool. Everyone clamored around the window to get a better look and imagine my surprise when I discovered it was you. I thought I made it clear that I want you to stay under the radar this week. I don't want you drawing any unnecessary attention to yourself."

"I wasn't trying to draw attention to myself, I just wanted to relax."

"Relax in something else," he says, turning to walk away from me.

"No." He is mid-stride when he stops and turns around to face me. If Prescott and I are going to work together we are going to have to set some boundaries. I'm not going to allow him to bully me—I'm through with men telling me what to do.

"Excuse me?"

"I said no, I'm tired of being bossed around. Nothing is wrong with the swimsuit I'm wearing and I'm not going to let you start to make me doubt myself and question my body." From his reaction you would swear I was walking around topless. My swimsuit may be sexy but I'm still covered. Prescott looks both furious and lost. Suddenly we are both aware of the looks we are receiving from the other patrons.

"Don't say another word." He takes my arm and leads me down a private hall. He stops at a room with no numbers on the outside and opens it with a key card. He crosses the threshold looking at me, probably expecting me to follow but I'm leery. I glance around and see it's a conference room. I take a deep breath and enter knowing I'm probably in for a fight.

I'm prepared for him to yell but instead he takes a much calmer approach.

"Look, the last thing I want to do is make you doubt yourself. Sometimes it's hard for me to believe that someone as beautiful as you still doesn't know it."

Hearing Prescott refer to me as beautiful still takes me by surprise. Hopefully one day I will be able to look at myself and see what he sees.

"You don't believe me do you?"

"Believe what?"

"Every time I tell you you're beautiful a look of doubt crosses your face."

This is what I hate. How is he able to read my mind? No matter how many times someone may say it, I still find it hard to believe. How can I be beautiful if I'm tainted? I feel foolish standing here in front of him half dressed. He's right; I need to go change.

"I'm sorry if I messed up your meeting this morning, I'll go up and change." Putting on this swimsuit was clearly a bad idea. I need to get out of here but before I can make it to the door he pulls me back slamming me against his chest.

"I can't give you the self-esteem you need but I would hope you know me well enough to know I would never bullshit you. If I say you're beautiful it's because it's true. I don't want you to walk out that door doubting yourself. I just want to make sure you stay safe this week and with all of the men ogling over you I don't know how to protect you without making things between us obvious to everyone around. Don't change what you're wearing, just promise me you'll be careful."

"I promise."

He still hasn't let me go. I don't think I will ever get tired of being in his arms. Neither one of us makes a move to part ways; this week is going to be more difficult than I thought. Without hesitation he leans forward and kisses me. I instantly react by opening to him and deepening our kiss.

"This is fucking crazy! I feel like I can't get enough of you."

Hearing him say that gives me a boost of confidence. I feel better knowing I'm not the only one who wants more. With one swift move he lifts me up and I wrap my legs around his waist. We are on borrowed time. We skip over all forms of foreplay in anticipation of the final act. He slips my bikini bottom to the side and enters me in one thrust.

How does he do that? Justin use to fumble all of the time but I swear Prescott has a GPS system in his cannon that leads him straight to my pussy. Quickly he moves inside of me, sliding my body up and down his beautiful shaft. I wrap my legs tighter around his waist and cling to his shoulders for balance. Gently I nibble and pull on his earlobe. Over the past two days I've learned he finds that to be a turn on. He is pounding into me now and I can feel how much his body needs this; he needs me and I need him. Faster and faster he thrusts into me, panting, trying to reach his release. I come first with my body shuddering in his arms.

"Oh Layla," he shouts pumping twice more before reaching his climax.

He's still holding me in his arms and I feel a release that I've secretly yearned for all morning. He kisses me on my neck before sliding out of me, reminding me I was already sore from last night.

"Spending this week without you is going to be harder than I thought," he says whispering in my ear.

"I know what you mean," I say finally, looking up at him.

"I don't like sneaking around."

"There are way too many people here from the office, someone will notice."

His expression says he doesn't care but even if he doesn't, I do. I don't want anyone to know I'm sleeping with my boss.

"If I think of a way for us to get some alone time together will you be up for it?"

I say yes without any hesitation. Spending the rest of the week with Prescott would be like winning the lottery.

"I'll take care of the details."

"What do you plan to do?"

"Don't worry, I'll work everything out."

What the hell is he up to? I decide against asking any more questions. If he can find a way for us to be together this week without anyone knowing, I'll be happy.

Chapter 18

I FEEL LIKE I have an extra pep in my step on my way back to meet my girls. In all my years with Justin, I don't think I've ever willingly done anything so kinky before. For most people, sex in a hotel conference room probably isn't a big deal but for me, it is. When I'm with Prescott I feel like nothing else matters. I wish this feeling could last forever.

When I arrive at the bar I see Carlos sitting in my seat.

"Layla! Where have you been? I've been waiting on you." I want to ask him why but decide against being rude. "I was told you were drinking rum punch so I went ahead and got you another round." Little does he know all of my drinks have already been covered for the week. That's one secret I will definitely be keeping to myself. If any of my girls found out they would have a ton of questions for me.

"Hey everyone," Georgina yells over the music, "I just got a text from Jonathan and it looks like he wants us all to gather for dinner in the main dining room tonight."

Dinner tonight? Prescott didn't mention anything about a

company dinner. This will be the first time we will be together with the staff and I need to make sure I don't do anything that will draw attention to myself.

"Hey Simone, do you mind if I borrow one of your dresses for dinner, everything Georgina packed for me is inappropriate and I'm not keen on looking like the company skank at dinner." Simone's not known for owning conservative dresses but out of all my girls, borrowing something from her is my best option. I could never fit into Georgina's or Pamela's clothes—they both look like they wear a size two and everything Stephanie owns is too masculine for my taste.

"Of course girl, I think I have just the dress for you," she says with a naughty smile on her face. Clearly Georgina had more help than I thought when it came to packing for me.

"Just remember after the incident at happy hour I need to keep a low profile."

"Don't worry, I'll take care of you." I don't trust the look on her face but before I can change my mind she links our arms together pulling me towards her room.

It turns out Simone's room is right next door to mine. She gives me a couple of dress options; I would prefer something a little more conservative but with limited choices I decide to borrow her white Chanel dress. It's cut a little shorter than I would have liked and the back is exposed but it still looks better than anything I currently have in my closet.

The more time I spend with my girls the more I learn. For instance today I learn Simone takes forever to get dressed. My patience is running thin. I yell out to her that I'm leaving and step into the hall closing the door behind me. In the hall I notice my room door is open and members of the staff are removing my bags.

"Excuse me," I say, getting the attention of a short Hispanic woman, "what's going on and where are you going with all my stuff?"

She smiles gracefully at me. The nametag on her shirt says Rosemary.

"Are you Ms. Layla Brown?"

"Yes." She digs into her apron pocket and hands me an envelope. I immediately rip it open; it's a note from Prescott.

I'm having your room moved to the suite next to mine.
If anyone asks, just tell them the A.C unit was not working and
management upgraded your room for your inconvenience.
See you after dinner.

This is probably as close to a love note as I will ever get from someone like Prescott. Of course he hadn't thought to ask me if I want to change rooms; as always he does what he wants. Rosemary is looking at me expectantly but I have nothing to say.

"You should be happy, Ms. Brown, your new room is lovely!"

"Thank you Rosemary," I say, smiling politely; it's not her fault Prescott doesn't know any better, "should I stop at the desk for a new key?"

"Here," she says, handing me another envelope. Inside is my new room key with my suite number. I'm glad Prescott wants me close but I'm nervous about being neighbors. I know he's going to watch my every move and I really don't want any more arguments. Rosemary told me not to worry about any of my belongings as the staff was ordered to unpack everything for me. I don't have time to check out my new room before dinner; I don't want to be late.

Inside the dining hall the entire marketing team is present and excitement is in the air. People are dispersed around the room laughing and talking amongst themselves. I see Georgina engaged in conversation with some of the senior staff. I continue my scan of the room and spot Stephanie and Pamela standing together. Simone, being the diva that she is, will undoubtedly make a grand entrance. On my way over to Steph and Pam I notice Veronica out the corner of my eye. She has on a tight, nude short dress.

The dress is so revealing I have to look twice to see it really isn't her skin showing—it left nothing to the imagination. And to think Prescott was concerned about my wardrobe. It's no secret who she's trying to impress.

"Hey, Layla, are you okay?" Pamela asks when I reach them both.

"What the hell is she wearing?" Pamela and Stephanie both look in the direction I'm staring in and spot Veronica. "She looks like a tramp!"

"I agree," Stephanie says, "but no need to get so upset about it. Everyone knows she's just trying to get attention from Mr. Prescott."

That's why I'm upset but I can't say anything. I remind myself that I need to play it cool if I don't want anyone to get suspicious—it's bad enough they already think I'm sleeping with someone on the resort.

I turn my attention away from Veronica and take in my surroundings. The dining room is massive with floor to ceiling windows overlooking the ocean. Through the doors is a large terrace with access to the beach. Just hearing the waves crash against the shore in the distance relaxes me. The lights dim and everyone moves to take their seats. The wait staff has placed several rectangular tables together so we can all sit at one massive table as a group. Of course Prescott is at the head of the table and Veronica is seated right next to him. Georgina takes the seat on the other side of him and I feel a pang of jealousy in my chest watching him surrounded by women. I already can't wait for dinner to be over.

Pamela, Stephanie and I are able to grab three chairs on the opposite end of the table. Simone finally makes her appearance and takes a seat closer to the head of the table by Prescott and Georgina. The seat next to me doesn't stay vacant long; Carlos grabs it before anyone else can. I look over at him in disgust—this is going to be a long dinner.

During dinner I casually glance down to the other end of the table and notice Prescott and Veronica engrossed in conversation. I wish I knew what they were talking about. I feel another pang of jealousy hit my chest and I'm reminded Prescott and I have no claims to each other. We are just two adults enjoying each other's company. Still, seeing her with him starts to piss me off. Veronica must be saying something funny because now the two of them are laughing. What the fuck! She's flirting with him and he doesn't seem to mind. I can't look anymore. Everyone around me is commenting on the food. Apparently it's delicious but I can't taste a thing; I'm too consumed with what's happening at the other end of the table. This is crazy, I'm getting jealous and I'm not even the jealous type. I need space. I need a night away from him.

"Do you all feel like hitting a club tonight?"

Not surprisingly, Carlos is the first to agree to go out. Pamela looks over at me surprised, "you mean you don't have to meet up with your new boy toy tonight?"

"Very funny, I'm serious, I feel like dancing tonight."

"I'm down," says Stephanie, "I'll ask Georgina after she finishes making a play for Mr. Prescott."

"Making a play for Prescott? What the hell are you talking about?"

"You don't know? Georgina would love to get her hands on that man but from the looks of things Veronica is giving her a run for her money."

Great! Keeping this secret is becoming more and more difficult. I definitely need to get away. "Let's leave right after dinner."

"What's the rush?" Stephanie asks.

"No rush," I say casually. "I just thought it would be fun to get out early that's all. We can meet in the lobby and catch a taxi."

"Sounds good to me," Carlos says smiling. Why the hell is he tagging along? Technically I hadn't invited him but it would be rude of me to tell him so, so I let it go.

After dinner Prescott makes a quick exit out of the dining room. I wonder if he's heading back up to his room. I immediately push the thought out of my mind. After the way he displayed himself with Veronica I'm not going to hang around the resort tonight waiting on him. I need some space to think. If I go back to my room and he's not there I will end up sitting by the door waiting for him and I refuse to become desperate.

Once the dining room starts to thin out Stephanie lets Georgina and Simone know about our plans to go out and they agree to join us. In the meantime, I make arrangements for the taxi at the front desk. As soon as the taxi pulls up Prescott comes strolling into the lobby with Veronica not far behind him. He looks over at me suspiciously but calls out to Georgina.

"You ladies heading out for the evening?" he asks nonchalantly.

"Layla wants to go dancing tonight. I don't suppose you would want to join us?" she asks smiling. Why the hell did she have to let him know that going out was my idea? Prescott glances at me quickly before turning away.

"No, you all have fun, I already made plans for the evening," he says looking directly at me. Shit, he's upset. To make matters worse, Carlos takes my hand to escort me to the taxi that's waiting for us. To no surprise I see the color start to rise in Prescott's face. Maybe this outing wasn't a good idea after all.

Chapter 19

IT'S NEARLY TWO o'clock in the morning before we get back to the hotel. The club was nice and the people were cool but my mind kept drifting back to Prescott. The sole purpose of me going out was to get space so I could clear my mind and think but instead I spent the entire evening wondering what he was up to. I'm tempted to knock on his door but think better of it and enter my room alone.

The one bright side to finally getting back to my room is that I can finally take off these damn shoes—my feet are killing me. I fumble for the light switch since this is my first time in my new suite but before I find it I catch a whiff of cologne—Prescott's. I immediately tense up, not knowing what to expect. Is he still here? Did he try to wait up for me? I leave my room in darkness as I slowly creep through the suite. It only takes a second for my eyes to adjust and see him sitting on a chair by the balcony with a glass in his hand. He reaches over and turns on a side lamp, the soft glow from the light does nothing to lessen his harsh features —he's pissed.

"Did you have a good time tonight?" His question may be simple but the lines on his forehead give away his true feelings. The last time I felt this nervous was when my father caught Cynthia and I sneaking out to a party.

"What are you doing here?" I ask. Yes, I wanted to see him but not if he's looking for an argument.

"I thought my note was pretty clear when I said that I wanted to meet you after dinner."

"If you had asked, I would have let you know that I wanted to go out tonight. I'm not here to take your orders." I'm not going to let him railroad me, no matter how much he may intimidate me.

"So, because I didn't say please meet me after dinner you decided to ditch me for Carlos? I'm not going to play games with you, if you want Carlos just fucking say so and we can end this thing right now."

"What are you talking about? I don't want Carlos; I didn't even invite him tonight, he invited himself. And secondly, I don't know why you're so upset, I'm not the one who spent half the night flirting with Veronica and Georgina." The audacity of this man!

"What the hell are you talking about? You actually think I'm interested in them? I already told you that I don't screw around with my employees. I've broken my rule for you and after tonight I will never let this shit happen again. And just so we are clear, if I were to ever date an employee those would be the last two women I would ever choose. Veronica is desperate for attention and needy as all hell and Georgina has fucked so many men I'm surprised she can even walk in an upright position."

Really? He has the gall to talk about how many men Georgina's been with when he's a swinger?

"This coming from a man who meets strangers over the internet for sex," I yell back. "You've probably fucked so many women I'm surprised you don't need a little blue pill to get yourself started!"

"Watch it!"

"Or what?!" I say challenging him.

"This is fucking crazy! I don't know why I let you irritate me the way you do."

Prescott stands and starts to pace with both hands in his hair. He rubs his face in frustration as a grunt escapes his lips.

"You know," he says, finally stopping, "I don't remember you being this combative with Justin."

"Was it not you who pulled me off him when I was kicking his ass?"

Prescott smirks and we both stop to laugh a little at the memory.

"I don't think I've ever been so proud of you than when I saw you beating him with your shoes."

"You never told me that, I thought you were upset."

"I was upset you did it at a company function but don't doubt for a minute I don't think he got what he deserved." I feel some of the anger starting to drain from my body. One thing for sure, together Prescott and I are explosive in more ways than one.

Finally he stops pacing and leans up against a cabinet with his arms crossed observing me.

"I don't remember the last time I've had anyone try to punish me."

"What are you talking about? I didn't punish you."

"You knew I was expecting to see you after dinner and because you didn't like me talking to Veronica you deliberately made plans to go out and not tell me. Call it what you want but that was your way of punishing me for doing something you didn't like."

I never thought about it like that; I guess in a way I was punishing him.

"I'm not admitting guilt but I can see your point."

"Coming from you I guess that's the closest thing to an apology I will ever receive." He's right but I'm not going to let him know that. All of the fight in me is gone. Sometimes I feel like our arguments are a form of foreplay. He's dressed down in a pair of shorts and a t-shirt but still looks sexy as all hell.

"Would you feel better if you got to punish me in return?" I say with a little devious smile.

"Be careful of what you ask for, you may just get it."

"I'm well aware of what I'm asking for."

"Are you sure about that?"

"Yes," I say with confidence. Prescott hasn't even done anything to me yet and I feel my body tingling all over. Without warning he scoops me up and carries me down the hall to what I can only assume is the bedroom. He opens the door and kicks it shut with his feet. Without missing a step he pushes me onto the bed.

"You have too many clothes on," he says and with both hands tugs my dress off over my head. He lies on top of me and immediately seeks out my lips as his hands roam my body. His hands feel rough for someone who sits in meetings and does paperwork all day.

"I've wanted you since dinner and you made me wait for you. I don't like being kept waiting." I'm learning to love it when he's aggressive. While kissing me he undoes his shorts, kicking them to the floor. Usually he's all about foreplay but not tonight.

"I'm going to take you right now," he pauses and looks at me for any sign of a flashback. When he feels confident that I'm okay he continues on. Moving my panties to the side I feel him insert two fingers, "I'm glad you're ready for me" and with one thrust he's inside of me. My body is shocked by his quick entrance. He gives me a moment to adjust before he starts to move. Faster and deeper his large muscle pumps within me, overtaking my body. His hips move faster and faster. I'm being fucked. I feel like my body is on the verge of exploding. He moves his hand to my throat and starts to squeeze as he continues to bury himself inside me. Holy shit, he's choking me, and more shockingly it feels good.

"The next time I leave you a note telling you to meet me, you are to do as you're told, do you understand?"

I nod my head yes. The feel of his hands wrapped around my throat only intensifies everything I'm feeling. My body is completely pinned beneath him and all I can do is feel him. Pounding away inside of me I hear him call my name "goddamn it Layla, what the fuck are you doing to me?" I would love to ask him the same question but I can't speak. His entire hand is covering my throat and his body feels delicious. The lack of air and the feel of his body is almost too intense for words. Two more thrusts and I have once again reached my climax, feeling my body drift into a state of euphoria. Prescott releases my neck and falls on top of me panting and shivering as he too has reached his climax. Who would have ever thought being choked could be so thrilling?

I wake up startled, realizing Prescott is still in my bed. I glance at the clock and see it's only five o'clock in the morning. Ever so gently I get up and search for the bathroom. I need a shower. As soon as I step into the bathroom I smile. This bathroom is probably every woman's dream. Everything is so modern it takes me a minute to figure out how to use the programmable shower.

Under the spray of the warm water a feeling of sadness overtakes my body. Not because of anything I've done with Prescott but because of what I can't have with him. No matter what we do, at the end of the day I'm still damaged goods. An image of Marcus enters my mind and I start scrubbing my skin harder and harder, trying desperately to scrub away my past. Why did Marcus have to touch me, why couldn't he just let me be? The rational side of me knows at the age of five it was not my fault but I still feel guilty. What did I do to bring this on myself? I stifle a cry, not wanting to wake Prescott. I slide to the floor of the shower stall and cry. My body shakes as I cry harder and harder. This isn't fair! Marcus is happily married with a child while I'm still trying to figure out a way to have sex without having a major breakdown. With my head buried in my hands I unleash everything within me.

Without any warning I hear the shower door open and before I know it I'm wrapped in Prescott's arms. He's getting soaked but neither of us says a word, he just lets me cry in his arms until I have nothing else left within me. Once my crying has died down he turns off the water, dries me off and carries me to bed.

"Don't worry," he says kissing me on the top of my head, "I'm never going to let anyone hurt you again." He speaks with authority and a part of me almost believes him.

Chapter 20

AFTER MY CRYING spell in the shower I pass out. Later in the morning when I finally wake up I look around the room and see Prescott is already dressed sitting in a chair across from the bed. He looks a little restless.

"Good morning."

"Good morning," I say eyeing him. I can tell by the creases in his forehead he's been in deep thought.

"How are you feeling?"

"I'm okay," I say shyly, not wanting to make eye contact. I'm not used to crying in front of anyone and I still feel a little embarrassed from last night.

"Layla, I think we should talk about last night."

"Please don't," I say, putting my hand up before he could go any further, "I don't want you to make a big deal out of this, I just had a moment but I feel better now."

"And what happens when you have another moment?"

"When that time comes I'll deal with it." He looks frustrated with me; he doesn't seem to understand that this is not his battle to fight. "What time is it?" I ask hoping to change the subject.

"It's a little after ten," he says getting up, "why don't you freshen up? I didn't know how long you would sleep so I ordered room service for you. When you're ready, meet me on the balcony for breakfast."

"Okay," I say getting up slowly. "Thank you for ordering breakfast." He gives me a brief nod in acknowledgement before leaving the room. Sometimes I find it alarming how thoughtful he can be; Justin would have never done anything like this for me.

I step out on the balcony and breathe in the fresh ocean air—this place is truly paradise. For breakfast Prescott has ordered us Belgian waffles with fresh strawberries, scrambled eggs and bacon. Before I take my seat he pulls me in for a warm embrace and all of the tension I feel evaporates. Stroking my hair he looks at me like I'm the most incredible woman in the world, which is crazy because that's the furthest thing from the truth. I'm damaged goods but when he looks at me this way I almost forget all of my baggage.

"Are you ready to eat?"

I nod my head yes and we take our seats across from each other. I truly do appreciate these moments with Prescott—I wish I could freeze them in time. The more time we spend together the harder it is for me to imagine going back to the way things were.

"Are you enjoying your breakfast?"

"Why yes—thank you," I say flirtatiously.

"I was thinking about last night," he says cautiously.

Here we go again, I hope he's not about to ruin this beautiful breakfast.

"Do I even want to know what you've been thinking?"

"Don't get defensive, I just want to propose something to you, something I would like for you to try."

Warning bells immediately go off in my head. The last time I tried something for a man I ended up meeting two swingers. My first instinct is to tell him to forget about whatever the hell he's thinking but Prescott is different from Justin and I can't imagine he would propose something I would be totally against. Whatever the case, he has my full attention. I just pray it doesn't end with us having a huge argument. I rest my fork on the plate and place my hands together in preparation for whatever it is he's about to say.

"You can put down your shield," he says smiling, "I'm not about to initiate war with you. I just want to run something by you."

"I'm listening."

"I'm not going to get into anything about last night but I have been thinking about your... episodes, for lack of a better word and I don't think we should continue on with the way things are."

Is he ending things with me? This sure sounds like the beginning of the end speech.

"If you don't want to see me anymore you don't need to make a long speech, just say what you need to say. I'm stronger than I look."

An incredulous expression takes over his face, "I'm not ending things; the opposite actually, I'm putting you in charge."

In charge? "What are you talking about?"

"I want you to be the one to initiate sex."

"Why?"

"I think if it's on your terms it will help you overcome some of your flashbacks. Also, if it's under your control, I'd be less likely to do something to turn you off."

"Is that what this is about, you think you did something to turn me off?"

"I shouldn't have done what I did to you last night."

"Are you kidding?! Last night was one of the most intense nights of my life," I say standing and coming to sit on his lap. I don't want him to ever think that any of my flashbacks are his fault. "I loved every minute with you, please don't ever doubt that."

"You may enjoy it but what about what happens to you when we're done? You don't understand what it does to me to see you break down the way you did last night."

"Prescott," I say, trying to interject but before I can finish he cuts me off.

"I don't want to get off track with what I'm proposing. I understand good sex is new to you," he says grinning, oh how proud he must be, cocky SOB, "and I want you to feel free to explore all of the possibilities under your own terms."

"What exactly does that mean?"

"It means I will be here for you whenever you want and we'll try whatever you like."

This is the last thing I would expect from him. I feel nervous at the thought yet I'm also intrigued. "So you'll do whatever I want, whenever I want it?"

"Yes, Ms. Brown. I will be at your beck and call." The sound of Prescott being at my beck and call is quite tantalizing.

"Not that I don't appreciate the gesture but I think you've forgotten we are on an island with everyone from the office. I can't exactly walk up to you and proposition you for sex."

"I already have a solution for that," he says reaching under the breakfast cart. He pulls out a smart phone and hands it over to me. "I have a special number programmed into the phone. It's not my office, home or cell number so no one will know that you're calling me. Just hold down the number one key for three seconds and it will take you to a special screen where you can either call or text me."

"What if I never call?"

"The choice is yours."

"So you're not ever going to initiate sex with me again?"

"If you want me to I will, but I really want you to try this. If it doesn't work out no harm done but I would like for you to try, just once."

Wow. I don't even know what to say. So rarely am I speechless but at the moment I have no words. Prescott is willing to relinquish all of his control and let me take charge. I've never been in charge during sex before, what if I mess up? What if I like it? It feels like a new challenge but I'm up for it. Besides, I know opportunities like this don't happen often. I feel comfortable with Prescott, so if I were to ever try something like this, he's the person I want it to be with.

"Where would we meet?"

"Everything is on your terms. Just send a text and I will meet you wherever you want."

"And you'll do whatever I say?" He's laughing now at the thought.

"I don't like pain so as long as it's not painful, yes, I will do whatever you want."

I don't have to look in the mirror to know I'm smiling from ear to ear. I feel like I just won the lottery. Sex on my terms whenever I want, wherever I want –Jackpot! I wrap my arms around him holding him close.

"I take it you like my idea."

"I love your idea," I say sweetly. This man is totally disarming me. I feel like I want to make love to him right now but I know I need time to plan our first escapade. This is the sweetest thing anyone has ever done for me, almost too sweet, and I start to feel a little skeptical.

"Are you going to sleep with other women while you're here?" If he says yes then I don't think this arrangement will work.

"No," he says without any hesitation, "I'm all yours for the rest of the week." I search his eyes but I don't see anything that makes me feel I should doubt him.

"You really are amazing."

"I try."

Prescott leaves after breakfast, leaving me to think about our new arrangement. I think about all of the things I could possibly try with him on my way to the pool.

When I meet up with the girls they're already gathered poolside with drinks in hand. Georgina and Pamela are lying in the sun while Simone and Stephanie have opted for seats in the shade. I notice a few male suiters surrounding the girls but thankfully as soon as I grab a lounge chair next to Simone they go away. I'm not seated for more than ten seconds before a server comes over and takes my drink order; that's when I notice all of the girls staring at me.

"Do you know how long we had to wait for a drink? How the hell did you get someone to take your order so quickly?" Simone asks.

"I don't know, I guess my timing is good," I don't see what the big deal is but they all look annoyed. My drink arrives in record time and I savor my first sip of rum punch for the day.

"What's the deal with you?" Georgina asks, "do you have dick repellent sprayed on you or something? Ever since you joined us all the men are staying away."

"What are you talking about?" I ask, readjusting my chair.

"Before you came we had to beat the men off with a stick but since you've come not one man has come this way."

Now that she mentions it, it is a little odd that all the men left as soon as I came over. I look around the pool and not one man has even glanced in our direction. As odd as it may seem, I'm still thankful; the men here can be little overbearing at times. An image of Paul comes to mind. I haven't seen him since he left me on the beach. Prescott would be happy to know I'm no longer drawing attention to myself. Maybe a little too happy; could he have something to do with this? Wait, what the hell am I thinking? I immediately dismiss the idea as soon as it comes to mind. He couldn't possibly arrange for all of the men to stay away, no-one has that type of power.

"Are you fucking some king-pin down here or something?" Georgina asks.

"You all need to stop talking crazy, besides I have an important question to ask."

"What's your question?"

"Well, if you were given complete control over a man sexually, what would you do to him? Oh, and whatever it is cannot involve pain."

"I'm not into men so I will leave that question to the rest of you ladies to answer," Stephanie says while reaching for another sip of her drink. I'm very curious about her; although she says she's a lesbian I've never even seen her so much as take a second look at a woman.

"That's your question?" asks Georgina. "That's an easy one; I would fuck him!"

"We know that Georgina, but what would you do to make it interesting?"

"Actually it depends on what type of experience you are looking for," Pamela says sitting up. "You need to decide if you have any fetishes that you would like to explore or if you want something romantic or you could even look into taking on a dominant or submissive role. Either way, there's a lot you can do with almost any scenario."

All of us freeze and look over at Pamela in surprise. She is the quietest in the bunch. If it weren't for her two kids you would think she's a virgin. Her mousy brown hair, thin frame and pale skin don't exactly scream sexual vixen, yet here she is asking me about fetishes, romance or some crazy dom/sub sexual experience. It makes me wonder what else she knows.

"And what do you know about sex?" Georgina asks giggling. "Do you have some slutty stories you would like to share?" she asks, egging Pamela on.

"Unlike you, I never kiss and tell."

"Well I think it's my civic duty to let women know if a man isn't worth fucking. If I can save one woman from making the same mistake I've made, I feel I've done my job as a good-Samaritan."

"That doesn't mean you go out and fuck every man you meet just so you can report on your experience," Stephanie says throwing a towel at Georgina, "besides this is not about your sexual escapades. Layla asked a question worthy of an answer. So Layla," Stephanie asks with a mischievous grin on her face, "I can't see you having some fetish so I'm going to assume you're either looking for romance or you're looking to be a dom or sub."

"What if I don't know what I like and I just want to explore some of the different possibilities?"

"There has to be something you like, something that you've found intriguing at some point in your life."

Pamela's right, there is one thing I've always been intrigued about. Saying it aloud seems silly though.

"Something's on your mind," Georgina says turning over. Since she's arrived in Jamaica she's at least three shades darker, "spill it."

"Do you all think role play is silly?"

"Are you kidding?! Some of my best experiences were through role play!" Georgina says laughing.

Could I actually role play with Prescott? Would he even go for it? I would love to become someone different in the bedroom, someone without a past. I remember the way Angela walked into the room the first night we all met. She was sexy and confident. I wonder if I'm capable of pulling off something like that.

"Well, well, well," Georgina says looking over at me, "ladies I think our little freak of the week has devised a role she would love to play."

I don't even bother to respond. I give her the finger while taking out my phone to text Prescott. As soon as I type my message and hit send he responds right back saying he'll meet me in my room in fifteen minutes. I guess he wasn't lying when he said he would be at my beck and call.

"Hey girls," I say gathering my things, "I'm going to head in for a little while it's hot out here. Want to meet up for dinner?"

"I bet it is hot, you horny little bitch," laughs Georgina. "Don't hold out on that good Jamaican sex Layla. Pay it forward!" I throw some ice from my drink at Georgina but she ducks.

"Why don't you try cooling off?" I say walking away. I can feel their eyes on me as I leave. I know they know what I'm up to. Truthfully I don't care if they know what I do. As long as they don't know who it's with.

Chapter 21

I HEAD STRAIGHT to my room knowing I don't have much time to prepare. Once again I'm thankful Georgina did indeed pack my bags. I dig through the drawers the staff have so nicely arranged and sure enough at the bottom I find a black leather lingerie set, complete with stockings and a garter belt. I don't know what the hell possessed Justin to buy this for me or for Georgina to even pack it in my bags but now I'm thankful.

I rush into the bathroom and freshen up before changing. I apply some make up and give my eyes a smoky seductive look. I stand back and take a look at myself in the mirror. I don't even recognize the woman staring back at me. She looks confident and sexy. I can do this, I say to myself. I slip on some heels and wait by the room door for Prescott to arrive when I hear what sounds like a door opening from the living room. I head in that direction and there he is dressed in slacks, a dress shirt and tie. We look at each other in surprise; he made sure we have connecting doors –how convenient.

Prescott's eyes never leave my body, "you look fucking amazing," he says and I smile, I need to be confident but his appearance has thrown me off. With his height and well-toned frame Prescott already has a very commanding appearance but when he's in work attire he can look downright ruthless and sexy.

"Why do you look like you just came from a meeting?"

"Because I did," he says loosening his tie.

"Is it over?"

"Nope," he says kicking of his shoes.

"You should have told me, we could have gotten together later."

"Are you crazy, you've been on my mind all day; I felt like a stupid teenage girl checking my phone every five minutes waiting for your call."

That's an image I can't imagine yet here he is.

"You look amazing."

"You already said that."

"Well, it is worth repeating."

I take a deep breath feeling anxious.

"So, Ms. Brown," he says with a hint of a smile, "what do you have in mind for us this afternoon?"

"I'd rather show you than tell you," I say with a little extra sass. I start our afternoon by sauntering over to the music station, *Game Changer* by Johnny Gill comes on and I slowly turn to face him. I've never seduced a man before but now more than anything I want to seduce him. I want to make him fall to his knees and beg me for my body. I want to experience what it feels like for a man to want you so badly he forgets everything and everyone and only focuses on you. Justin used other women to supplement our sex life and I don't ever want to go through that again. I want to be enough, fuck that, I want to be more than enough.

I take my time swaying my hips as I take a seductive stroll back towards Prescott.

"I love your tie," I say wrapping it around my hand and pulling him closer. I waste no time in plunging into him with a kiss. My hands are all over him at once and I feel an extra boost of confidence as he moans into my mouth and whispers my name.

"If you don't want things to be over before we start, I'm going to need you to slow down," he says, but I dismiss his suggestion.

"I'm in charge," I say pushing him down onto the couch. I rip his shirt open and kiss his glorious pecs while rubbing his broad shoulders.

"Layla," he says my name again but I ignore him. I'm having too much fun being in control. I strip him out of his shirt and immediately get started on the task of removing his pants. A huge tent has formed in his groin area thanks to his erection. A smile crosses my face knowing I'm the one who has turned him on, no porn or cheap magazine, just me. I need both of my hands to encase his erection. I slowly start to stroke him and another moan escapes his lips. Holding him like this makes me feel powerful. Now I understand why he refers to it as a cannon. I want to make him explode. I can feel the blood in his muscle pumping and watch as his eyes close and his head falls back as he continues to whisper my name. Feeling brave and confident I decide to lick the tip of him. His eyes shoot open in awe when he feels my lips touch him. I know he's wanted this from me for a long time but I didn't have the confidence. Marcus use to hold my head over him until I would lick him and the memory was so strong I couldn't imagine ever doing it again. I did try once with Justin but that too turned out to be a disaster. Today I have the confidence to do this for Prescott. The old Layla is not available; whoever is taking over is completely different and she's really starting to grow on me.

Call it instinct if you like but I know exactly what to do to make Prescott cum. I stroke and take him all in until his muscle hits the back of my throat. Over and over I continue to take him deeper and deeper, tasting his salty sweetness. I can tell he's close to erupting when he says, "Holy Shit!" Then as if he is saving me from a bomb that is about to erupt he pulls my head back and we both watch as he spills his seed all over my breasts. I don't think I've ever felt so alive before.

"I should have given you control a long time ago," he says out of breath.

"I think your timing was perfect," I reply smiling. I straddle his hips and lean in for a kiss. Our tongues immediately meet each other and intertwine in an exotic dance of their own. His strong arms grip my waist and I feel his muscle coming alive below me.

"I need you," he whispers, which is exactly what I wanted to hear. I rock back and forth over his groin feeling him harden more and more.

When grinding on him is no longer enough I ask him to take me to bed and fuck me senseless. He looks at me in amazement, probably because he's never heard me talk that way before. With no effort he stands lifting me up off the couch with him and heads straight for the bedroom.

I hadn't realized the music from the living room also played in the bedroom. It makes for a perfect scene. The curtains are drawn open and the weather outside has changed significantly. Dark rain clouds fill the sky while Carl Thomas's *Summer Rain* plays in the background.

"You okay?" Prescott asks.

"Take me now." I need him—the ache between my thighs is growing. I watch as he puts on a condom and slides into my folds filling me to the rim. I gasp at how hard he feels. I don't know if I will ever get used to him entering me. He moves to the pace of the music as he rocks back and forth inside of me. With our arms wrapped around each other, the sweat from our bodies inter-twined. This is different. The intensity between us is changing. I no longer feel in control but neither is he—our bodies have taken over. I'm not sure how long this session lasts, but when we erupt we do it together. Both of our orgasms are powerful, leaving us spent and out of breath.

Chapter 22

PRESCOTT AND I don't leave my room for the rest of the day. Usually rain showers in the islands don't last long but it rains all afternoon and into the evening which is fine by me because it is the perfect excuse to stay in bed. We have dinner brought up to my room and spend the night talking and making love.

I sleep in his arms through the night and as the sun starts to rise, I realize I don't want him to let me go. My attachment towards him is starting to grow which will make returning to the office that much harder. I already know once I get back to my apartment I'm going to have sleepless nights. It's hard to go from one extreme to the other. I wonder if he'll miss me.

"What are you thinking about?" I look up and smile at the sight of his beautiful blue eyes and ruffled hair.

"Nothing in particular, I was just letting my mind wander."

"Layla, you're a terrible liar," he says sitting up. "This little line right here," he says touching the space between my eyebrows, "only furrows when you're deep in thought."

"Are you always this observant?"

"Yes."

I don't really want him to know what's on my mind. Men tend to act differently if they even suspect you're developing feelings towards them. Yet if he can notice a simple line when I'm in thought then he has to know he's growing on me. Still, I'm not going to take a chance on ruining the rest of this trip so I opt for a half truth.

"I was just thinking it would've been nice to spend the day together."

"I'm glad you said that," he says getting out of bed to stretch. "I want to take you some place special this afternoon."

My whole body comes alive, "you do?"

"Yes. Do you think you can escape from your girls for a few hours unnoticed?"

"That won't be a problem. They already suspect I'm seeing someone. Don't worry, they don't suspect you," I quickly add.

"Who do they think it is? Has someone been hanging around you?" A flash of rage crosses his face.

"No, nothing like that. Georgina says I look like a woman who has been thoroughly fucked and the others agree."

"You okay with not telling them?"

Is this a test? Does he think I would really spill our secret?

"You don't have to worry, I'm not going to say anything."

"I know you all are growing close, you must feel the need to tell someone."

"You don't need to worry," I reiterate, "I'm good at keeping secrets."

"This is not a secret I'm worried about you keeping," he says casually while pulling his shirt over his head. What the hell does that mean?

"You're not concerned about this coming out?" I ask a little confused. Wasn't he the one who made a big deal about never sleeping with his employees?

"I was, but I'm not anymore." He leans in and swiftly kisses me before grabbing his shoes. "I'm sending a car to pick you up in the hotel lobby at twelve. Wear something comfortable and don't eat lunch, I'm having something prepared for us."

Before I can even form a sentence Prescott leaves the bedroom closing the door behind him. A few seconds later I hear the adjoining door between our rooms close as well. What just happened? Are we actually going on an official date?

I spend the morning prepping for my afternoon with Prescott. I don't leave my room until it's time for the car to arrive in fear I'll have to answer a ton of questions if any of the girls see me leaving the resort. I don't mind lying to them, but I also don't want to make a habit of it.

I feel a nervous energy build inside me when I'm in the lobby. I don't have to wait long, a black stretch limo pulls up and the driver runs around to open the door for me. I'm so stunned it takes a few seconds for me to actually move, I can't believe he sent a limo to pick me up.

Prescott is waiting for me in the limo with a single red rose in his hand. Is he giving me romance? I take a seat next to him, smiling.

"You did all of this for me?" I ask, smelling the rose.

"I think it's time you have the full Jonathan Prescott experience," he says pulling me in closer.

"I don't know if I'm ready for that."

"You may not be ready but you're definitely worth it." The limo pulls off and I rest my head on his shoulders and enjoy the ride. The country scenery is beautiful but the limo looks out of place on the dirt roads. The locals stand by and watch, probably thinking someone famous is in the car. Some of the smaller kids actually chase after the limo in hopes of getting a glimpse at who's inside. They would be disappointed to see Prescott and I in the backseat. We make our way up a steep incline and stop outside of what looks like a stable.

"Come on," he says, taking my hand as we exit the limo. We needed a limo to take us to a stable? I hope this isn't his big surprise. I can tell from the way he's holding my hand his excitement is growing. When we reach the stable I notice a white horse waiting for us. I stop and look at him, "I don't know how to ride a horse."

"That's why you'll be riding with me." I'm not sure about this but I continue to follow him. The closer we get the larger the horse appears. Between the horse and Prescott I feel like a dwarf in my flats. I should have asked more questions about his plans for the day; I'm wearing a dress and I'm not sure if I want my crotch sitting on top of a horse.

Out of no-where a shirtless man dressed in dusty overalls appears with a saddle in hand. He preps the horse and hands the reins over to Prescott. Prescott mounts the horse like a pro and extends his arm to help me up.

"Are you sure about this?" I ask with hesitation, "I don't even know where we are going."

"We can only get to where I'm taking you by horseback, trust me," he says, extending his hand further. I do trust him and take hold of his arm as he helps me settle in behind him. "I'll take it slow until you're comfortable." Prescott lets the man in overalls know we will return at sun down. He doesn't say anything, he just grunts and we take off in a slow trot through an open field. Soon we are traveling up a mountain. Sure the scenery is beautiful but I must have never mentioned my fear of heights in un-secured opens spaces. I know he feels my death grip around his midsection however he doesn't seem to mind. When the land finally flattens out thick brush gives way to a rain forest.

"Where exactly are you taking me?"

"We're almost there," I can hear the amusement in his voice. He knows I'm scared but I have every right to be. We both duck as we pass through massive trees with long limbs. I'm terrified that something will jump out from all of the thick foliage but Prescott seems to be at ease. The horse starts to slow as we approach what sounds like rumbling water. We enter a cave and come out behind the most beautiful waterfall I've ever seen.

"This is it," he says proudly. I have no words. I've never been behind a waterfall before.

"This is beautiful," I say in awe of my surroundings. Who would have thought our journey would lead us to such a beautiful place? Prescott dismounts the horse and takes hold of my waist helping me down. That's when I notice a picnic set out for us.

My eyes fill with water, "you did this for us?"

"This land is privately owned but I wanted you to experience this with me."

"Prescott, I don't know what to say, this is beautiful."

"I'm glad you like it. Come on, I'm famished," he says, leading me towards the picnic. All words escape me. Never in a million years would I have ever thought he would be capable of anything so romantic.

"Thank you for sharing this with me."

He works on setting out lunch but my eyes keep going back to the beautiful waterfall. I walk to the edge of the cave so I can get a better view. The body of water below us is calm and very tempting. I look back at Prescott and notice he's watching me with a satisfied look on his face.

"Come, let's eat and then we'll go for a swim."

"A swim? I didn't bring a bathing suit or change of clothes."

"I have it all taken care of."

Why am I not surprised? We eat lunch at the edge of the cave, which is fascinating because I can literally stick my hand out into the rushing water. We eat in peaceful silence but my mind is not at rest. I don't want to read into anything but this is not the type of place you take someone you're just casually screwing. At the same time, the thought of having more with someone like Prescott terrifies me. We come from two different worlds and my family would never accept him. I can already see grandpa referring to him as the blue-eyed devil and that shit would not go over well with Prescott. I need to focus on enjoying the here and now. In a few days all of this will be over and it will be back to work as normal.

"I see that line forming again."

"Sorry, I guess I spaced out for a second," I say taking a sip of my wine. "So what's next?"

"You're still not going to tell me what's on your mind?"

I shake my head no. I'm not going to do anything to ruin this beautiful moment. Sometimes silence truly is golden.

"Have it your way," he says standing up. "Let's go for a swim."

I follow Prescott down a path where the current is a little calmer. He discards all of his clothes and wastes no time diving in. I love watching him when he's so carefree. I follow suit and jump in after him. We spend all afternoon swimming and chasing each other in the water. When he catches me he wraps me in his arms and pulls me in close for the softest most erotic kiss. He holds me in his arms as he treads water keeping us both afloat. Caught up in the moment I ask him to make love to me. Carrying me out of the water he lays me on a huge boulder where he pleasures me in the way only he can. When he finally enters me the experience is like nothing I've ever experienced before. He made love to me in nature's garden and it's a memory that will be with me always.

When the sun starts to set we pack up our lunch and make our way back to the stable. The ride back is a lot faster, most likely due to my new familiarity with the area. I see the stable in the distance but I'm a little sad that our perfect day is coming to an end.

"Thank you for this afternoon; I couldn't have imagined anything better."

"My pleasure."

When we reach the stable I notice the limo driver has a panicked expression on his face.

"Mr. Prescott," he says approaching us, "there is an urgent matter that needs your attention." He passes Prescott a note and as soon as he reads it he immediately changes color. Whatever it is, it must be really bad.

"Get my bags packed and make sure the plane is ready for takeoff."

"Yes sir," the driver says opening the door.

"What's going on?" I ask as we take our seats in the back of the limo. His entire demeanor has changed.

"Nothing, it's work related."

"Well in case you forgot I do work for your company, is there something I can help with?" The expression Prescott gives me is unexplainable. You would think I didn't work for him at all. What could be going on in the world of marketing that would make him cut his trip short? Most urgent matters can be defused by a simple conference call and why would he need to leave if the majority of the executive staff is on the island with us?

"It's nothing to concern yourself with," he says staring out the window. Now he's not even making eye contact with me.

"Are you sure I can't help in some way?"

"No." The finality in his voice lets me know the topic is no longer up for discussion. We reach the resort in record time but I feel conflicted on leaving him this way.

"I'm sorry I have to cut our evening short," he says, trying to regain some of his composure. "I'll give you a call when I get back into town."

"Back in town? Aren't you heading home to Chicago?"

Prescott doesn't answer and the driver is waiting for me to exit the car. "Prescott, what's going on?"

"I'll call you when I can."

"Fine," I say getting out of the car. Our perfect afternoon has definitely been ruined. I don't know why he's acting as if I can't be trusted but whatever the reason, it hurts.

Chapter 23

MY MAGICAL WEEK in Jamaica is over and now it's back to reality. I got shit from my girls for the remainder of our
vacation. They all noticed a visible change in my mood; it was
clear my love interest was gone. Thankfully no-one realized the
change came at the same time as Prescott's departure.

Sadly I have to fly home with the rest of the staff. Although we
are seated in first class, nothing beats flying in a private plane. When
we arrive in Chicago shuttle buses are waiting to take us home. I'm
the only one out of my girls who still lives in corporate housing so
we all split ways. When I board the shuttle Carlos grabs the seat next
to me; that's when I discover that he not only lives in my building
but we both live on the same floor. I notice his behavior around me
has changed since returning home. He's still funny and playful but
he no longer tries to hit on me, which is a welcome change.

When I enter the building the doorman rushes to take my
bags while I grab a weeks-worth of mail from the bank of mail-
boxes. I'm on my way to the elevators when out of nowhere Justin
emerges.

He opens his mouth to speak but then stops as he looks me over.

"Layla you look… different, you look alive."

"It's amazing what can happen when you don't have someone sucking the life out of you. Justin what are you doing here? I was told you already moved out."

"I did. Your mother called my mom who then called me. No-one has heard from you all week and everyone's been worried."

I immediately smack myself in the forehead. How could I forget to call my mom and tell her I would be in Jamaica? Everything happened so quickly I didn't even have time to think about my family.

"I'll give her a call right now—I know she must be worried."

"She called your office and found out you would be returning from Jamaica today so she's calmed down a little, however she still wanted me to make sure you arrived home safely."

I look at him and it's still crazy to think just a week ago I assaulted him in public. My behavior may have been bad but the outcome was well worth it. If we didn't fight I would have never had those two days alone with Prescott in Jamaica.

"Well, thanks for checking, I'll give her a call and put her mind to rest. Take care," I say as I turn to walk away.

"Layla," he calls after me.

I turn to face him.

"Yes."

"I'm sorry about how everything turned out."

"Me too," that's as close to an apology as he'll ever get. I turn and continue towards the elevators.

"Was that your ex?" Carlos asks appearing at my side.

"Yep."

"A word of advice," he says. "Don't let Jonathan find out he was here."

I look over at him, shocked.

"Don't worry, your secret is safe with me."

The elevator door slides open and we both get on in silence. When we part ways in the hall I rush to my apartment. How the hell did Carlos find out?

I spend the majority of the weekend deep in thought. My mind races in every direction possible. When I finally call my mother she is furious with me which results in me promising to go home for a visit in a week. She knows Justin moved out but she doesn't know the details behind the break-up. I'm not surprised he never mentioned his cheating to anyone.

Then there's the way I left things with Prescott. I still have no clue as to his whereabouts and I haven't heard from him since we parted ways in the limo. What's even more complicated is trying to figure out exactly what Carlos knows. His observation on Friday was unnerving but he's right; Prescott would blow a gasket if he found out Justin came to see me. And then there's Justin. Ever since he came to check on me for my mother he's been calling and texting me non-stop using any excuse he can think of to lure me into meeting him. I'm sure he's shocked I've declined every invitation.

Needless to say, my weekend has been a restless one but the one thing that bothers me the most is how Prescott and I left things. Is our romantic escapade over? I would be lying if I didn't admit I would love to extend our arrangement but he hasn't mentioned anything about wanting more. I feel like we have unfinished business and its driving me crazy. I need to do something to take my mind off things. I decide to go out for a walk, maybe some fresh air will help me relax.

The summer heat in Chicago can be intense but I'm learning to take advantage of it due to the brutal winter months. I hit the concrete at a vigorous pace. I don't have a specific destination in mind; I'll just walk until I burn off some of my excess energy.

"So where are you headed?"

I'm so focused on thoughts of Prescott I don't hear Carlos approach. He's jogging at a slow pace next to me.

"Where did you come from?" I ask looking around.

"I jog every evening around this time; I've never seen you out here before."

"I was bored so I decided some fresh air and exercise would be good for me. You really jog out here every day?"

"Why do you look so surprised?"

"I never took you to be a runner."

"And I never took you to be a speed walker," he says with a hint of sarcasm.

"Have you ever thought about jogging?"

"Not really, I prefer walking."

"Where are you headed?"

"Nowhere in particular" I say, taking note of the cross streets. I didn't intend on walking this far from the building.

"We live in a good neighborhood however there are some unsavory parts, so I suggest you be mindful on how far you stray from the building, especially at night by yourself."

He's right, the sun is starting to descend and I'm passing storefronts with bars on them, which is never a good sign. "I should probably turn around now."

"I'll walk with you," he says, wiping the sweat from his forehead. "What the hell are you wearing?" he asks looking down at me, "did you borrow those shorts from your grandmother?"

"Ha ha, very funny," I say dryly, "I believe workout clothes should be comfortable, not sexy."

"In that case you look very comfortable."

We talk about work and some of the people in our office during our walk back to the building but neither of us mentions Prescott's name. When we make it back to the building we agree to meet around the same time tomorrow. Carlos offers to show me some cool walking trails in a park not too far from our building that's well-lit and patrolled often.

My walk has not done much to subdue my mood. I realize it's not nervous energy but sexual tension that has me on edge and without Prescott I have no way of releasing it. The sun has set and the city below me is calm and quiet. I turn on a movie and order Chinese for dinner. Exactly ten minutes after I place my order there's a knock at the door.

I grab my purse off the counter and open the door, "how much do I owe you?" I ask digging through my purse.

"My services are always free to you." My head snaps up—it's one thing to wish someone is with you but when that person actually appears it can knock the wind out of you. Finally the blood pumps to my brain and I'm able to regain my cognitive abilities.

"What are you doing here?" I ask, still in disbelief.

"How could you open the door without checking to see who it is first?" he asks, visibly angry with me.

"I thought you were the delivery man."

"That's no excuse, you should never open the door without checking to see who's on the other side."

"Fine but that still doesn't answer my question, what are you doing here? I haven't heard from you since you left the resort."

"Sorry about that, I was in an area with poor reception," he says moving past me to enter the apartment. Does he really think I'm going to buy that lame excuse in this day and age?

"You're a freaking millionaire and you're going to tell me you couldn't get a working phone or internet connection?"

"I didn't mean to make you worry about me," he says calmly, too calmly. I'm prepared to lay into him some more when there's a knock at the door. I move to answer it but he beats me to it.

"You're answering my door now?"

"What did you order?" he asks bypassing my question and accepting the takeout bag from the delivery man.

"Chinese for one," I say, snatching the bag from him. Prescott pulls out his wallet and pays for the food and then he places his own order but requests that it be sent up in two hours.

"You're staying?"

"Yes," he says kicking the door shut, "I need to make up for some lost time."

"Don't you think we should talk first?"

We're no longer in Jamaica and I don't want to get confused about what's going on between us.

"If you insist, what's on your mind?" he asks making himself comfortable on the couch.

"Well," I start pacing nervously, "we're no longer in Jamaica yet here you are," I say stopping in front of him.

"I thought you wanted this?" he asks, looking confused.

"You said we couldn't go any further beyond our vacation. Has that changed?"

"I would hope so."

"What about work?"

"What about it?"

"Aren't you going to tell me that you can't see me because I work for you?"

"No."

"No," I repeat, shocked by his aloof behavior, "what do you mean no, you said yourself our affair couldn't go anywhere."

"In that case we're no longer having an affair, we're dating and as to everyone in the office, I could give two shits about what any of them think."

"You may not care but I do; I don't want to be seen as the office skank. My professional career is just beginning and I can't start it off by sleeping with my boss."

"Then you should have thought about that before you slept with me."

Damn...that shut me up. I hate it when he's right—what the hell am I supposed to say to that?

"Look, I know you just got out of your relationship with Justin and everything between us is new so we'll take it slow and see what happens."

"That's easy for you to say. If things don't work out I'm the one who's screwed, not you."

"What are you saying? You think if things end I'll fire you or make your life hell?" he looks angry but neither of us can pretend he's not capable of both.

"At the end of the day I still work for you and I live in an apartment provided by your company," I say motioning around the apartment, "so yes if things end badly forgive me for being concerned about what would happen to me."

"I wouldn't fuck with your livelihood, end of discussion."

"No, not end of discussion," from his expression I can tell he's used to getting his way, "Prescott I'm serious, I don't want anyone to know what's going on between us which also means you can't just pop up whenever you want. What if I had company?"

"This is a first," he says getting off the couch, "women usually lie about being with me just so they can gain notoriety yet here you are wanting to keep it a secret. You really are a complex creature but I'll tell you what; until you are ready to let everyone know I'll do my best to be discreet. Does that make you happy?"

"Yes."

"Good, I'm hungry and it's time to eat."

"But your food's not here yet."

Seductively he approaches, "I'm looking at my meal right now." A smile creeps over each of our faces as we make our way to the bedroom. The Chinese food will have to wait.

Chapter 24

I'T'S MONDAY MORNING, my first day back in the office from Jamaica and I feel exhausted. Prescott stretched my body in every position imaginable. He spent the night but left first thing in the morning to go home and change. I have a ton of work waiting for me on my desk and over a thousand emails in my inbox, which is ridiculous considering most of us were away. Some of my emails are from Georgina; when in hell did she make time to work?

I work diligently through the morning but receive a surprise at lunch when Justin shows up with a dozen red roses. Before I can even acknowledge his presence, Stephanie and Simone come crashing into my office at the same time.

"What the hell are you doing here?" Simone asks. I pray Justin doesn't say or do anything stupid because she looks like she's ready for a fight.

"I came to see Layla," he says, looking confused by her attitude towards him.

I finally regain my voice and step out from around my desk. "Justin, you need to leave, I don't want any drama at work."

"I didn't come to fight with you; I was just hoping to take you out to lunch."

At that exact moment Georgina comes into my office and her eyes practically bulge out of her head at the sight of Justin.

"What the hell is he doing here?" she asks, looking at me with an accusatory glare.

"Don't look at me like that, I didn't invite him."

"Invited or not we need to get his ass out of here before Jonathan sees him."

She's right, just the mere mention of Justin's name has him changing color. I practically shove Justin out of my office and usher him to the back stairwell.

"Layla, I'm not walking down twenty flights of stairs," he says trying to halt me from shoving him.

"I'm giving you the chance to leave this building without injury. If Prescott sees you he may toss your ass down all twenty flights."

"Who the hell is Prescott?"

"Jonathan Prescott, my boss," I say, giving him one final push before slamming the door to the stairwell behind me. I lean back against the door in an attempt to regain my composure. Why the hell does he keep showing up? Could he be so delusional to think I would ever entertain taking him back?

When I get back to my office Pamela has joined the party and they all look at me expectantly.

"No secrets this time Layla, what the hell is going on and why was he here?" Stephanie asks. We order lunch and I go over the details of Justin's reappearance in my life.

"So what are you going to do?"

"Nothing, I know Justin. He'll lose interest soon enough when he sees he's not getting anywhere with me."

"I hope you're–" before Pamela could finish her sentence Prescott strolls into my office but halts when he see's everyone gathered around my desk with their feet up eating lunch.

"Jonathan!" Georgina says standing up, "did you need me for something?"

"No," he replies curtly, surveying the room before his eyes finally lands on me.

"Layla, can I see you for a moment?"

"Sure," I say, putting my sandwich down. We step into the adjoining conference room for privacy. That's when I realize that although the room is private you can still hear everything from my office. My girls take the moment to start gossiping about Prescott, which gets his full attention.

"I swear I would love to fuck the shit out of him." That would be Georgina—I shake my head at her bluntness.

"He is cute," Pamela says giggling like a school-girl with a crush.

"Cute!" Georgina says sounding appalled, "puppy dogs are cute, little babies with no teeth are cute, couples taking carriage rides around the park are cute. You don't describe a beautiful male specimen like Jonathan Prescott as cute. He needs a totally new definition."

I look over at Prescott as he smirks.

"Well, what's the proper definition?"

I hear some shuffling but I can't tell what she's doing; "we need a thesaurus," I finally hear her say. Is she serious? She's really about to look up words to describe Prescott?

"Okay, I got it. Jonathan Prescott can be defined as a mature, robust, well-developed astute male with a body to die for and face I would love to sit on every day of the week."

Jonathan turns three shades brighter while I cover my mouth to try to stifle my laugh. Georgina would die if she knew he was hearing every word she was saying. I'll save her the embarrassment and keep this to myself.

"Looks like you have quite the fan club," I say smiling.

"Hey, does anyone find it strange that he didn't even knock on Layla's door?" Stephanie asks the group.

"I know, I thought it was weird too. I hope he's not about to ask her about Justin. I can't believe he's still calling her—and thank God she got him out of the office before he showed up."

Fuck! I'm so dead. I don't have to look up at Prescott to know his eyes are on me. I risk taking a glance up; just as I suspected, he is furious.

"What the fuck was Justin doing in my building?"

"Will you lower your voice?" I say whispering. "If we can hear them I'm sure they can hear us."

"You think I give a fuck about anyone hearing me? Answer me, what hell was he doing in my goddamn building?"

"He came to ask me out to lunch which I obviously refused."

"And the phone calls?"

"What about the phone calls?"

"Why didn't you tell me about this yesterday?"

"Because of the way you're acting right now. You'd just come back into town and I wasn't going to bother you with stupid stuff. You don't have to worry about Justin; I'll take care of him."

"No!" he shouts. "You don't do shit, I'll take care of it!"

"No!" I say, barking right back at him, "he's my problem and I said I'll handle it."

His mouth opens to say something but then his features relax. I can tell he's still stewing but he's trying to regain the last of his composure.

"Fine, but if I find out it's not taken care of I'm stepping in and I will do things my way."

I'm tempted to ask what he means by doing things his way but think better of it and decide to keep my mouth shut. It's time for a change in topic.

"What brought you down to my office?"

"What?" he looks confused but then quickly refocuses, "oh, James Bradford called and he wants to meet with you tonight over dinner."

This would be my first dinner meeting. "Will you be there?" I ask, filled with hope.

"No, unfortunately I have another meeting already scheduled but I moved my location so I won't be far from you."

"Where am I meeting him?"

"At the Four Seasons, I'll have a car waiting to take you."

Something about Prescott's appearance is off center. He looks nervous and I don't think I've ever seen nervous Prescott before.

"I've been meaning to ask you, do you still have the phone I gave you in Jamaica?"

"Yes," I say. He knows I still have it. Come to think of it, I now have two of his phones. I really should return the phone I snatched from the coffee shop.

"Make sure you take it with you this evening. If James says or does anything to make you feel the least bit uncomfortable, call me right away and I'll be there."

"Is there something I should know?" He's making me nervous.

"Just promise me you will call me if you need me, I'm serious."

"Fine, I'll call but under one condition."

"What?"

"After dinner will you tell me why you're acting so weird?"

Prescott ignores my request and heads for the door that leads to the hallway.

"Make sure you're in the lobby by five o'clock sharp, after your meeting I'll arrange for the car to bring you back to my place."

"Wait, we can't meet at your place."

He stops with his hand resting on the doorknob. "Why not?"

"Because Georgina lives in your building and whether you're aware of it or not she watches your every move." I learned that bit of information in Jamaica.

"Don't be late for your meeting with James," he says closing the door tightly behind him. I hate it when he leaves things unfinished between us.

If the girls heard our conversation no one says a word when I return from my private meeting. After lunch I spend the remainder of the afternoon tying up loose ends on the Bradford account. Just as Prescott said, the car arrived promptly at five o'clock to take me to the Four Seasons.

My dinner with Mr. Bradford turns out to be uneventful. He asks a lot of questions about my background and experience in marketing but he doesn't say or do anything inappropriate at all. I don't know what Prescott was so paranoid about.

Stepping out of the hotel I can feel the drop in temperature; this will be a perfect evening to check out the park with Carlos. I send him a quick text letting him know I'm on my way home. When I get to my door I notice my deadbolt is undone; I could have sworn I locked it this morning but think nothing of it until I enter my apartment and find Prescott lounging on my couch.

"What are you doing here?" I thought we talked about his unannounced visits yesterday but clearly he missed that part of the conversation.

"I came to see you. Is that a problem now?"

He looks at home in my apartment, which is a little alarming. Then again since he owns the building and practically everything in it I guess it's technically his place. His shoes are by the door and his tie is hanging loosely around his neck. Even when he's disheveled he still looks sexy.

"Of course not, but a heads-up would be nice," I reply a little panicky. "I thought we talked about us being discreet."

"Not this shit again, what do you want me to do?"

"Did anyone see you come in?" The last thing I need is for one of my neighbors to have seen Prescott enter my apartment. I hear how the women in the office gossip.

"If this is going to be an issue I'll get you an apartment somewhere else."

"What? I don't want to move!"

"You don't want to go to my place in fear you'll run into Georgina and you don't want me to visit you in fear someone will see me. I can't figure you out, so you're going to have to tell me what the hell you want."

I don't have time to have this debate with him, Carlos is on his way over and to be honest I'm not sure how he'll respond to that bit of news.

Prescott watches me closely as I hang up my keys and purse.

"You look nervous—did everything go okay with James?" he asks, coming towards me and wrapping me in his arms. How do I tell him James is not the issue at the moment?

"You promise to not get upset?" I ask cautiously.

"What is it?" Uh oh, I can feel his grasp tighten, maybe I should put a little distance between us.

"Nothing serious… Carlos is on his way over so we can go jogging," I say as fast as possible.

Prescott holds me at arm's length and his eyebrows furrow in response to my news.

"Since when have you taken up jogging and why the hell are you jogging with Carlos?"

"We ran into each other last night and he offered to show me the neighborhood park. He suggested it would be safer for me if I decide to exercise in the evening."

"When were you going to tell me about this?"

Probably never I think to myself.

"I don't know," I say, stepping out of his grasp, "I wasn't trying to hide it from you or anything, I just didn't have time yet."

"I could show you the park if you weren't so against being seen with me."

Not this argument again.

"I thought we both agreed it would be best to be discreet right now."

"Forgive me for not being used to sneaking around with someone I'm supposed to be dating. Not to sound arrogant but usually women are all too thrilled to announce to the world they are dating me. This is the first time I've ever been with someone who doesn't want anyone to know."

"I don't know how I can make you understand; if things go south between us I'm the one who loses, not you. Have you forgotten your own company policy about dating in the workplace?" I'm stalling but I need an excuse to keep him at bay until I can figure things out. He may not care about the world knowing about us but I have a feeling the minute everyone finds out my life will never be the same and I'm not ready for more changes just yet.

"Layla, who the fuck is going to question me about my goddamn policy? The only one concerned about it is you. If you like I will have a whole new employee handbook printed tomorrow, would that make you happy?"

"That's not necessary and I don't want to argue with you right now." I glance at the clock on the wall, I don't have much time.

"What time is he coming?"

"He should be here in ten minutes."

"Why is he coming up to your place? There's a beautiful lobby he could wait for you in downstairs."

"He lives down the hall so it just makes sense to head out together."

"Carlos lives on this floor!" he says yelling. "Why did I not know about this?" Okay this he can't blame on me; Carlos lived in this building way before I even moved in.

"I don't know how you want me to answer you! He worked for your company well before I came on board and he's been living in his apartment for the past three years now."

"Does it really terrify you that much to be seen with me?"

"I'm not scared to be seen with you," I say, moving closer towards him, "I've just lost so much recently and I don't want to add this job to the list. I know you said you wouldn't fire me if things between us don't work out but I just couldn't imagine working for you if things ended after we made our relationship public. The women in the office are vicious. You don't know the type of scrutiny I would face on a day-to-day basis."

Prescott takes a quick look down at his watch, "looks like we only have a few minutes." I was getting ready to ask for what when he unbuttons his shirt and removes his slacks.

"What are you doing?"

"Reminding you of one of the benefits of being with me," he says proudly. He then grabs both of my wrists and walks backwards towards the couch taking me with him. Once he's seated he pulls me onto his lap facing him and places his hands up my skirt and ever so slowly removes my panties. My breath starts to quicken as I feel him slide first one and then a second finger inside of me.

"Looks like you're ready for me."

"I'm always ready for you," I say breathlessly. With the clock ticking he lowers me onto his long thick cock and starts to give me the ride of my life. I lose all self-control. I find his lips and kiss him in hopes it will convey how much I truly care for him. Not long into our love making I hear Carlos knocking on the door,

"Layla, are you ready to go?"

"Shit! Prescott, we have to stop, he's here," I say breathlessly.

"Fuck him, make his ass wait, I'm not done with you yet." Prescott then flips me over and takes me from behind. He knows this is one of my favorite positions.

Knock, knock, knock, "Layla, are you okay in there?"

Shit! "I'm okay Carlos, just give me a sec," I call out.

"You're mine, you understand," Prescott whispers in my ear.

"Yes, I'm yours." I say, panting as he increases his rhythm.

"Layla, what are you doing, you sound out of breath and we haven't even started our run yet." Why couldn't Carlos be late? The more he talks the faster Prescott moves within me.

"I'm just getting dressed, I'll be out in a sec," I yell back.

"Okay... make sure you wear those little black shorts I like," he says chuckling. I know he only meant that as a joke but that's the last thing Prescott needed to hear. He flips me over onto my back and tosses both of my legs over his shoulders. I'm never frightened when I'm with him but the murderous look in his eyes has me terrified. Why the hell did Carlos have to make that comment? Prescott takes no mercy on me; my body is going to ache for days when he's done. We are treading a fine line between pleasure and pain but pleasure wins as an intense orgasm racks through my body. As soon as I cum Prescott lets out a loud grunt and crashes down on me. We are both hot, sweaty and out of breath. The last thing I want to do at the moment is go for a run. Prescott immediately slides out of me and I wince at the pain.

"Would you prefer that I hide in the closet or bathroom?"

"Please don't do this," I whisper.

"I'm not going to tolerate this shit much longer, just know that," he says as he gathers his clothes and heads for the bathroom slamming the door behind him.

Chapter 25

My run with Carlos doesn't last long. I lie and say dinner didn't agree with me when truthfully I'm dealing with the soreness between my legs courtesy of Prescott. By the time I get home he is gone, only his boxers remain on my living room floor. I guess he went home commando. I know leaving them behind is his way of marking his territory. I should probably be annoyed but instead I feel a small smile creep over my face—how cute.

I try reaching out to Prescott later in the evening but I don't get a response. I guess he's still pissed at me.

The next day at work he doesn't respond to any of my text messages or emails—how long is he going to give me the silent treatment? His behavior is childish. Part of me wants to go up to his office and put an end to his foolishness but I decide against it. When he's ready to talk to me he knows where to find me, until then I'll give him his space.

I stay late in the office hoping to see him but still nothing. I know he's been in the building for the majority of the day which is un-nerving. He's so close yet I feel like we are worlds apart. When I get home from work and off the elevator an eerie feeling sets in. The hallway is empty, too empty. Not to say people hang out in the halls, this isn't that type of building however in the evening people are always coming and going. The building is full of a lot of young professionals and the majority of them have very active social lives. There has never been an occasion where I've come home from work and no-one could be spotted. I shake the feeling and go into my apartment.

Part of me is hoping Prescott will be waiting—no such luck. He must be really mad at me. I wonder how long this is going to last?

I haven't lived alone long enough to develop any type of rou-tine. With no-one here I start to feel restless. If I'm going to live alone I'm going to have to find different ways to occupy my time, especially after work.

I change out of my clothes and grab a book I've been meaning to read since I was in Jamaica. I make myself comfortable on the window seat and look out at the city below me. The lights are shining bright which gives me hope for a better day tomorrow.

I try to focus on my book but I notice I keep re-reading the same pages over and over again; I just can't concentrate. I hear a rumble of thunder in the distance and see a flash of lightening in the sky. I love to watch summer storms and from up here I have the perfect view. Another large bolt of lightning flashes through the sky and then the power goes out. Great, now I'm alone in the dark. I never bought any flashlights so I'll just have to sit here and wait for the power to return.

I look out my peephole and can see the emergency lights on in the hall. I open the door to see if I can catch anyone. I've never experienced a power outage in this building and I'm wondering how long it will last but the only person I see is Ralph the front desk attendant.

"Good evening, Ms. Brown," Ralph is such a sweet old man. The creases around his eyes remind me of my grandpa. He has a ton of laugh lines around his mouth which can be expected since he always has a funny story to share.

"Hi Ralph, any idea on how long the power will be out?"

"It shouldn't be too long. I wanted to check on you since you're on the floor by yourself now."

By myself? What is he talking about? "I'm not by myself, I'm sure my neighbors will return home at some point tonight."

"You didn't hear?"

"Hear what?"

"Everyone on your floor had to relocate, something about some major electrical overhaul in all of the apartments. Amazingly yours was the only unit not affected."

Amazing indeed! This has Prescott's name written all over it! I can't believe he would do something like this. He's not avoiding me because he's mad at me, he's avoiding me because he knew I would strangle him once I found out he had everyone on my floor relocated.

"Everything okay, Ms. Brown?"

"Yes, thanks Ralph," I say closing the door behind me. What the hell makes him think I would want to live on the floor by myself? He's gone too far this time and I'm going to let him know about it. When I call his phone I'm sent straight to voice mail. Ugh! He is so frustrating. Well two can play this game! I'm going to confront him first thing in the morning.

Chapter 26

THE NEXT MORNING I literally leave my apartment at the crack of dawn in hopes of catching Prescott before he leaves for his 5a.m. run. I could never imagine waking up at such an ungodly hour every morning just to work out but he does so religiously. I feel like a spy lurking in the shadows of his building waiting to catch a glimpse of him. Thankfully I'm not kept waiting long. When he emerges I feel my pulse quicken; he's shirtless and looks delicious. For a second I forget why I'm even here and find myself enjoying the view.

"Who are you looking for?"

I spin around and Justin is watching me. "What the hell are you doing here?"

"I followed you here."

"What the hell are you doing following me?" Has he lost his mind?

"You haven't been accepting any of my calls and you practically threw me out of your building when I came to see you at work. I thought you were maybe seeing someone and wanted to find out who you had in your life trying to take my place."

I can't believe this shit.

"Justin, my love life is none of your concern so why don't you back the hell off and go find the little redheaded chick you've been fucking."

"I made a mistake in leaving you for Sylvia and I'm man enough to admit it. I didn't follow you to argue, I just think we should give things a second try; you owe me that much."

"I owe you?" I yell viciously, "I don't owe you shit!"

"What's going on here? Ma'am, are you okay?" The man approaching us looks like a marine on steroids. His poor shirt looks to be hanging on for dear life; if he flexes one muscle it will probably rip open.

So much for me being discreet. I was hoping to get to Prescott undetected but, thanks to Justin, my plan is now ruined.

"I'm sorry, we were just having a little debate," I say scrambling, "we'll be leaving now." I try to leave but the security guard stops me.

"Are you Layla Brown?" the guard asks.

Dammit! I say nothing. If the guard knows who I am it's because of Prescott. He reaches into his back pocket and pulls out a walkie talkie, "please alert Mr. Prescott of Ms. Brown's arrival."

"Mr. Prescott?" Justin asks in confusion. "Isn't that the name of your boss?"

I ignore Justin's question. "You don't need to alert anyone of my arrival, I'm leaving." My plan was to catch Prescott off guard but clearly he was expecting my arrival. I don't know what pisses me off more, Prescott being able to predict my actions or Justin following me.

"I'm sorry, Ms. Brown, but I can't let you leave. Mr. Prescott has been contacted and we are under orders to keep you here until he returns."

"What!? You can't keep me here against my will."

"Please don't make this difficult ma'am, he should be back any second now."

I am so fucked! Justin has a cocky grin on his face—little does he know he's in serious danger.

"So, Layla" he says with a smirk on his face "what's your boss going to do when he finds out you've been stalking him? You can probably kiss your job goodbye now but don't worry; I'll help you pick up the pieces."

"That won't be necessary."

Prescott has returned. His hair is damp and his abs are glistening with sweat.

"Layla, I know why you're here," he says looking in my direction, "but Justin, for the life of me I can't figure out what the fuck you're doing here. I thought my directions were pretty simple—stay away from Layla."

"Layla, what the hell's going on? I thought your boss was on his way. What the hell is William doing here?"

I don't have the energy for this shit. "William is Jonathan Prescott—my boss." Prescott steps closer to me and places a protective arm around my waist.

"She's mine now and if I catch your ass around her again you'll be begging me to show you mercy."

"Wait a minute," Justin says looking between the two of us confused, "Layla, you're sleeping with him?"

I don't bother to answer. I turn to Prescott "we need to talk and preferably somewhere where we can be alone." The security guard has given us all a little space but he's still within earshot.

"We'll talk later."

"Why not now?" I can't take him putting me off any longer.

"Because right now I'm pissed and probably won't hear anything you have to say."

"You're not the only one who's upset," I say stepping out of his arms. "How could you move everyone off my floor without consulting me?"

"My building, my floor and I'll do whatever I want. Furthermore if you weren't so bent on keeping us a secret none of this shit would be happening. I wouldn't have had to go through all of the trouble and expense of moving everyone and I wouldn't have to deal with your stupid ex-boyfriend randomly popping up on my property. My guess is that you came here to see me, which I anticipated, but you didn't tell me he's been following you."

"I didn't know he was following me."

"I don't believe you."

That hurt more than a slap in the face. "If you don't trust me to tell you the truth then what's the point of us dating?" I don't wait for him to answer me. I turn and sprint from the building; I don't want him or Justin to see me cry.

When I get to my building I race to my apartment and lock the door tightly behind me. I strip out of my clothes and take the longest shower ever. I always think better in the shower. Slowly the warm water starts to calm me. In the end I rationalize what I have with Prescott can't work. He wants more than I'm willing to give. He blames me for not wanting to make our relationship public and I blame him for being too demanding to soon. It hasn't even been a full week since our return from Jamaica and already things are falling apart. It's better to just end things now before they get even crazier.

With a brave face and a false sense of strength I march into the office prepared for whatever comes my way. When I log onto my computer the first thing I do is check my email. It wouldn't surprise me if he has sent an email demanding I meet him in his office but instead there is just a reminder notice about a lunch meeting I have scheduled with Georgina and the other marketing executives. Prescott's name is not on the attendee list so it looks like I may make it through the day without running into him. Eventually we are going to have to clear the air but I don't feel strong enough to face him yet. His words hurt; after everything I've shared with him how could he not trust me to be honest with him? He knows more about me than anyone else I know. From the moment we met I trusted him. Clearly that trust was never reciprocated.

When I get to the conference room for my meeting Veronica is already seated. We both make it a point to never speak to each other. I take a seat on the other end of the table as far away from her as possible. Soon the room fills up and Georgina hands out the afternoon agenda.

Roughly twenty minutes into the meeting Prescott strolls in. I should have known there was no such thing as a Prescott-free day. He wasn't scheduled to attend, yet here he is.

"Jonathan," Georgina says, startled by his presence, "I didn't expect you."

"My last meeting ended early so I decided to join you."

"Wonderful," she says, clasping her hands together. Georgina gets busy gathering a copy of the meeting agenda for him and makes the seat next to her available for him. Simultaneously Veronica grabs an empty chair from the back wall and moves it next to her for Prescott. I'm immediately annoyed by the both of them. All of the other women in the room perk up at his arrival but at least everyone else is discreet. Although two seats have become available for him he walks past them both towards me.

"Do you mind scooting down?" he asks Valerie, the woman sitting next to me. What the hell is he doing? Both Veronica and Georgina look at me in surprise but no-one dares say a word. That's when I realize he's proving his point: everyone could think whatever they want but no-one would ever question him.

Georgina continues on with the agenda but with Prescott so close I don't hear a word she says. His close proximity reminds my body of how badly I need his touch. There's no way in hell I can pass him every day in the halls or see him at meetings and pretend I don't want him. I do want him, I want him badly and we're going to have to come to some type of resolution—fast.

When the meeting is over I head straight for my office; I know he will follow me. I don't bother to close my door in anticipation of his arrival. He takes a little longer than I expect but he shows up and closes the door, locking it behind him.

"We need to talk," he says, taking a seat on the other side of my desk. I nod my head in agreement and wait for him to start. Before he can get his first word out my desk phone rings; I send the caller to voice mail; whoever it is will have to wait. But the unknown caller is persistent—the person just hangs up and calls again. The only person who has been calling me back to back like this is Justin and from the look on Prescott's face he's thinking the same thing.

"Answer your phone and put it on speaker in case it's him."

I do as he asks, hoping I can rush Justin off the phone but have no such luck when I realize it's my mother on the other end.

"Layla Brown, what the hell is going on with you?"

"Hi mom." This is bad; she only uses my full name when she's mad as hell. "I was going to give you a call later this evening, is it okay if I call you back?"

"Don't you even think of getting me off this phone—I just received a disturbing call from Justin."

That little snitch! I can't believe he called my mother of all people.

"Mom, I don't know what he told you but I'm sure it's all lies." Prescott and I make eye contact; he looks a little amused at my discomfort.

"So he lied when he said that you're having an affair with your boss?" Prescott moves to the edge of his seat and looks me directly in the eye. This is it. If I lie to my mom about him I know he'll get up and walk out of my office never to return. If I tell the truth I'm going to have to face a ton of backlash from my family. Time stands still as I weigh my options but I already know what I have to do.

"Mom, I'm not having an affair with my boss," I say pausing, "we're dating."

I can see the visible sigh of relief in his eyes and I know I've made the right decision.

"Little girl, have you gone to Chicago and lost your mind? I thought I raised you better than this!"

And so the backlash begins. Whenever she thinks I'm in the wrong she has no problem jumping all over me. It's everyone else who gets away with murder around her. I look up at Prescott and I can see the creases in his forehead. Definitely not a good sign.

"Mom, can I give you a call back in a few minutes? I'm in the middle of something."

"Why, is he there with you right now?" I should never have answered my phone while it's on speaker, lesson learned.

"Mom, I promise I will call you later." I've never hung up on her before but it's clear that's what I may have to do just to get her off the phone.

"Layla, put him on the phone."

What?! Has she lost her mind? There is no way in hell I'm letting my mom talk to Prescott; it's bad enough he can hear our entire conversation. I reach to pick up the receiver but he grabs my hand and gives me a warning look. He wants to hear my conversation in its entirety. Nothing good could ever come from this.

"Mom, now is not a good time. Can I please call you back in a few minutes?"

"What's the matter, you afraid of hearing the truth?"

"And what truth is that?"

"After I got off the phone with Justin I did some digging and googled Jonathan Prescott. After reading his profile I had to stop and ask myself, what does a 40-year-old white man want with my 24-year-old black daughter? The two of you have absolutely nothing in common. Layla, the man is a multi-millionaire with a string of anorexic ex-girlfriends. From some of the things I've read he's known to be a hard ass. Men like him like to possess things and when they're done they throw them away. Wise up child, you have two degrees yet you're acting like you have no sense! He doesn't want you, he's just having fun with you and when he's done you're going to be left with nothing. Aside from what's between your legs you have nothing to offer a man like that and if you think otherwise you're more foolish than I thought. Your father and I did not invest so much money into your education for you to go and throw your future away. You and Justin are a perfect match and the sooner you realize that the better."

Hearing my mother's words makes me feel like a cheap whore. I look up at Prescott and I can't even describe the color on his face; I've never seen him turn this shade before. I hate to admit it but my mother's words sting and I start to wonder, what do I do for him? He's already accomplished so much, it's not like we can grow together. Aside from good sex, what do we really have?

"Layla, are you there?"

Damn, I must have spaced out, "yes, I'm here mom," I wish I weren't but I am.

"Well, are you going to end this crazy affair with your boss?"

"First answer my question, why is it so hard for you to believe that he may actually want me?" All my life she told me how beautiful I am and how proud she is of the young woman I've become yet the minute she finds out I'm dating Jonathan Prescott it's as if I'm not good enough for him.

"I don't doubt he wants you, you're beautiful. What I'm trying to get you to realize is that relationships with men like him don't last long. Men like Jonathan Prescott think the world and everyone in it is at their disposal. They take what they want and when they're finished they move on. I'm not speaking out of ignorance, I'm speaking from experience. You may be having fun now but when it's time to stop sneaking around and actually make your relationship public, that's when they go running in the opposite direction."

My mother couldn't be more wrong about Prescott if she tried. How ironic, he wants to tell the world we're dating and I'm the one who isn't ready to divulge that secret yet.

"Trust me Layla, when it's time for him to come around and meet your family he'll start making excuses as to why he can't."

"Actually, Mrs. Brown, I would love the opportunity to meet you and your family."

There is silence on both ends. I can't believe he just opened his mouth confirming my mother's suspicions that I wasn't alone.

"Mrs. Brown, are you there?" he probably stunned her into silence.

"I'm here," she finally answers.

"I'm not sure if you heard me but I just said that I would accept an invitation to meet you and your family."

"Will you now?" she answers sarcastically. "Layla, have you had me on speaker this entire time?" She's pissed; I'm never going to hear the end of this –ever! Thankfully Prescott covers for me.

"Sorry Mrs. Brown, I just walked into Layla's office and overheard you talking about all of us meeting."

Smooth.

"In that case, Layla is scheduled to come home for a visit this weekend, if you're free you can join us for dinner on Saturday."

"You didn't tell me you were going home this weekend," he says looking at me with an accusatory glare.

"Not now," I whisper to him. I can only handle one crisis at a time. "Mom, we'll see you on Saturday," I say rushing her off the phone. I don't wait for her response, I immediately end the call and slump back in my chair releasing the breath I've been holding since I first answered the phone.

Prescott glances down at his watch, "shit, I'm late for a meeting," he says rising from his chair, "I will have to re-arrange my schedule this weekend but it shouldn't be a big deal," he says casually on his way to the door. "I'll arrange for Loraine to have the plane ready this weekend. I hope you don't mind but we'll need to fly back out Sunday morning, I have to fly out of the country on Monday and will be gone for a few days."

Fly? I can't even think about travel arrangements right now. The thought of Prescott meeting my family has already increased my stress level. He seems so casual about everything, how can he stay calm at a time like this?

"Prescott, I don't think you know what you just signed up for."

"I know exactly what I signed up for."

"No, you don't. My family will never approve of you and they will do everything in their power to make you as uncomfortable as possible during dinner. I appreciate you wanting to prove a point to my mother but this will only end in disaster. Why don't you let me go home first and smooth things out with them? When things settle down, and if we're still together, maybe then you can all meet."

"Are you ashamed of me?"

"Of course not!"

"Then what is it with you and all of this sneaking around?"

As much as it pains me I'm going to have to be blunt. "Prescott, my family members don't really care for white people."

"So your family is racist."

"They're not racist, they're just hurt," I say in their defense.

"I didn't do anything to them."

"I never told you this but Cynthia is not my only sibling and I'm not the oldest." Prescott steps away from the door and takes a seat.

"I'm listening."

"I had an older brother, his name was Craig." Telling this story always pains me. Even after all of these years the mere mention of his name brings tears to my eyes. "My parents used to own a house in a subdivision called Lancaster Estates in Virginia. The community was predominately white. One day when Craig was on his way home from school some cops stopped him. They didn't believe he was walking home; they didn't believe a black family could ever afford to live in that neighborhood. From the witness reports the cops took him down fast. When he insisted he was on his way home they decided to beat him until he told the truth. Since he wasn't lying they ended up beating him to death."

Prescott walks around to hold me but I step out of his reach; I need space so I can finish this story.

"When we went to trial the cops received a slap on the wrist for excessive force and were suspended for six months without pay. My family was distraught and no-one in the neighborhood seemed to care. People started making arguments that racial profiling is necessary in order to keep their neighborhoods safe. Things got even worse the following year when our neighbor's son brutally raped their housekeeper's daughter. She ran to our house for help and we called the cops for her. The cops didn't even question him. She was from El Salvador and they were more worried about whether or not she was here illegally than the crime that was committed. At that point my family had had enough and we moved."

"I'm not making excuses for how they feel but I want you to understand, no-one just decided to wake up and distrust white people but when you experience what our family has, and hear about cases like Trevon Martin and Michael Brown, it's hard to not have your heart harden."

"And how do you feel?"

"Marcus taught me at an early age not to trust anyone, no matter what they look like. I take people as they come and decide for myself."

"Then why all the secrecy with us?"

"I already told you, if things don't work I have a lot more to lose than you. You're Jonathan Prescott; no-one questions you or your actions. Things are different for me."

"I don't want you to think I'm oblivious to the world we live in. I see a lot of ugly shit on a day-to-day basis and I always do everything in my power to make things right."

"Yes, I'm sure the world of marketing can be very ugly at times," I say sarcastically. He probably has no clue about all of the shit that goes on. When you can afford to live in a bubble it's hard to not have your views distorted.

"Thank you for telling me about your brother, I know it was hard for you."

"I know my family isn't perfect but I love them, they mean a lot to me."

"I'll remember that," he says walking out of my office.

Chapter 27

EVER SINCE PRESCOTT confirmed dinner with my mother I've been a wreck. I've done everything in my power to convince him this is not a good idea but he's hell bent on meeting my family. He's tried his best to reassure me things will be okay but I know better. D-day is quickly approaching and it doesn't look like I'll be able to do anything to stop it.

At times like this I wish I could talk to my girls but I would probably spend more time answering their questions about our relationship versus actually solving my problem.

D-day has arrived. I'm so nervous my hands are sweaty and my heart is beating unusually fast.

"Calm down Layla. It's not like dinner will end in a blood bath."

That's what he thinks. Prescott tries to be reassuring but he just doesn't know my family. After everything they've all been through no-one is going to appreciate me bringing a white man home for dinner.

When we pull up outside I take a deep breath. Prescott squeezes my hand reassuringly as we approach the front door. I could use my key to enter but I decide to ring the doorbell instead.

"Nice home," he says looking around. The house looks immaculate with the plush lawn that resembles green carpet and a garden of various flowers that have always been the envy of our neighbors. The path leading to the front door is made of cobblestone and the huge double door entrance can be seen as intimidating. My parents have done well for themselves and I've always admired them for their many accomplishments. I ring the doorbell again and hear the commotion inside as my mother shouts, "Layla is here!"

My mom opens the door and extends both arms to embrace me in a hug. That's when she looks up and sees Prescott standing behind me. She takes her time in looking him over.

"So I see you made it," she finally says.

"Mrs. Brown," Prescott says extending his hand, "it's a pleasure to meet you."

My mom looks at his hand for a few seconds before finally deciding to shake it. I exhale in relief. At least she's willing to try.

"Susan, let that man through the door so we can get a good look at him!" Aunt Janet! My mom didn't mention she was having any of the other family members over. I thought it would just be the four of us. I feel a panic attack coming on. If Aunt Janet is here then Marcus and his family are probably here as well.

Stepping aside my mom ushers us into the family room where several of my aunts, uncles and cousins are seated. I feel like we just walked into an ambush.

"Are you okay?" Prescott asks whispering in my ear.

I have cotton mouth and am unable to speak. I only mentioned Marcus by name once and I'm praying he doesn't remember. As soon as Marcus sees me he makes his way over

"Hey baby girl," he says wrapping me in his arms.

He then looks up at Prescott acknowledging his presence, "Hey, how are you?" he says shaking Prescott's hand, "I'm Layla's cousin, Marcus, and this is my wife Tracy and daughter Amanda."

The introduction took Prescott by surprise. "I'm sorry, did you say your name was Marcus?"

Shit! I grab Prescott's hand and squeeze it as tight as possible. He looks down at me as I silently plead with him to not make a scene. He takes mercy on me and acts cordially. As soon as the introduction is over I quickly pull him away to other side of the room, as far away from Marcus as possible.

"You didn't tell me your cousin would be here," he says soft enough so only I could hear him.

"I thought it would just be the four of us," I reply quickly.

Now I'm nervous for an entirely new reason. I pray Prescott won't cause a scene at dinner. I'm about to reiterate my need for him to stay calm when my father enters the room.

I can feel the room grow tense and all conversation dies down when he makes his way towards us.

"Hi daddy, I say nervously. He lets out a grunt, barely acknowledging my presence. Prescott extends his hands to greet my father but my dad doesn't return the handshake.

"Hello Mr. Brown," Prescott says sounding stiff and formal. I know he doesn't think highly of my parents but so far he's at least putting on a decent front.

"Good evening," my dad finally says with a disapproving glance in my direction.

Not even a knife could cut through the tension in this room. Sensing everyone's unease my mom announces dinner. Maybe if I don't bother to chew I can get us out of here in record time.

It's not uncommon for my family to have formal Saturday dinners. We used to get together after church on Sunday but as the family grew and everyone started attending different services, it was easier to just meet on Saturday instead. The first thing anyone would notice when entering the dining room is the large cherry wood table. My parents had a custom table built to accommodate the growing family. There are also two large bay windows that provide an excellent view of the gardens out back.

My mom put out her best China and everyone's place setting is immaculate. Fresh flowers grace the table with a row of small softly lit candles that run down the length of the table. My parents take their seat at the head while everyone fills the remaining chairs. I always take the seat to my father's left and in hopes of restoring some normalcy to our relationship, I don't stray from tradition. Prescott quickly takes the seat next to me and we all hold hands and say grace before delving into our delicious meal.

My mother has prepared a traditional soul food dinner with roasted chicken, macaroni and cheese, collard greens and candied yams. God I miss her cooking.

We are only a few minutes into the meal when my dad starts to drill me about work.

"So, Layla," he starts off in between bites, "how do your co-workers feel about you sleeping with your boss?" Oh shit! I drop my fork in shock. The room has grown silent. Everyone looks between my father and I waiting for my response. Prescott turns beat red and I frantically look for my water glass to take a sip. My dad never held any punches but he's never been this rude to me either. I do my best to side-step his question.

"Work is great dad, and I get along well with my co-workers. Thanks for asking."

"I find that hard to believe," he says putting his fork down and clasping his hands together, "I've been retired for some time now but if memory serves me correctly, when a girl is sleeping with the boss she is usually labeled several things that I won't say aloud since we are at the dinner table."

Prescott clears his throat.

"Mr. Brown, I understand your concerns, however Layla and I are two professionals who happen to be dating. Our personal and professional relationships do not interfere with each other."

"I find that hard to believe. You think because you are wealthy and white you can go into your office, select the first naive little black girl you find, take her out a few times and fuck her? Then come and sit at my goddamn table and tell me how your personal and professional lives don't interfere with each other?"

"Dad, please stop!" I scream horrified at how this conversation is going, "I didn't come here for an argument; why won't you even give him a chance before passing judgment?!"

"Little girl, you have no experience in these matters. When he is finished with you, your mom and I will be the ones left to help you pick up the pieces while he continues with business as usual. You should never have gotten involved with this man and to say I'm disappointed in you is an understatement."

My eyes fill with water. I don't remember ever feeling this embarrassed.

Anger is seething from Prescott as he turns his head looking at me and my father.

"Mr. Brown, I don't have children however I can understand your concern, which is why I am here. Layla is very important to me and I want nothing more than to make our relationship work."

"What kind of bullshit are you trying to sell me boy? You think I'm stupid or something? I know how your people work and trust me when I say that I know nothing good can come from this!"

"Brandon!" my mom yells out trying to make my dad stop.

"Susan, this needs to be said. I know how you high roller men think. You think because you are willing to have dinner with us it's supposed to impress me? You don't give a crap about me or my family and as soon as you break my little girl's heart this dinner will be nothing but a distant memory. Maybe you can go and tell your white friends about the time you sat and had dinner with some colored folk."

"Fuck this shit!" Prescott blurts out.

"Prescott! No!" I yell.

"Did you just curse at my table boy!?"

"Layla, I'm sorry but I'm not going to sit here for this shit." He then turns to my dad,

"To be honest Mr. Brown, I was never enthusiastic about meeting you but not for the reasons you think. You let that son of a bitch Marcus sit at your table after what he did to your daughter but you want to question me about my intensions because I'm white?!"

Everyone's jaws drop, including my dad's.

"Layla told me what happened to her and how you and your wife did nothing to help or protect her. Not only did you know about this asshole molesting your daughter, but you continued to invite him into your home, not giving a fuck about what effect it would have on your own child. So don't sit here and act like you give a shit now. You want to play over-protective daddy because she's dating a white man? Well don't bother—she's got a new daddy now."

Prescott stands and reaches out to me, "Layla, let's go!"

My body is frozen and unable to move. Prescott bends to look me in my eyes.

"I'm sorry but it had to be said."

He may say he's sorry but no part of him looks apologetic. No one says a word as we leave the table and head for the front door. The room is so quiet you can literally hear a pin drop.

As we get into Prescott's car my body starts to shake. I feel my face and I'm surprised to find that I haven't shed a tear. He starts to pull out of the driveway but I know I need to stop him. If I'm ever going to confront my family and speak up for myself it's now or never.

"Wait!" I yell. His foot pumps the brake, jerking my body forward.

"Wait here, okay," I ask with a new sense of determination.

"Okay."

I rush back inside to confront my parents. It's time for me to speak up for myself.

"Layla!" My mom screams as soon as she sees me. "How could you tell a stranger about our personal family business? What are you trying to do? Ruin our family? Don't you think we've been through enough?"

"You don't get it do you? Since I can remember I have done

exactly what's been expected of me no matter how much it hurts but no more! I'm not going to pretend like everything is okay when it's not. I'm too old for this. I know you and dad are both disappointed in me but truth be told I'm also disappointed in you. My love life is always in a shambles and it's because of him," I say pointing to Marcus.

"Not this shit again," yells my mother.

"Yes, this shit again. You are my parents and you didn't do shit. I know what happened is not your fault but when you found out you simply wiped my tears away and told me everything will be okay but it's not! The shit is still in my head and no matter how hard I try I can't get it out. I still remember and I know I'll never forget."

I turn and quickly walk over to Marcus and spit in his face.

"You are a low piece of shit and your sick ass needs help! You think I don't remember but I do! I remember everything you did to me and I will never forget. No more pretending it didn't happen."

I pick up a steak knife from the table and point it at his crotch.

"I can change you from a man to a bitch with one flick of my wrist. You are never to come near me ever again or so help me God I'll cut it off and no doc on this planet will be able to reattach it!"

I drop the knife in his lap and head for the door. When I'm finally outside I take a deep breath for the first time since I'd gone back inside the house. I slide into the passenger seat of Prescott's car and order him to drive. He takes off driving faster than he should down the residential streets, both of us sitting in complete silence.

Chapter 28

AFTER THE DINNER fiasco the flight back to Chicago is dreadful. Prescott is still steaming mad and I am an emotional wreck. When we land he wants me to go back to his place but I need time alone to think.

My sister Cynthia wastes no time in calling me. As soon as I see her number across my cell I turn my phone off. I don't want to talk to anyone right now. When I get back to my apartment and check my messages, I discover I have over fifty missed calls and thirty messages. In Cynthia's last voice mail she threatens to show up un-announced if I don't answer. Needless to say, that got my attention. I know I can no longer postpone the inevitable so when the phone rings again and the caller ID flashes her number this time I answer it.

"Layla, it's me Cynthia, I'm not calling to fight with you but I have to ask, why are you willing to give up on your family for this man? Don't you have any sense of loyalty to us?"

What?! I guess we are going to pass all telephone etiquette and get right to the argument that is undoubtedly looming ahead.

"Where is the family's sense of loyalty to me?" I ask. "I'm not the bad guy in all of this yet everyone wants to make me out to be the villain. The only person on my side is Prescott."

"You know what your problem is Layla? You need to get over yourself. Marcus touched you, big deal!" She yells into the phone. "You make Marcus out to be some kind of monster and he's not. I know for a fact his touch doesn't hurt so why can't you just get over it?"

"What do you mean you know his touch doesn't hurt?"

"Just what I said."

Oh. My. God!

"Are you telling me he molested you too?"

Has one of my worst fears become a reality? I tried my best to keep Marcus away from my little sister. Did all of my efforts fail?

"People experiment all the time Layla, it's no big deal. He realized what he was doing was wrong and it never happened again. Why can't you just let this go?"

Am I hearing correctly? Am I really talking to my baby sister? My heart is breaking in two. With each word that comes from Cynthia's mouth I feel like bashing Marcus' head into the ground. How could I have missed the signs? Granted I was a child myself but still, I should have protected her. The bastard fucked us both up, and what's worse, she doesn't even know it. She still idolizes him. How will I ever get her to see Marcus for what he truly is? How will I ever get anyone in my family to understand the long term damage his actions have caused?

"Cynthia, why didn't you ever tell anyone?"

"What for? You opened your mouth and it almost destroyed our family. You know what your problem is Layla? You don't like to take responsibility for your own actions. I don't remember hearing stories of you screaming down the house begging him to stop. As a matter of fact, Aunty Janet was home the first time anything happened and you didn't even tell her. If you were so scared, and if what he did was so hurtful, why didn't you immediately go tell someone? Why did you let it happen over and over again? Don't you think you bear some of the responsibility in this?"

"I was a child!" I say shouting, "I was scared and confused."

"I'm not saying you weren't a child and I'm not saying what he did was right. I just wish you would stop putting all of the blame on him. Growing up anytime you hurt yourself you had no problem running to mom and dad for help, yet it took you years to admit what Marcus was doing. Why is that?"

"You don't think I struggle with this?"

"Well I think you struggle because you know you could have stopped it a long time ago and you didn't and now you want the family to pay for your own weakness. What he did was wrong but you need to forgive him and move on. We are a family and we are supposed to stick together, no matter what. How could you tell a stranger about what happened? And what about his wife and child?" she says continuing her rant, "did you ever stop to think about what this is doing to his marriage? This happened years ago and because of your big ass mouth Marcus could end up in some serious trouble."

"So what, I should care more about what happens to Marcus than myself?"

I love my baby sister but I don't have the strength for this shit anymore. I'm tired of fighting everyone. I battle myself and my family and so far it hasn't gotten any of us anywhere. I can't continue to go through this. I wish they could understand that I want to move on and forget the past more than anyone but I can't. Granted since being with Prescott things have gotten better but I want to feel whole. I want to feel clean. No matter how much I wash I still feel stained and dirty. When will that feeling ever go away?

She thinks I don't question myself about this but I do, I question myself all the time. Why didn't I scream at the top of my lungs for Aunty Janet? No matter how many times I question myself, I still don't have an answer. All I know is that one day I woke up an innocent five-year-old girl and by bedtime I had been stained and tainted for the rest of my life.

The only thing I know for sure is this conversation with Cynthia has to end.

"Cynthia, I'm sorry we don't see eye to eye on this. More than anything I'm sorry the same thing happened to you. Maybe you are stronger than me, I don't know, all I do know is that what happened bothers me and it has affected me and my relationships. I should be able to be intimate with whomever I choose and not have images of my cousin spilling his sperm all over my body. If that bothers everyone then maybe it's a good thing I stay away for a while."

"So once again you're bailing on your family."

"No, for the first time I'm going to do what I should have done a long time ago and put myself first. I need to take time to decide on how I want to handle things. Not just for me but for the sake of our family. I love you baby sis. Talk to you soon," and with that I hang up.

After my phone call with Cynthia I feel like I need a shower. Everything we talked about has made me feel dirty. As soon as the warm water hits my body I immediately start to relax. Thank God for spa showers. Water jets are hitting me from every direction and it reminds of me of the many directions my family pulls me in. Am I wrong in the way I feel? No. I have every right to feel the way I feel and I don't have to justify anything to anyone. I'm so tired of my family expecting me to put their feelings in front of my own. Maybe it's a blessing no-one is talking to me right now. This way I don't have to deal with any of their demands. This is my time. This is the time for me to fully discover myself; no more doing things everyone else's way, it's time for me to do things my way.

After my shower I wander around my apartment in a bit of a daze. How can one person cause so much destruction in a family? The crazy part is that no one is putting the blame where it belongs. Cynthia and I should be comforting each other, not arguing with one another.

I keep going over events from my childhood in my head until the sound of the phone ringing pulls me back into reality. I don't even look to see who is calling, I'm just happy for the distraction.

"Hello."

"Hey, I've been trying to reach you, are you okay?" Just hearing his voice makes me feel better.

"Not really. I'm having a shitty evening." I should have gone back to his place, at least then I wouldn't be alone. "How are you doing?" I ask. Hopefully his evening is better than mine.

"You want to talk about it?"

"No."

"I'm here if you change your mind."

"Thanks." It still shocks me how attentive he is.

"Not to change the subject, but I just received an invitation for a political fundraiser in New York this weekend for Congressman Gordon and I thought maybe we could make a weekend of it."

"Your timing is perfect," I say perking up.

"My timing is better than you think."

I'm about to ask him what he means by that when I hear a knock at my door. He's here! My body feels revived. This is the effect he has on me. A smile graces my face when I see him. He's leaning against the door jamb in that GQ pose I love. I rush into his arms and exhale; when I'm with Prescott I know everything will be okay.

Chapter 29

P RESCOTT HAS BEEN away on business all week. With him gone
I've spent a lot of time with my girls. Tonight we're heading
out to dinner. Georgina knows the owner of some trendy over-
priced restaurant that just opened. The restaurant is not far from
the office, so we all decide to meet in the lobby after work and
walk over together.

When I step off the elevator, the sight of Simone in the lobby
stops me dead in my tracks. I'm not shocked she's changed—it's
what she's changed into that gives me a reason to pause. Stephanie approaches the lobby from the opposite direction. I laugh to
myself when I see the look of disgust on her face. Tonight will
definitely be an interesting evening.

"Simone, what the hell are you wearing?" Stephanie asks.

I have t-shirts that are longer than Simone's dress.

"Cute right?" she asks.

Wrong, I think to myself, but I know better than to say anything. I give Stephanie a look, urging her to let it go. Thankfully,
she takes the hint and remains quiet.

"Has anyone seen Georgina or Pamela?"

"Georgina is wrapping up a conference call and Pamela is on her way down," Stephanie says tightening her bun.

"They better hurry up; I'm excited to see this new spot. I heard a lot of athletes hang out there."

Inwardly I laugh at Simone. She's always excited at the prospect of meeting a man with deep pockets.

"Stephanie, why do you always have to look so serious?" Simone asks, after inspecting her man suit.

I don't know why Simone even bothers to give Stephanie a hard time about her wardrobe. She's dedicated herself to dressing like a man; yet no matter how masculine her clothes may be, she can't escape her feminine beauty.

"Why don't you take your hair down tonight?" Simone suggests.

"Why don't you wear something that doesn't expose your chest and ass?" Stephanie asks in return. Those two could go back and forth for forever. I've learned to stay quiet when they get started. There's no point in intervening; in the end Stephanie's hair will stay in its customary bun and Simone's ass and chest will continue to be exposed.

I hear the ding of the elevator and smile when I see Georgina and Pamela approaching—it's time to get our lady's night out started!

I laugh as we walk and gossip all the way to the restaurant. We're having a debate on important matters like, should a woman wear shoes that are comfortable or stylish? Tonight style won out for me. My feet may be killing me but my Louboutin's are well worth the pain.

There's a line outside the restaurant, but thanks to Georgina's connections, we're able to get seated right away. This place almost reminds me of Hancock's, except they only cater to a certain clientele. We take our seats at the table and order our first round of drinks. As always, Simone starts the evening off by scanning the room for available men. I thought Stephanie and Pamela were joking about her one-night stands. Who knew they were telling the truth?

"He's cute," she says, eyeing some guy at the bar. I pay no attention to her. As far as I'm concerned if Prescott's not in a room, there's no one worth paying attention to.

"Layla, don't you think he's cute?" I don't know why she's asking me. My opinion never matters to Simone, however I indulge her, and take a look at the man who's captured her attention. Our eyes don't meet but I could never forget that face. It's the same guy I saw Prescott talking to at the bar in Jamaica.

"Layla, stop staring!"

"Oh-oh," Georgina says. "The last time Layla stared across the room like that, she caught Justin cheating and we ended up having to break up a fight."

"I can assure you there's no one in this place worth fighting over."

Simone continues to check out Prescott's friend at the bar. I make a mental note to ask Prescott about him tomorrow.

"I think I'm about to reel him in girls!"

"I don't know Simone," Pamela says, "looks to me like he's staring at Layla."

I was thinking the same thing; however I didn't want to voice my observation in case I was wrong.

"Layla, you should go talk to him."

The look I give Pamela immediately shuts her up. The last thing I need is for Prescott to think I'm trying to make a move on his friend.

"Forget him," Georgina says taking a sip of her drink. "There are plenty of sexy ass men for the taking in this place."

"Whatever!" Stephanie says looking annoyed.

"Why the hell do you bother coming out with us if you're just going to get annoyed when we start checking out men?" Simone asks, irritated with Stephanie.

"Someone's got to make sure you and Georgina don't get into trouble."

"Do we look like we need a chaperone?"

"No, you look like you need a dress that fits!"

"Whatever!" Simone says plucking an appetizer from the tray in front of her.

"Everyone just relax!" Georgina says taking another sip from her drink.

"We're here to have a good time."

Single Ladies by Beyonce starts to play and Georgina practically jumps out of her seat. "Let's dance!" she shouts over the music.

There's not much of a dance floor however under Georgina's persistence and with the fuel of alcohol, we take over the dance floor and do the Uh-Oh dance. The music is blazing, the alcohol is intoxicating and my girls are all here. We do our best to make Queen B—aka Sasha Fierce—proud!

As the night progresses Simone and Georgina engage in conversation with some of the guys lurking around our table. A couple of guys try to get my attention but I don't entertain anyone's advances. Not that I'm concerned, but Prescott's friend is still here and I don't want him going back and reporting anything.

Pamela is her normal quiet self. Nights like this Pamela and Stephanie usually end up keeping each other company. I watch as Georgina works the room. She's so confident. She knows just about every man in the room would love the opportunity to take her home tonight. I know there are a lot of stereotypes about blondes. Georgina definitely knows how to have a good time, but that's where the stereotype ends. Her head for business still amazes me. No matter how she may act outside of the office, I understand why Prescott made her his VP—she knows how to get shit done and her work ethic is something to admire.

Georgina and Simone are similar. They are both natural social butterflies. However, one big difference I've observed is while Georgina has men wanting to commit to her left and right; Simone always ends up with men who use her for her body. No matter how much we talk to Simone about closing her legs, she refuses to believe she doesn't have to sleep with a man in order for him to be genuinely interested in her. I watch her closely at the bar. She's leaning up against some ungodly tall guy. From the way she's flirting his pockets must be deep. She takes out her phone and I watch as the two exchange numbers. She's heading back to our table with a giddy expression on her face.

"OMG! Girls do you know who that is?"

"Enlighten us," Stephanie says dryly.

"Girl, that's Alonzo Woods," she says gathering her purse.

"Simone, where are you going?" I ask.

"Home with Alonzo. I've never had a NBA player before," she says excitedly.

"Are you crazy?!" I ask. "You just met him."

"So? Men do it all the time. Why can a man pick up any woman he wants, yet if a woman does the same thing she's considered cheap?"

"Simone, you can't allow every man that smiles in your direction entrance into your temple. There are some things worth keeping sacred."

"What?"

"Let me put it this way; who's dumber: the thief that breaks in and continues to get away with it or the homeowner who refuses to lock their door?"

"What?"

I swear, sometimes I think talking to a brick wall would be easier!

"I'm saying it's okay to lock your door sometimes."

"Too late," she says smiling. "I already gave him the keys."

Chapter 30

MY WEEKEND AWAY with Prescott finally arrives. This weekend symbolizes a lot. This is the first time we will be around his friends and business partners and I'm anxious to see how he plans to introduce me. I'm also looking forward to maybe learning a little more about his family; he rarely mentions them and I get the feeling he does that on purpose.

Prescott arranges for a private car to pick me up. The fundraiser is tonight so I leave work a little early. I haven't seen him since he came over last Sunday after I had my call with Cynthia. I never filled him in on that conversation—just thinking about it still disturbs me.

When I reach the airport anticipation builds; I'm looking forward to our flight. I would never admit this to Prescott but I love flying in his plane. I don't have to worry about lines, security checks or making sure all of my toiletries are in travel-size containers. After 9/11, traveling has become a real pain in the ass.

When I board the plane I see Prescott is already seated with his phone glued to his ear. I notice his laptop is open and what looks like blueprints spread out around him. I immediately feel like an ass for not bringing any work with me. Foolish of me to think this weekend was all about us. I take the seat next to him and notice as soon as I'm seated he ends his call. He does that often and I find it a little unsettling. Why won't he hold a conversation around me? Is he hiding something?

"Sorry about that," he says, leaning in for a kiss. "I was hoping to relax during the flight but it looks like I need to go over a few things before we arrive."

Disappointment sets in. I haven't seen him all week and I'm starving for his attention. He's done his due diligence in calling and checking on me but I was hoping he could make me a member of the mile high club on this trip. He always works when we're in flight and today is no different. I remind myself to not be so needy. He has a company to run and I refuse to become some nagging girlfriend.

"It's no problem. I should have brought my laptop with me so I could get some work done as well."

"This is not a working weekend. Just sit back and relax during the flight, we'll be in New York before you know it. I promise to wrap everything up as soon as we touch down, deal?"

"Deal," I say, reaching for a magazine. I guess I'll use this time to get caught up on celebrity gossip. I pick up a copy of People and start flipping through some of the pics until I come across an article entitled *"10 Ways You Know You've Met the One."* I usually don't read crap like this but today the article grabs my attention. I laugh aloud when one of the guys quoted says he'll propose to the first woman who sees him cry; how absurd!

"What's so funny?"

"Nothing, just a ridiculous article I'm reading."

"About what?"

"10 Ways You Know You've Met the One." One of the guys they interviewed said he'll marry the first woman to see him cry."

Prescott smirks, "I guess I'll never get married."

"Are you seriously going to sit here and say you honestly never cry, not even when you're alone?"

"Tears don't make anything better."

"I disagree, sometimes a good cry can cleanse your soul."

"I'll let you believe that," he says, returning his attention back to the work in front of him.

True to his word Prescott closes up his laptop and puts all of his reports away as soon as we get into the city. I thought we would be staying at some fancy hotel but it turns out he owns a condo in Manhattan. To describe the place as gorgeous would be an understatement. Everything is ultra-sleek, modern and white. Doesn't he believe in pops of color?

There is a large bank of windows on one side of his condo with a fabulous view of the city. I immediately gravitate to the window and look out. Part of me still wants to pinch myself. I can't believe I'm standing here in all of this luxury with a man I'm falling for. Before, I couldn't picture my life outside of Justin and now my relationship with Justin seems like a lifetime ago. I feel Prescott's presence behind me. He wraps both of his arms around me and we stand in silence together staring out at the beautiful skyline.

It doesn't take long for our moment of silence to be interrupted by the phone. The call is from the concierge service letting us know the car will arrive to pick us up at seven o'clock.

"Layla, let's start to get dressed, I don't want to be late."

"Okay, which way to the bathroom? I need to shower and get started on my hair." I was hoping for a tour of the condo but I guess that will have to wait since we are definitely on a time crunch.

"I'll join you in the shower."

"Are you asking or telling me?"

"I have to ask for permission to join you in my shower?" he says crossing him arms in amusement.

"I'm not on the clock so I don't have to take any of your orders. While we are out of the office you're going to have to widen your vocabulary to include words like may I, please and thank you," I say smartly.

"Ms. Layla Brown, may I join you in the shower... please." Watching Prescott ask for permission is like watching someone getting their teeth pulled at the dentist—painful.

"You may join me but only if you promise to keep your hands to yourself, I'm not going to let you blame me for us running late."

"You should know I could never make such a promise," he says, taking my hand and leading me to the bathroom. The bathroom, if you could call it that, is enormous.

We manage to shower without incident but it isn't for a lack of him trying. His cannon stood in the firing position the whole time. After we shower, I start on my hair while he shaves.

"So, how's the Bradford account coming along?" he asks, looking in the mirror.

Really, he wants to discuss the Bradford account now? I thought we were going to put work behind us.

"Everything is coming along fine. I have a meeting with him next week."

"How is he treating you?'"

"Treating me? Fine I guess. We haven't had any issues."

"Has he introduced you to his wife?" he asks, looking uneasy.

"No, why do you ask?"

"Just curious," he says rinsing out his razor.

Bullshit. Something's up. Every time we talk about Mr. Bradford Prescott starts acting all weird and I'm tired of it; it's time for me to get to the bottom of this.

I turn towards him placing my curling iron on the counter.

"Why do you keep asking me questions about Mr. Bradford?"

"What are you talking about?"

"You know exactly what I'm talking about. Every time I have a meeting with him you start acting weird and ask me a ton of questions; what's the deal and for once please be straight with me." The look on his face lets me know he's contemplating whether he wants to actually tell me the truth. Whatever the case I've got to get to the bottom of this, I know something is up and I will not let it rest until I get the truth.

"I'll come straight with you but only if you promise to keep a cool head."

"I promise," I say quickly.

"Well, remember how we first met?"

"I don't think I will ever forget that night, but what does that have to do with Mr. Bradford?"

"Many people don't know this, but James and I are good friends outside of work, we have similar tastes and are members at most of the same clubs."

"Really?" I would have never thought they had anything in common outside of work. "If you two are friends, why do you freak out every time I have a meeting with him?"

"We have a unique friendship."

I'm not liking the sound of this. "What kind of unique friendship?"

"James is a swinger."

"WHAT?! James Bradford is a swinger?" I yell.

"Yes," is all he says, but I know there is more to this story. The thought of that overweight balding white man getting it on with anyone makes my skin crawl.

"Okay," I say, trying to keep my cool, "well that still doesn't explain why you act the way you do."

"James was in D.C. the night we met and he knows how we met."

"WHAT!!!" This is not happening. "How does he know? Did you tell him?"

"He saw Melony and I at Clyde's and I may have casually mentioned we were scouting out a new couple. He had mentioned you looked familiar but it wasn't until after your presentation he remembered where he recognized you from."

Oh. My. God. I feel like such an ass.

"You knew I was going into meeting after meeting with this man and you never thought to tell me he knew about my past? How could you keep a secret like that from me?"

"Because I knew you would freak out like you're doing right now."

"Damn right I'm freaking out! This is a nightmare." How could I be so stupid as to think that night would never come back to bite me in the ass? Sure, I'm happy I met Prescott, but this is the type of scandal that always comes back to haunt you.

"Is there anything else I should know?"

He said no but he said it too quickly. I watch him as he starts getting dressed and notice he's paying way too much attention to the buttons on his shirt. He's definitely hiding something.

"Does it bother you that I'm not into the swinging lifestyle?" I blurt the question out quickly in hopes he has the answer I want to hear.

"No."

"Do you think you can change my mind about being a swinger?"

"What do I look like, a fucking recruiter?" Whoa, clearly I've offended him.

"I didn't mean to upset you, I just want to make it clear to you I have no interest in becoming a swinger and I would never sleep with Mr. Bradford or anyone else for that matter."

"Layla, I'm not a pimp. The lifestyle is for consenting adults who like to add spice to their relationships. I know you're not interested and that's fine with me, now can we PLEASE change the subject."

"Only because you said please," I say smiling at him in the mirror. Jonathan Prescott is definitely a work in progress.

Chapter 31

THE SET-UP FOR the party is everything I imagined it would be. All of the tables are decorated with beautiful bouquets of flowers and candles. The lights from the crystal chandeliers shine brightly and compliment what look to be Italian marble floors. Prescott and I arrive in time for the cocktail hour so people are scattered all throughout the room with servers bustling by with appetizers and champagne.

I look over at Prescott and admire how handsome he looks in his tux. He glances down at me and gives me a quick smile and kiss on the lips before taking my hand as we walk further into the ballroom.

"Come," he says, "there are some people I would like for you to meet."

Clearly he's already forgotten our conversation about me not taking orders however this time I'm not offended. I'm interested in meeting some of the people he socializes with.

Usually at functions like this you have to work the room but I guess that doesn't apply to Prescott. We barely take two steps before people start randomly coming up to us. How the hell does someone in marketing hold such a commanding presence? I can't imagine why members of congress are standing around waiting for a turn to talk to him—shouldn't it be the other way around?

When he first asked me to join him I wondered why we were attending a political fundraiser since our firm doesn't have any clients in politics, but in the end I was so happy he wanted to bring me I didn't question why we were attending. I figured maybe he was trying to branch out but now I'm not so sure. None of our competitors are here and I can't follow any of his conversations, it's like everyone is talking in code. I appreciate the fact that he wants to keep me close but I'm starting to feel more like an accessory than his date.

He's in the middle of wrapping up his conversation with House Representative Charles Banks when a woman in a very revealing red dress approaches.

"Jonathan, here you are, I've been looking all over for you!" Prescott turns and greets the woman with a warm smile, something he doesn't do often. They must be good friends I tell myself.

"Hi Deb," he says, bending to give the woman who can't be more than five feet with heels on a warm embrace. This is the first time he's let go of my hand all evening. I stand silent waiting for him to make the introductions.

"Deborah, I would like you to meet my…" Prescott takes a long pause, what the hell is he waiting for? "I would like for you to meet my girlfriend, Layla… Layla, this is Mrs. Deborah Mayweather."

Girlfriend! This is the first time he referred to me as his girlfriend all evening.

"Girlfriend!" Deborah exclaims, "oh how wonderful Jonathan. How long have the two of you been dating?"

Prescott looks at me and smiles before answering, "we've been an item for a few weeks now."

He's trying to make me uncomfortable and its working. Deborah on the other hand seems elated by the news.

"I always knew you would find someone special and it looks like you have."

I notice while she's talking she grabs his biceps and squeezes. This man just told her we are in a relationship and she takes this opportunity to openly flirt? What the hell is she after? I try to not be the possessive type but everything in me wants to grab him and pull him away from her but before I get the chance she gives Prescott a quick hug telling him how nice it is to see him and excuses herself. I look at Prescott watching Deborah walk away and I feel the heat rising inside of me. I need to get a grip. He hasn't given me a reason to be jealous but I can't help the quiver in my stomach. I don't want to ruin our evening with my insecurities. Maybe this is a good time for a bathroom break. I quickly excuse myself to find a restroom but before I can get away Prescott grabs a hold of my hand and pulls me closer to him.

"You okay?" He looks concerned.

"I'm fine, I just need the ladies room," I say making my escape. On my way I notice Mr. Bradford is here. We lock eyes for a moment and I immediately think back to my earlier conversation. I shudder at the thought of him having sex. I should go over and say hello but instead I just smile politely and hurry to the bathroom.

I don't really need to use the restroom; I just need some space. I would love to splash cold water on my face but that would ruin my makeup. This night is nothing like I expected. This is a fundraiser for Congressman Gordon but you wouldn't know it. For some reason Jonathan Prescott has become the king of the ball.

I walk over to the large mirrors to inspect my appearance. I took special care in getting dressed. It was a little difficult to stay focused, especially after Prescott shared the news about Mr. Bradford, but considering everything I think I did an excellent job. I selected a royal blue floor length dress that nicely accentuates all of my assets. I knew I chose well when I saw Prescott's reaction to my dress. The only mishap came when I asked him to help me with my necklace. He took one look at it and refused to let me wear it. He walked out of the dressing room and made two phone calls. Thirty minutes later someone from the concierge desk appeared with several jewelry selections for me to choose from. I felt a little offended at his reaction, I mean every woman I know owns costume jewelry but I took one look at the sparkling jewels and all was forgiven.

I spend so much time admiring my necklace I don't notice Deborah until I see her reflection in the mirror, watching me.

"Hi," I say with a strained smile.

"Layla, you look absolutely breathtaking in that dress." She's looking at me as if I literally take her breath away, *please God*, I silently pray, *don't let me have another incident like the one on the plane*.

"Thank you…you also look lovely in your dress." It's not a lie; I wish I could pull off wearing something so revealing in a classy way.

"Why thank you. So…what time will you and Jonathan arrive at the after party?"

After party? Prescott never mentioned anything to me. I got the impression we would be heading back to his place once the event was over. I don't want to let her know he never told me, so I lie instead.

"I'm not sure if we are attending."

"Not sure?" she says with her eyes widening. "You two have to be there." She sounds adamant about us attending. What could be so important about an after party? I always thought the main event was the most important.

"Is there another party you two are considering?"

She's a nosy little thing. I'll have to watch her. "We're just keeping our options open," I say, opening my purse to powder my nose. Without warning Deborah grabs me by the waist and pushes me into a stall.

"What the hell are you doing?" Her eyes grow wide as she licks her lips.

"I'm giving you a reason to come to our party instead." Deborah then pulls me so we are chest to chest and tries to kiss me while caressing my breast.

Totally caught off guard by her actions I drop my purse to the floor. I turn my head just in time to avoid her kiss. "Deborah stop!" I scream and finally she unhands me. For such a small woman she sure is strong as hell. I open the stall door and order her to get out.

"I'm sorry Layla, was I too rough?" she asks looking apologetic. "Jonathan's girls usually like it a little rough but I can be gentle if you like."

This is fucking crazy! Is every woman he comes into contact with a freak?

"I'm not a swinger," I say, stooping down to collect all of the items that fell out of my purse.

"Excuse me?" she asks, taking a step away from me as if she's scared she'll catch the 'I don't fuck everyone' disease.

"I'm not bi-playful, bi-sexual or a swinger," I say angrily. "I'm just plain old Layla Brown who believes that sex is between one man and one woman. Can you handle that?" I ask, shoving the last of the fallen contents back into my purse.

"I'm sorry Layla, I didn't know. Jonathan's never dated a vanilla girl before."

Vanilla girl? That's a new one!

"Well, sorry to disappoint you, however I'm not a swinger and Prescott is out of the lifestyle."

"Layla, are you telling me Jonathan Prescott is dating you even though you're not a swinger?"

"Is that so shocking?" What the hell is she getting at? There is more to a relationship than sex. What Prescott and I share may have started with sex but it is growing into so much more. What we share is something none of these freaks will ever understand.

"I don't mean to come across as cruel; it's just that Jonathan is like the prize bull in our club. Ever since he joined the lifestyle I don't think he's ever dated anyone who wasn't a bi-playful swinger. Don't get me wrong, I'm happy for the two of you really, it just comes as a surprise that's all... boy, there are going to be a lot of heartbroken women tonight."

"Just how many hearts will he be breaking out there?" I ask out of curiosity.

"It may be hard to swallow but just about every woman out there is going to be saddened when I tell them we won't be able to see our stallion in action."

"Isn't anyone happily married anymore?" I mumble to myself.

"Quite the contrary dear, we are all happily married," she says taking a step closer to me. "You haven't had much experience with this have you?"

"I haven't had any experience with this," I say lying. She doesn't need to know how we met.

"Well, all I can say is don't judge us. Who knows," she says smiling, "you may just like it."

"I like conventional relationships. Besides, the lifestyle goes against everything I've ever been taught."

"In that case, I do apologize for my actions and our little misunderstanding but I must ask, being that the lifestyle is a part of who Jonathan is, how long do you actually expect this relationship of yours to last?"

"Are you implying our relationship won't last because I'm not a swinger?"

"I give Jonathan credit for trying something new Layla, but at the end of the day, a leopard can't change its spots."

She's voicing one of my biggest fears but I'm not going to let her know that.

"Jonathan and I will last for as long as we are meant to last." With that I turn and exit the bathroom in search of Prescott. He has a lot of explaining to do.

As soon as I'm out of the restroom I take a deep breath and count to ten. I need to have a word with Prescott and even though now is not the time or place I can't sit with this shit on my chest all evening. I immediately seek him out but I don't have to look long. With long strides I see him heading my way.

"I was wondering what was taking you so long; are you okay?"

Once he's in earshot I waste no time in getting straight to the point, "how could you?" I ask. I feel myself getting more and more upset by the second.

"How could I what?"

"You brought me to a place filled with your horny ass swinger friends and you didn't even warn me!? How many of these women have you fucked?" I ask looking around. His entire demeanor changes as he does a quick scan of the room to make sure nobody can overhear our conversation.

"We're not doing this here."

"Oh yes we are—how many?" I ask with persistence. It's time for me to know exactly what the hell I'm getting myself into.

"Fuck Layla, I don't know," he says running his fingers through his hair: a sign of pure frustration.

Is he kidding me? "What do you mean you don't know?"

"I don't keep track. I'm not some fucking frat boy that keeps notches in his belt."

"Deborah mentioned you have a membership at some club; is that how the two of you met?"

"You had a conversation with Deborah about the swinger club? What the hell happened in the bathroom?"

"Your little friend Deborah started asking me about some after-party. When I let her know that I wasn't sure if we would be attending she pulled me into a stall and groped me."

"Shit," I hear him whisper under his breath. "I'm sorry," he says softening his tone, "I didn't think she would do something like that."

"Really? I tell you that your little playmate just accosted me in the bathroom and all you can say is that you didn't think she would do something like that? I'm tired of being felt up by your little swinger freaks. All of you need to get your shit together and learn how to fuck one person at a time." I didn't mean to cause a scene but from the way Prescott keeps looking around, that's exactly what I'm starting to do.

"I'm only going to tell you this once; watch what you say."

"Or what?" I ask, folding my arms in a defensive posture.

"This is not the time to test me so change the subject—now."

"Is that a threat?"

"It's a warning and if you're smart you'll take heed of it."

"To hell with you and your warning, I'm not going to let you intimidate me."

Prescott lets out a grunt in frustration but his attention is diverted when a tall Middle-Eastern man approaches us. He's five feet away and the men seem to be communicating without uttering one word. Finally Prescott looks at me and he looks like he's been hit with a ton of bricks. The Middle-Eastern man backs away and Prescott takes my hand leading me out to the terrace. The terrace is full of couples mingling but when we step outside and he asks for some privacy, without question everyone heads back inside. I stand still in shock. Again, how the hell does a man in marketing hold so much power over people who clearly should have more clout than he does? This doesn't make sense.

"Layla..." he says my name while pacing, which is never a good sign, "I'm not used to this."

"Not used to what?"

"Arguing."

"I don't like arguing either but with you it feels like it's inevitable."

"Why is that?" he asks, stopping to stand in front of me.

"Because you act like I can't bring up certain subjects unless you want to talk about it and that's now how it works. If I ask you a question all I want is a truthful answer but instead you try to use intimidation to shut me up which, if you haven't noticed, only makes me more upset."

"I never start arguments, I always end them but I just realized I can't use my tactics on you so we're going to have to figure something out."

"What tactics do you normally use?" I wonder if this has anything to do with the tall Middle-Eastern gentleman who approached us.

"Let's address one issue at a time. Correct me if I'm wrong," he says while continuing to pace, "you're upset with me because of a lifestyle I engaged in when I was single. I understand you're not into it, which is fine, but everyone who is a swinger is not some weird freak. Swingers are people who enjoy sexual freedom and feel free to explore their sexuality with trusted partners. I know it may be hard to believe after your experience but most of the swingers I engage with are some of the most honest and trustworthy people I know."

"I hear what you're saying but I still find that hard to believe."

"Why don't you see for yourself?" he asks looking at me pointedly.

"What do you mean see for myself?" I hope he's not thinking what I think he's thinking.

"On our way home lets swing by the after party so you can see things for yourself. Maybe then you can understand that everyone is normal, they just enjoy a sexual freedom society labels as taboo."

"Before I answer I have one question." Depending on how he answers this, tonight could be the last time Prescott and I see each other, "would you like to see me with another man?"

"No," he responds quickly. "I know I'm contradicting everything I just said but there's no man walking this earth who's worthy enough for me to share you with."

"Okay," I say smiling, "when the fundraiser is over we'll stop by the after party."

"That's it?" he asks surprised.

"I'm just as eager as you are to put all of this behind us and if you think going to the after party will help me to understand then I'm willing to go—I trust you."

"I've never been one to talk things out before but I can see how in some circumstances it truly can work."

That's an odd thing to say. "What do you normally do? Beat someone up if they don't agree with you?" I ask jokingly.

"I'll fill you in soon enough," he says, taking my arm to escort me back into the hotel. Prescott is definitely full of secrets.

Chapter 32

THE REMAINDER OF the fundraiser goes by in a flash and before I know it we're in the backseat of Prescott's limo. During the car ride he coaches me on how to conduct myself while we are at the party; who knew the freaks had so many rules?

After a thirty minute drive towards the city limits we pull up to a huge building that looks like it houses executive offices.

"Is this an office building?" I ask, trying to take in my surroundings.

"You'd be surprised to find out what happens in a lot of these offices after dark," he says with a wink.

How devious. Prescott uses a special key card to gain access to the building. Two security guards that look like secret service with their ear pieces, stand blocking the entrance to the elevators. He reaches into his wallet and pulls out a black-titanium looking card with the word DISCREET in all caps engraved in gold on it. The security guards swipe the card and the elevators open; both men step aside giving us access. No-one speaks a word through the entire transaction.

Prescott holds down the number twelve and fourteen button simultaneously on the elevator panel until they both blink three times before letting go. I stay quiet while watching him. I can't believe I'm doing this. Of course this time things are different but still, do I really need to see this with my own eyes?

The elevator stops midway between the twelfth and fourteenth floors.

"Lucky number thirteen," he says with a smile.

I look at the buttons on the elevator panel and there is no number 13 listed. "This building has a thirteenth floor?"

"I'll tell you a little secret," he says smiling. "Whether it's above ground or below, all government buildings have a thirteenth floor; it's just about knowing how to access it."

I feel like I'm on some top secret mission. What else do these buildings hide I wonder? The elevator starts making a grinding noise and suddenly what I thought was a solid wall of wood paneling gives way to steal doors opening on the opposite side. Was this place always intended to be a swinger hideout? This is crazy! The technology alone must have cost a pretty penny but if these people have money like Prescott I guess the extra security is worth it.

As soon as I step off the elevator I feel my eyes about to bulge out of my head. Pastor Rawlings and Senator Williams!

"Prescott," I say whispering, "what the hell are they doing here?!"

"Don't be so surprised by who you see here tonight, try to act casual and for heaven's sake stop staring!"

"I can't help it. I watch Pastor Rawlings on TV every Sunday and if I lived in New York I would have voted for Senator Williams." He just looks at me and shakes his head. "Prescott, this is serious, these men are married!"

"I know… their wives are very close, if you catch my drift."

Holy shit! The pastor and senator are swingers. This is way too much. I immediately start scanning the room looking for more people I may recognize. I wish I could tell someone about this but no-one would ever believe me. That, and I would never want anyone to know I was here.

"Come on, let's head into that room over there."

The room Prescott is pointing to is large with four king size beds on each side. It has velvet red walls and all the beds are made with white linens. I notice a laundry basket in the corner and clean sheets stacked on a shelf. At least they make sure things are clean.

When Pastor Rawlings steps inside the room we are heading to I stop dead in my tracks, "we can't go in there."

"Why not?"

"I'm not going to look at Pastor Rawlings have sex. It's bad enough I will probably never get the image of him in his boxers out of my mind."

"Layla, he's just another man."

"He's not just another man, he's a pastor and the answer is no." From the expression on Prescott's face he thinks this whole thing is amusing.

"If you're going to have fun tonight you will have to loosen up. This room is filled with open-minded adults who enjoy sharing in the pleasures of intimacy, nothing more."

"That's easy for you to say."

"Why don't you wait here while I get us a drink, maybe that will help you relax a little."

"Don't leave me alone in here."

"Layla calm down. No-one's going to do anything to you. I'll be right back."

Before I can protest any further Prescott walks away heading to a bar on the other end of the floor. Left alone I anxiously look around feeling nervous and over-dressed. My eyes are darting all around the room trying to take everything in when I hear a woman moaning from what I can only assume is pleasure. I don't have to wonder what's going on. Before I can stop myself my legs start moving in the direction of the moaning as a woman pleads for more. I stop at the entrance of the room where she is being ravished by a man with a small audience surrounding them. I should look away but I can't. What I'm witnessing is both appalling and appealing. She looks to be having the time of her life. I feel my palms start to sweat and my body begins to tingle. Oh. My. God, am I turned on by this? No, no, no, pull it together Layla. Suddenly another couple joins in and everyone switches partners. This is so wrong. I shouldn't be watching this but I can't help my body's reaction. I make eye connect with one of the guys on the bed and I swear he is daring me to join them. With every stroke his eyes pierce through my body. Holy shit, what is happening?

"Going somewhere?"

I jump at the sound of Prescott's voice.

"Pretty erotic isn't it?"

"If you're into that type of thing I guess it could be considered erotic," I say fanning my face. Did someone just turn up the heat in here? I'm hot as hell! My body is tingling as tiny beads of sweat slide down my chest. Everyone is enjoying themselves. All of the moaning from pleasure is getting to me. I know I shouldn't stare but it's like watching a train wreck. Words can't describe all of the things I'm seeing. There are women pleasing other women and couples swapping partners all over the room. I feel like I'm in some type of erotic trance. My body heat rises as I feel the moistness increase between my thighs. All of my home training is telling me I should leave this place at once but it's as if someone else is taking over.

"Come," Prescott says pulling me closer to him. I take a sip of my drink hoping it would help to cool me down but the warm rum only intensifies the heat coursing through my body. I find myself holding on to Prescott for dear life in fear of what may happen to me if I'm left alone. I don't think I've ever wanted sex as bad as I do right now. Prescott grips my waist tightly and his touch makes me throb. I need to find a way to release myself from this high I'm feeling. If I don't find a release soon I'm afraid my body will combust. I can't believe I'm turned on by this. I look over at Prescott and lick my lips—I can already taste the salty sweetness of him in my mouth. He catches me staring and a knowing look crosses his face.

"I'll get us a room," he whispers in my ear. I nod my head in agreement—fearful speaking would break the trance I seem to be in.

I move to a corner to wait for him while I fan myself, trying to cool down. I scan the room surprised to see how many people I recognize. This place looks more like a Republican convention than a swinger party; so much for them being the conservative party.

An eerie feeling comes over me as if I'm being watched. That's when I notice the man from the private room heading my way.

"You look lovely tonight," he says when I'm in earshot.

I want to thank him but he's completely naked and I find it hard to gather my thoughts. He waves his hand in my face and thankfully that snaps me out of my thoughts, "th-thank y-you," I say stumbling over my words. I would normally reciprocate the compliment, but given the fact he's naked, complimenting him would seem rather awkward.

"So, what do you think of the club?" the stranger asks.

"Um…it's nice," I manage to say, trying to clear my throat.

"This must be your first time here."

"Am I that obvious?"

"You are too beautiful for me to not have noticed you before." I smile at his compliment. "Can I give you some advice for the evening?"

"Okay."

What is he going to do? Give me a pep talk?

"Keep an open mind. While you're here you can become any-one you want, no-one will judge you."

"Excuse me?" An open mind is a good thing to have but this is extreme.

"Try to enjoy the freedom of being whoever you want to be tonight. Let your inhibitions free and let your imagination run wild. I have a feeling there is a sexual vixen hiding inside of you; don't be afraid to let her out once in a while."

The stranger then takes my hand and raises it to his lips before leaving. I never got his name but that's probably for the best. I'm still stewing over what he said when Prescott returns.

"Ready?" he asks. The strangers words still play in my mind, maybe letting go for one night isn't such a bad thing, a lot of people have alter egos. I look around and everyone is having a great time. They are free and relaxed. I don't need the freedom to be with other people but I do want to feel free with Prescott. Suddenly the name Sasha enters my mind. Where the hell did that name come from?

"Layla, are you ready?"

I nod my head yes. I feel a strange sensation start to take over. I've been horny before but this is different. I've wanted sex before but tonight I'm yearning for it. It's as if I won't be able to survive if I'm not fucked senseless. What the hell is wrong with me?

"You okay?"

"I'm fine," I say slightly distracted. I'm trying to hold onto some sense of decorum but I feel it fading quickly.

"Our room should be ready."

"They have private rooms here?"

"Nothing's private here but I'll make sure we're not disturbed."

Excitement courses through my body as I follow Prescott down a dim corridor. The hall is lined with open doors. I peek inside every room we pass—they all have different exotic themes. We stop at the entrance of a Caribbean-themed room.

"I thought we could take a stroll down memory lane," he says, stepping aside so I can take a look around. The walls are covered in tropical style wall paper. There's even a fake palm tree with coconuts in the corner. I notice the bed is freshly made and there is a bedside table stacked with condoms and an assortment of lubricants. Everything you could possibly need is right here.

I feel Prescott's arms wrap around me from behind. "Are you sure you're okay with this? We can easily go back to my place."

I turn around facing him, "I'm right where I want to be."

I hear the stranger's words playing in my head, *"I have a feeling there's a sexual vixen within you."* I'm starting to think he's right. I feel an internal struggle within. I'm always up for having sex with Prescott but tonight I want more than just sex. I fight for control yet I feel it slowly slipping away. Sasha wants to be free and I'm tempted to let her loose. I don't feel like being decent tonight. Tonight I want to do all the things good girls don't do. Tonight I want to be Sasha.

Sasha immediately takes charge, pushing Prescott onto the bed. She slides her hand up his torso and slowly starts the task of removing his shirt.

"Layla, are you okay? You seem different."

Sasha nor I answer. With one look we order his silence and he obeys. Next she gets started on his pants. The huge tent that has formed looks delicious. Without hesitation she takes in all of him, swallowing him whole. He groans in pleasure which only increases the moistness between Sasha's thighs. Prescott cusses and grunts as Sasha moistens him with her saliva then starts the task of licking him clean. She continues the pattern, watching in awe, as he comes undone in her mouth. She takes him in her hands and strokes him while teasing the base of his cannon. Prescott grunts and she knows he's close. He tries to stop her but she's determined to taste all of him. Sasha opens wide until his erection hits the back of her throat. She fucks him with her mouth until he can no longer hold on. With one final thrust Prescott spills his seed down Sasha's throat and she greedily swallows all of him, taking great pleasure in licking him clean. Sasha smiles knowing this is something good girls never do. When she finally stops his cannon glistens. Her actions are aggressive. She's definitely all about control.

Next, without a second thought, Sasha gracefully removes my dress but she keeps my heels, lingerie and jewelry on. I'm sure I'm quite the sight to behold. Climbing back on the bed she starts a total body exploration of Prescott. I've admired his body from a distance but Sasha, being the curious vixen that she is, wants an up close and personal touch. Slowly she kisses, bites and playfully nibbles on every inch of his body. When she reaches his lips he wastes no time in opening for her, allowing Sasha full access. The taste of champagne on Prescott's tongue is intoxicating. I can sense he's trying to keep up with her but she's clearly still in control.

A small audience has gathered outside the door but no one has made a move to enter the room. They watch in awe as their prize bull Jonathan Prescott is dominated by a woman. Without hesitation Sasha climbs on top of Prescott and puts her second set of lips right on his face. No decent girl would ever do such a thing but Sasha doesn't believe in being decent. Greedily Prescott eats. This is where he gets his power. With each lick and plunge of his tongue he takes back the control Sasha once had. She comes undone all over him spreading her wetness all over his lips. If she ever wants to keep up with Prescott she's going to have to work on her stamina. Fully revived and in control Prescott flips Sasha over onto her back and spreads her like an eagle.

"I like the way you took control but now it's time for me to show you how it's done." With that said Prescott slides inside filling her to the hilt. It's as if he has laid down his anchor and declared her body his own. With each stroke he becomes more and more powerful. Sasha closes her eyes while his strong hand and even stronger muscle caresses her body inside and out. He's rough in a delicious way but then she feels softness. A soft delicate hand is caressing her. Sasha's eyes fly open; she's no longer the only woman in the room. The other woman boldly sits on the bed but her eyes are not on Prescott, they're on Sasha. Gently she caresses Sasha. The smooth rhythm in her touch is calming, a stark contrast to Prescott's rough hands.

Prescott whispers to Sasha, "I can tell her to leave," but she shakes her head no. The woman isn't aggressive and her gentle touch brings on a whole new feeling. The woman bravely comes closer and takes Sasha's nipple into her mouth and starts to suckle. Both Prescott and Sasha moan for different reasons. Prescott is clearly excited by the scene taking place right in front of him and Sasha moans from the pleasure she is finding in the stranger's touch. Gently she massages and suckles on Sasha until Sasha's body can no longer hold on. Prescott vigorously thrusts while the stranger moves back and forth suckling on one nipple and then the other, paying close attention to them both. Sasha screams out in pleasure as the most intense orgasm she has ever experienced racks through her body. Prescott grunts like a wild animal as he spills his seed. Even with a table full of condoms right next to him he never put one on and he never pulled out. Sasha lies on the bed spent, with Prescott on top of her. As quietly as the strange woman entered the room she leaves with a satisfied look on her face.

Chapter 33

WAS LAST NIGHT a dream? I stretch out in my seat on the plane and my sore muscles remind me that no, last night was not a dream. Originally Prescott and I were going to spend the entire weekend in New York but early this morning he got a call and said he needed to get back to Chicago ASAP. Our time away may have been short but I still had a great time. I'm still shocked by my behavior. Watching all of those people have sex made me horny as hell yet no matter what I saw, I can only hold myself responsible for my actions. The most amazing part is that I don't feel an ounce of guilt.

We put on quite a show. The room filled with spectators, including Pastor Rawlings who, when we were leaving, let me know he would love the chance to see me again. Knowing how I felt about seeing him there, Prescott pulled me away before I had the opportunity to scold him. All in all it was a great experience, something I look forward to doing again and again and again, I think to myself with a smile.

The sun isn't quite up yet and the city streets are quiet as we make our way back to his place. I've never spent time in Prescott's condo before. Since our weekend was cut short he insists I accompany him home and to his surprise I don't argue. I feel closer to him and I'm not ready for our weekend together to end. He travels a lot so I'm learning to cherish our time together, especially when it's without interruption.

When we arrive at his building he escorts me up through a private elevator. I watch as he swipes his key card. I'm not surprised to learn his unit is the only one on his floor. It's funny how time changes everything. A few weeks ago I would have been looking for the nearest exit but not today. Today I'm looking forward to our privacy.

Prescott's home is not exactly what I expected. His condo looks more like a command center than a home. Even his furniture is tech friendly; you can program your comfort level on his couch before sitting down. I've never seen anything like it. With a press of a button he can change the displays on his wall to match whatever mood he's in. I almost feel like I'm in an episode of the Jetsons. All that's missing is a robotic dog.

He gives me a quick tour, showing me only the essential rooms. That's when I notice there are several doors that require a biometric scan of your hand before you can enter. Is he paranoid or something? I can't imagine why he needs so much security within his own home.

The only room in his entire condo I've seen so far that is actually relaxing is his bedroom. It has a cozy rustic feel with a bed that has so many pillows it makes you want to just fall in. I notice there are no pictures on the wall but with a view like the one he has you really don't need any wall art. From up here everything below looks perfect.

"Can I get you anything?" he asks, putting my bag in his closet.

"No, I'm fine." His bed has my full attention. I rub my hands over the sheets wondering what the expensive silk is going to feel like on my skin. It's like his bed just calls out to you and invites you to get in, so I do.

"I'll show you what this baby can do," he says, patting his mattress with a smile. When Prescott said he was going to show me what his bed can do I didn't take him seriously. It not only vibrates but the damn thing can move up and down as well as side to side. It's like the bed was made to mimic his body movements during sex. The control panel has so many options I am scared to press anything. From the smile on his face Prescott is clearly very proud of his gadget bed. There is a childlike gleam in his eyes as he shows me the cool down feature for when he gets hot and sweaty. I don't even want to know how much something like this cost. Once he's finished fidgeting with all of its features he curls up next to me. The warmth from his body combined with the gentle way he caresses my body puts me to sleep.

I'm not sure how long I'm out but I wake up as soon as I feel a cool draft against my skin. I roll towards his side of the bed expecting to feel the warmth from his body but he's gone. Sitting up I listen for him. I think I hear voices down the hall. I grab Prescott's t-shirt and head towards his foyer. Prescott is in nothing but a towel wrapped around his waist while five beautiful half dressed women surround him.

None of them notice me. A Happy Birthday card on the table in the foyer catches my attention; it wasn't there earlier. Is today his birthday? I pick up the card to read it,

Happy Birthday J,
I hand-picked each one for you and threw in a little
extra chocolate since that seems to be your flavor lately.

Enjoy,
B. Fletcher

"Are you fucking kidding me?" I yell aloud, after reading the note. All chatter stops. Prescott's blue eyes grow wide as he approaches me.

"Layla, it's not what you think."

I immediately turn and leave the room in disgust.

I'm just starting to accept the fact that he has sex on his plane and in private clubs; now this? We all have or pasts but his is too much! I don't even want to think about all of the women he's probably fucked in his bed, the same bed we just got out of.

I head straight for his closet and start tossing all my things into my bag. I'm getting the hell out of here. Prescott will have to have his little fuck fest without me.

"What are you doing?"

"I'm leaving," I say zipping my bag shut.

"Layla, stop overreacting."

"What?! How dare you tell me to stop overreacting when you have five half dressed women delivered to your home ready to fuck you!"

"You're acting like I invited them. I had no clue they were coming."

"Whatever...oh, by the way, Happy Birthday," I say, moving past him on my way to the door.

"Today's not my birthday," he says following me. "The Saturday we had your family dinner was my birthday."

"Why didn't you say anything?"

"I didn't want you to use my birthday as a reason to postpone me meeting your family. Layla, don't leave over this. It's just a misunderstanding."

"This is way more than a misunderstanding. You're the one that pushed me into having a relationship with you but clearly you still operate as if you're single behind my back!"

"I haven't done shit behind your back!"

"What would have happened if I wasn't here? Do you expect me to believe you would have sent them all home?"

Silence.

"Your silence speaks volumes," I say reaching for the door but Prescott blocks my path.

"I already told you I didn't plan for the girls to come. Nothing happened, therefore there's no need for you to make a big deal out of anything."

"When I was with Justin our biggest issue was bad sex. With you the sex may be great but look at all of the other shit we have to deal with. You fuck women in clubs, on planes and have friends who send them to your home unannounced. How can sleeping with me ever be enough for you?"

"You are more than enough."

"I don't see how. I'm never going to be like those women you sent home. I'm not going to arrange private parties for you to fuck different women. Last night at the club was fun but I'm not looking to make that some new lifestyle."

"I already told you, I'm okay with that."

"You say that now but eventually you're going to want more and I'm not going to be able to give it to you."

"I'm not asking for more. I've only asked for you. Why is that so difficult for you to understand?"

"Because our relationship doesn't make any sense. How can you be okay with going from sleeping with multiple women to just sleeping with me?"

"It may not make sense to you but it makes perfect sense to me."

"I'm sorry but I need time to think. I'm not sure if I can handle your lifestyle."

Prescott remains quiet.

I grab my bag and this time when I reach for the door he doesn't stop me. He stands in the foyer watching me as I close the door behind me—possibly for the last time.

Outside in the hall I exhale. I can't let good sex cloud my judgement. There are too many secrets between us: some that bring us closer together and others that tear us further apart. I need someone to talk to. There's only one person I can think of right now but I'm scared to make the call. All I can do is hope that she'll answer.

Chapter 34

BACK HOME IN the safe confines of my apartment I start to pace. Just when things between Prescott and I seem to be going in the right direction I discover just how much I don't know. As much as it may hurt I should end things with him. My head is telling me to run but my heart is telling me to be patient. Could I live my life with someone who has so many secrets? Would we be able to come together and have a normal family? The thought of starting a family with Prescott reminds me of how careless we've been when it comes to using protection. If I ever do end up in his bed again, I'm going to make protected sex mandatory.

I need someone to talk to. My mother said she knew about men like Prescott from experience and I'm eager to find out exactly what she knows. I'm in need of guidance. If I stay with him I know my life will never be the same. My fingers itch to dial home but I'm scared. I haven't spoken to my mom since the blow-up at dinner. I go to the kitchen and start raiding my cabinets in hopes I can find something strong enough to calm my nerves. I need liquid courage to make this call. Thankfully my girls didn't drink everything. I pour myself a stiff drink and call home.

The phone only rings once before she answers.

"Hi Mom."

"Layla!"

From the tone of her voice I can tell she's surprised to hear from me.

"How are you?"

Silence. She doesn't hang up which is a good sign. "Mom, are you there?"

"Yes."

"I miss you," I say, breaking down. Despite everything I still love her. I hate the way she handles shit but that has never stopped me from loving her.

"I miss you too. I was going to call you but things have been so crazy around here."

"What's going on? Is everyone okay?" I've never been out of the loop when it came to my family's wellbeing. For the first time I feel like an outsider.

"A lot has happened since we last spoke." She takes a long pause and I start to wonder if she's going to fill me in. "Marcus' wife left him. After dinner Amanda came out and told her he's been coming into her room at night."

"What!" I scream into the phone.

"I know," my mother says, "we are all mortified, I mean who would have ever thought he would molest his own child. Your Aunt Janet has gone into a state of depression and no-one can reach her."

"I don't know what to say," I say, slumping down onto my couch. My problems with Prescott are minutiae compared to what's going on with the family. "Why didn't you call me?"

"For what? There's nothing you can do."

"So is Marcus in jail? Is there going to be a trial?"

"Jail! Layla Brown, do you really expect us to call the police on your cousin? This is family business. Besides he needs help not a jail cell. We've called Reverend Thomas and he's been praying with him."

"The same Reverend who supposedly cured him the last time we went through all of this?"

"I don't appreciate your tone young lady. Whether you believe it or not, prayer works. It healed Marcus before and it will heal him again. Prayer will not only heal your cousin but it will also heal this family, you wait and see."

I can't believe this shit! Prayer has done nothing to heal Marcus. She probably still doesn't know about him molesting Cynthia, and although I'm tempted to tell her, it's not my secret to share.

I wanted to come home but after hearing all of the shit that's going on, home is the last place I need to go.

"For the sake of the family I hope you're right mom; I'll call you in a few days," I say hanging up. Thinking about what Marcus has put Amanda through makes me sick to my stomach. If Prescott didn't come to dinner Marcus may have never been exposed. Though I hate the way things are now, for Amanda's sake it's all worth it.

I still feel like crap and I need someone to talk to. I send a mass text to my girls telling them I need their help. I'm hoping at least one of them is available. Shortly thereafter my phone starts beeping with reply messages; they're on their way. Of course Georgina's text is vulgar; she needs to let me know that I'm interrupting a "good fuck" as she calls it but she's still coming.

I have at least thirty minutes to myself before anyone arrives. I head to the bathroom to pull myself together. I look like shit. I wash my face and freshen up while thinking things through. As upset as I am by everyone keeping secrets, I'm still not sure if I'm ready to divulge the extent of my relationship with Prescott. Just as I finish drying my face I hear the first knock at the door.

I open the door and immediately regret not checking to see who it is first.

"Marcus! What the hell are you doing here?"

Chapter 35

MY EYES KEEP readjusting at the sight of Marcus. He looks like shit. Before I can react he barges into my apartment, slamming the door closed behind him and locking it.

"You couldn't leave well enough alone could you? You just had to go and bring that old shit up."

"Marcus, you need to leave right now!"

"I'm not leaving until I get what I want. You ruined my fucking life. My wife is divorcing me and my daughter wants nothing to do with me."

"You molested your own child!" I yell in disbelief. Is he really blaming me for his shit?

"None of this would be happening if you simply left that shit alone. I told you to keep your mouth shut, you didn't listen and now you're going to pay!" he says menacingly.

I look around the apartment frantically for a weapon. Shit! God I wish I had a gun... I would blow his fucking brains out! A knife! I need a knife! I scramble for the kitchen but as if he is reading my mind he lunges for me. He lands a blow with his fist right to my temple, knocking me down.

"Marcus stop!" I scream at the top of my lungs. This is bad; thanks to Prescott I'm the only one living on this floor so no-one's going to hear me cry out for help.

"Let's see what you have between those sweet thighs of yours now that you're all grown up."

"Marcus, stop!" I yell but he covers my mouth with his hand while I fight vigorously beneath him. My arms are whaling but he's too big and too strong. This can't be happening. I fight as best I can but he still manages to rip my clothes. Oh my god, he's trying to rape me. I must fight. With everything in me I must fight. I reach up trying to grab anything I can from the nearby table to hit him with but everything is out of my reach. Please God, I pray, please don't let this happen. Marcus tries to hold me down while simultaneously removing his pants. I take this opportunity to swing my arms but he thwarts my attempts and punches me in the face. I can taste my blood mixing with my tears.

"I'm going to have you the way I've always wanted you Layla, and this time you will shut your fucking mouth."

"Marcus, please don't do this," I beg but he doesn't stop.

He manages to undo his pants and rips my underwear.

"Shit! You're bleeding," he says stunned.

My period! It's here!

Marcus looks down at me with a new menacing expression. The last words I remember him saying are "you little bitch" before he starts punching me over and over again. I feel myself drift in and out of consciousness as my body is assaulted with one blow after the other. This is it. He's going to kill me. This is how I'm going to die. I don't want to hurt anymore. God, if you're listening please take me... take me now, I want to go to heaven so I don't hurt anymore.

Chapter 36

Wʜᴀᴛ's ᴛʜᴀᴛ sᴏᴜɴᴅ? Why does heaven have loud banging noises? I hear someone calling my name. Is it an angel?

"Layla, are you home?"

Someone is shouting frantically but I can't make out everything being said.

"Well open the fucking door."

I hear keys. I try to open my eyes but they are swollen shut. I try to move but my body literally feels broken. Someone bursts through the door. Has he come to finish me off?

"Oh-my-God, Layla!" someone shouts. Don't they know to be quiet? My head is ringing. I hear another voice, "call an ambulance quick!"

More shouting. My body is being moved.

"It's okay Layla, help is here."

"Layla, who did this to you?" someone shouts. Why do they keep yelling? I
need quiet.

"Layla, stay with me."

With who? Why isn't anyone answering my questions?

"We're all here Layla. You're safe now. The ambulance is here, just stay with us."

My girls, my girls are all here.

I hear arguing and threats of being kicked out of the room. Is there chaos in heaven? I try to sit up but my body can't move. I hurt. I hurt all over and then I remember; Marcus. My body may feel broken but my tear ducts are still intact. The salty water makes its descent down my cheeks. How could I have been so stupid as to open my door without looking? No time to blame myself, I can do that later. My throat is parched; I need water. I try to open my mouth to speak but I can't. Something is keeping me from talking. When I try to open my eyes all I see is darkness.

"Layla, can you hear me?"

Who's that?

"She may not be alert yet but all of her vitals show she should come around soon. You're going to have to pay attention to any movement you may see. Her eyes are swollen shut and her jaw is wired shut while we work to reset it. We are giving her pain medication so she shouldn't feel too much discomfort but she doesn't have much control over her limbs right now so she won't be able to respond to anyone. The good news is that she's strong and I expect for her to make a full recovery."

I hear sobbing. I can recognize that cry anywhere; my mom is here. I feel her soft hands on me rubbing my arm, "Layla, sweetie, please wake up okay. Just please wake up for mommy. I love you."

"I love you too mom." She can't hear me. Wait, how can my mother be here already? How long have I been out? I hear other voices throughout the room. It sounds like the whole family is here.

"When I find that son of a bitch I'm going to fucking kill him." That's my dad. He must be talking about Marcus.

"Stop staying that. We need to focus on praying for Layla to have a quick recovery. Talking about killing Marcus is not going to heal our daughter any quicker."

An argument erupts. I hear my girls siding with my father about finding and killing Marcus. My mom and other voices I don't recognize—probably friends from her church—are talking about staying in prayer and letting God right my wrongs. It's funny. I haven't prayed, I mean really prayed, since I was a little girl. I'm sure I called on God to get me out of a jam once or twice but not because I really believed in him, only because there was no one else to help me at the time. The first time I do pray I ask for him to end my life yet here I am. If Marcus were to come back, what would I do? My eyes are swollen shut so I can't see him coming. My mouth is wired shut so I can't call out for help. My body feels like it's literally broken so there is no way I can possibly physically defend myself; long story short I'm a sitting duck. If Marcus, or anyone for that matter, came into this room and tried to attack me they could do whatever they wanted and I wouldn't be able to do a damn thing about it. The only thing I can do is... pray.

This is the crux of human existence. Whether I want to believe in God or not I have no choice. I can sit here and do nothing or I can pray. I can pray that when I'm blind, speechless and without control over my flesh God will still protect me. God, if you can hear me I ask that you get everyone out of my room. All of their arguing is making it hard for me to rest.

I hear the door open. "I need everyone to clear the room."

Do you always work this fast God? A voice I don't recognize, probably a staff member from the hospital, is putting everyone out. Maybe prayer really can work. I feel soft kisses and hear whispers of "I'll see you soon" in my ear as everyone leaves the room. I'm thankful for the quiet. I hear the door close. Finally I can enjoy some peace.

No one is in the room but I hear a voice. It feels like it's coming from within and a warm sense of peace washes over me. Maybe the hospital is dosing me up too much. How can I possibly feel good at a time like this? I may be losing my mind but something is telling me everything will be okay. It's not a voice I can literally hear, just a feeling from within. Whatever it is it's enough to calm my entire spirit.

Shortly thereafter I hear the door to my room open. His scent takes over. Prescott is here.

"Don't interrupt us unless it's absolutely necessary."

"Yes sir," someone says.

My hands yearn to touch him but I can't move. He picks up my hand and places it in his. No telling what he's thinking right now but I can tell from his touch he's scared. Even after all of the trauma I've suffered, I can still feel his eyes on me piercing through my soul. I try to squeeze his hand but my body is too weak.

"I know you're awake," he says calmly. "I want you to know I'll take care of this."

You can't fix this, I think to myself. Then the same voice that gave me peace within speaks again: *don't let him turn to darkness.* What does that mean?

Silence.

God, if you're listening, I need clarification. What do you mean don't let him turn to darkness?

Still nothing.

If I'm going to turn to you we're going to have to work on our communication. I can't even get upset; the sense of peace over my body is still strong.

I wait for Prescott to talk but he sits holding my hand in silence. Sleep wants to take over but I struggle to stay awake.

"Stop fighting the sleep, you need your rest."

How the hell does he know I'm fighting to stay awake?

"Just do as I say. I'll be right here." Knowing Prescott plans to stay close gives me an extra sense of security. I rest easy knowing both God and Prescott are watching over me.

Chapter 37

WHAT DAY IS IT? It takes some maneuvering but I'm finally able to open my eyes. I'm no longer in the hospital. I feel warm and comfortable. I'm somewhere familiar: in Prescott's bed. How the hell did I get here and where is Prescott? The room is dim; it must be late. I try moving my body and surprisingly I'm finally able to control my hands and legs. I also notice my jaw is no longer wired shut. Ever since my attack everything's been very vague. I know my parents were by my side. I don't think I've ever heard my mother pray so much in my life. I remember her asking the Holy Spirit to watch over and protect me; I think it's the Holy Spirit that gave me peace.

I also remember my girls staying by my side. It feels good to know so many people care for me. I could be mistaken but I think even Justin came to see me. Now that I think about it, he did. His visit prompted a huge argument. I remember all of the shouting. Prescott's voice sounded like thunder when he ordered him out of my room. None of that explains how the hell I ended up here. Not that I'm complaining, I love this bed.

What time is it? I try looking around. My vision is a little blurry but if my eyes are correct it looks like it's one o'clock in the morning. Why isn't Prescott here with me? Something has me feeling uneasy. I don't feel like I'm in danger but something's wrong. That's when I hear a faint sound. I think the noise is coming from the bathroom. I listen closely, it sounds like someone's in pain.

Every part of my body hurts but I need to at least try and move. Someone may be in trouble. It takes everything out of me but I slowly slide out of bed. Slowly I walk towards the sound; it's definitely coming from the bathroom. I pray Prescott's okay. I hurt like hell but I finally reach the bathroom and manage to push the door open. The sight in front of me stops me from taking another step. Prescott is in the shower punching the wall. His hands are all bloodied. I watch in horror as light pink water washes down the bathroom drain. He doesn't notice me and my attempt to shout is futile.

With renewed strength I walk to the shower door and yank it open. He stops his assault against the tile wall as soon as he sees me.

"What the hell are you doing in here?" he asks, picking me up and cradling me in his arms.

"What are you doing?" I mumble. His hands are bruised and his eyes are red. I don't think I ever imagined the day I would see Prescott cry. His body is dripping wet but with great care he carries me back to bed.

"I don't want you getting out of bed, you need your rest."

"Please don't," I mumble, taking his hand in mine. His knuckles are bruised and bloodied. His animalistic anger makes him appear even more dangerous than before. "Don't shut me out, tell me what's going on?" I reach up and wipe away the tears from his eyes. He doesn't move. He just stares at me. Under his gaze I start to feel self-conscious.

"Do I look that bad?" I can tell from his expression I must look like shit.

"Don't ever worry about the way you look, you're always beautiful."

"I guess it's your turn to be the terrible liar." My speech is still slurred but I'm happy to finally be able to communicate.

"I'm getting you all wet. I'll go dry off, stay here."

He doesn't need to order me to stay in bed. My walk to the bathroom was exhausting enough. I couldn't move even if I wanted to. I lay in bed patiently waiting for his return. When he emerges from the bathroom he's only wearing pajama bottoms. Even after everything I've been through, I still yearn to be with him. With more care than necessary he climbs into bed beside me and wraps me in his arms.

"I didn't mean to wake you," he says, kissing my cheek.

"Why were you crying?" I know he's not going to want to admit I saw him cry but my eyes were not mistaken, I know what I saw.

"You have to ask?"

"In case you've forgotten I've been out of it for a while so you're going to have to bring me up to speed."

"He could have killed you," he says, holding me tighter. "I was so worried about seeing you whenever I wanted I put you in danger. It's my fault this happened but I swear to you I will make it right. You have my word—you will never have to worry about Marcus ever again."

I try to turn around in his arms to face him but I don't have the strength. "You can't blame yourself for Marcus' actions. None of this is your fault."

Prescott remains silent. I can't have him going around blaming himself for what happened. No one could have ever expected Marcus to lose it the way he did. Just talking about him sends a chill through my spine.

I'm scared to hear the truth but I have to ask, "has anyone found him?"

"Yes... His body was found two days ago."

"His body! He's dead?" I don't know why that scares me. If Marcus is gone that means my nightmare is over yet I still find no comfort in the news. After everything that's transpired I still would have preferred for him to be in jail.

"There was a man hunt for him after your attack. He couldn't call on anyone he knew to stay with and all of his accounts were frozen so he didn't have any access to money. The police knew it was only a matter of time before they flushed him out. He went into hiding and was living on the street. It looks like he was mugged and beaten to death by a street gang."

"How has my family reacted to the news?"

"Mixed emotions but at the end of the day everyone is more concerned with your safety. I don't want you to concern yourself with any of this. Just focus on getting better for me... can you do that?"

"Of course."

"Are you in any pain?"

"It hurts all over." That's the truth. My body still feels broken.

"Here, take these," he says reaching towards the nightstand and handing me two pills with a glass of water. "Your jaw has healed so the doctor took your IV out this morning. You can take your pain meds orally now."

I gladly accept the medication. This almost reminds me of our first night together. From the beginning he's always taken care of me.

"The medication should kick in soon. In the meantime get some rest."

For once I do as I'm told. My eyelids feel heavy and in the safety of Prescott's arms I fall back to sleep.

Chapter 38

SHHH, I'M SLEEPING. I hear a voice telling me to get up. That uneasy feeling I felt earlier starts to take over. Maybe Prescott's home is not the best place for me to rest.

"What is it?" I mumble.

Wait, what am I doing? Who am I even talking to?

I look over at Prescott's side of the bed—he's gone. Where the hell is he? I look at the clock on the night stand; it's three o'clock in the morning. Maybe he's working I tell myself. I lie back down and fuse my eyes closed in hopes sleep will take over...nothing. I feel restless. In the pit of my stomach I know something's not right. I pray Prescott's not doing something to hurt himself again. The image of him bashing his hands against the tile wall still disturbs me. I don't like the fact that he feels guilty for what's happened to me. There's only one person to blame for all of this and he's already dead.

Still, maybe I should look for him and make sure he's okay. Thanks to the pain medication I took a couple hours ago, it doesn't hurt as much to get up. I notice a robe lying on Prescott's side of the bed. I grab it and push my feet into his slippers. On shaky legs I go in search of him.

I walk around the condo but come up empty. Something's telling me he's not here but I can feel he's close. Am I crazy? I may need to talk to my doctor about my medication; they're definitely dosing me up too much. I wander off into the hall and take the elevator to the lobby. Maybe someone at the front desk has seen him. I must look ridiculous in Prescott's robe and slippers. I haven't seen my face in days and I have no desire to take a look.

Stepping off the elevator I walk towards the front desk.

"Excuse me, have you seen Jonathan Prescott?"

"Ms. Brown, what are you doing out of bed?"

The front desk attendant is an elderly gentleman. He rushes around the desk to take hold of me. The man looks so fragile, I feel like I should be the one assisting him.

"Please don't worry about me, I'm fine," I say, swatting his hands away. "I'm looking for Mr. Prescott."

"I haven't seen him all night. Do you need help with anything? I can get someone down here ASAP if you need me to."

"No, it's okay, I'll just give him a call on his cell."

"Okay ma'am, let me know if I can be of any assistance."

"Thank you."

I head back towards the elevators; I'll try reaching him on his cell. If I had any sense that's the first thing I should have done. I could have saved myself the trip and embarrassment of being seen like this.

In no time the elevator arrives. I press the button for the penthouse but it doesn't light up. Shit! I forgot to take the key card with me. At times like this all of the extra security in his home can be a real pain. He's always so cautious. I survey the control panel to see if there are any other options. If I can't find a way to get upstairs I'll have to go back to the front desk.

The control panel in this elevator reminds me of the one in the office building where the swinger party was held. I still can't believe what Prescott shared with me about all government building

having a 13th floor. Just for the hell of it I check out all of the
floors listed in the elevator—no lucky number 13 spotted. I
shouldn't do it I tell myself, but ever since I was in the elevator
with him back in New York, I've been dying to try the same thing.
Of course it won't work in this elevator; this is a luxury high-rise
not a government building but the urge to try is strong. What's
the worst that can happen?

Mimicking Prescott, I hold both buttons simultaneously and
they actually flash three times. Instead of going up the elevator
starts going down to the basement. I watch, shocked, as the display panel goes past all five levels in the parking garage until
finally stopping.

Shit! I already wish this didn't work. I should go back upstairs
right now and forget about this. If Prescott finds out I've been
poking around his building he'll be furious. Still, I can't help but
wonder if he's down here?

My feet feel like lead as I move through the hall. The hallway
is bare. I don't hear anything. I walk to the end of the hall and
stop at a biometric scan. It looks like the ones in his apartment.
Did he scan me into his system? I thought it was just a dream but
now I'm not sure. With all the pain killers I've been on my
memory is foggy.

Just for the hell of it I place my hand on the scanner. A green
laser light passes over my palm and quickly thereafter the door in
front of me slides open. My heart starts to pound. What the hell
is this place? I feel like one of those stupid girls in those low
budget horror flicks that go looking for trouble. I have no business being here.

I should go back upstairs. If anything I'll ask Prescott about this
place when I get better. I have a sick feeling in the pit of my stomach. Knowing him, this hall is probably lined with cameras. I'm
sure he'll be giving me an earful soon enough. On my way back to
the elevator I hear a scream. The sound startles me. I feel a surge of
adrenalin take over my body. I know that voice. He's screaming out
in pain over and over again. I cringe at the sound but I have to see

for myself. I stop at the door where I hear the crying. My hand has a death grip on the doorknob. The voice cries out again and the hairs on the back of my neck stand at full attention. I push the door open and the scene in front of me makes me freeze. I look between the both of them in horror. Prescott looks wild. His hair is tousled and his chest is sweaty. Strung up on steel chains I see Marcus. His body is severely beaten and bruised.

What the hell is going on?! Marcus is supposed to be dead!

Prescott's eyes lock in on mine. He's probably wondering what I'm thinking and I'm wondering the same thing. I don't know how to feel right now. The scene in front of me is frightening. I will admit most women get off knowing their man would do anything to protect them. Men fight all time to protect their women. If Prescott walked in on Marcus attacking me and beat him up I wouldn't have a problem with that but this is different. I don't know if I can handle this. The only sound in the room is Marcus' cry for help. I can't be here I rationalize to myself. I don't want to see this.

I back out of the room aware that all eyes are on me. Prescott has made no move to come closer to me and his silence is deafening. I retreat as fast as I can back to the elevators. The doors can't slide open fast enough for me. I remember the voice I heard in the hospital: *keep him away from the darkness*. I didn't understand at first but now I get it. Prescott's dark side is worse than anything I could have ever imagined.

I take the elevator back to the lobby. I still need access to the penthouse. All of my stuff is there. I can't walk out on the street in the middle of the night dressed in a robe and bedroom slippers. The cops would probably pick me up and have me admitted to a psyche ward.

"Are you okay Ms. Brown?"

Even the front desk attendant is looking at me like I'm crazy. Little does he know I'm not the only crazy one in the building.

"I'm fine. I just realized I don't have the card that allows me access to the penthouse."

"No problem," he says coming out from behind the desk. The doorman escorts me to the elevator and uses his key card so I can gain access.

"Do you need anything else ma'am?"

"No, that will be all thank you."

I should get my stuff and leave. That would be the smart thing to do but I already know that's the last thing I want to do. Why the hell didn't he just turn Marcus over to the cops? I'm not ready to walk out, not without an explanation. I'll have to wait and talk to him. I need to understand his rationale for all of this. I make myself comfortable on the couch as I wait. I watch as the clock above the mantel keeps ticking away. I feel my eyelids growing heavy. Maybe I'll close them for just a few...

Chapter 39

KNOCK, KNOCK, KNOCK. My eyes fly open. I look around the room in a panic. How the hell did I end up in Prescott's bed? I look at the clock on the nightstand, it's after 8a.m.

Knock, knock, knock.

"Come in," I yell. I wipe the crust out of my eyes and sit up. Loretta, the nurse Prescott hired to take care of me, comes into the room with a tray of pancakes, eggs and sausage. I'm in no mood to eat.

"Good morning Ms. Brown."

Loretta has always been very kind to me. She's truly a natural nurturer.

"Good morning Loretta. Have you seen Prescott?"

"He left about an hour ago," she says, setting up the tray.

"Sorry Loretta, I think I'm going to skip breakfast this morning."

"You need to eat. Mr. Prescott has quite the day planned for you and you'll need your energy."

"What are you talking about?"

"Mr. Prescott has arranged for you to be pampered today. You have someone coming over to take care of your hair and nails. He's even arranged for a full body massage and facial," she says excitedly.

Is he stupid? Does he really think a day of pampering will erase what the hell I just saw last night?

"Loretta, please cancel all of the appointments and tell Prescott I need to talk to him ASAP!"

"Sorry sweetie but he can't be reached today."

Leave it to Prescott to keep me stewing. How does he expect me to relax and get pampered while Marcus hangs in chains in the basement? I grab my cell from the drawer in the nightstand.

"If you're trying to call him don't bother, he said he won't be able to be reached by phone today."

"Did he say where he'll be?"

"No. He just made me promise to take good care of you today. Don't worry; he'll be back this evening."

I hate it when he avoids me. He knows we need to talk.

"Loretta, please cancel all of the appointments."

"Are you sure? You should at least consider getting your hair and nails taken care of."

I look down at my feet and sigh. They look terrible. All of me looks terrible. Anyone would after taking the beating I took a few days ago. Come to think of it, I don't remember the last time I was able to wash my hair.

"Fine, I'll take the hair and nail appointment but cancel my massage and facial."

"Sure thing Ms. Brown," she says excitedly.

On most days Loretta is actually good company but not today. She keeps going on and on about how nice it is of Prescott to arrange all of this for me. I really want to tell her shut up but instead I bite my tongue. With each hour that passes my patience thins. My mind keeps going back to what I witnessed in the basement and one thought has been racing through my mind all day…is Marcus still alive? I'm not brave enough to go downstairs and check. I tried my hand on some of the scanners in his home and it works. He definitely gave me access to everything. After last night I've learned my lesson about poking around. If I want to see anything I'll wait for Prescott to show me himself.

My hair and nail appointments don't take long. I don't allow the hairdresser to do anything fancy. Loretta wants me to get dolled up for Prescott but that's not happening. Ever since the attack I've been living in t-shirts and sweats. Today is no different. I watch mindless TV while I wait for him to return home. Finally at five o'clock Loretta comes into the den.

"He's here," she says with a brilliant smile. Why the hell is she so excited?

"He's asked that you meet him on the roof-top."

"Roof-top?" I repeat.

"Yes, and for the last time are you sure you don't want to change?"

"No." I respond firmly. We've had this debate all day.

"Fine but don't say I didn't try."

I've never been on the roof-top before. The elevator slides open and the scene in front of me takes my breath away. Candles are lit all around. There's a beautiful table set for two next to the pool which is filled with white and red rose petals. The sun setting against the evening sky makes the perfect backdrop. I'll give him credit for trying but if he thinks all of this will make me forget last night he's mistaken. No way in hell he's getting off that easy.

I take two steps but stop when I hear a beautiful voice sing "hello." I look over to my left and Adele is here with a mike in her hand. I watch in awe as she starts to sing her latest single "Hello." The lyrics speak to me and my eyes swell with tears. When she reaches the chorus and sings *"hello from the other side,"* Prescott comes into view. Dressed in a black tux, he takes long purposeful steps towards me. I want nothing more than to run into his arms but I stand firm and wait. How can someone so ruthless also be so sweet?

He takes my hand in his and holds me close as we both stand together and watch as Adele belts out her latest hit. Her voice captivates us. Neither of us move until the song ends. Prescott gives her a signal and she leaves giving us privacy.

I can't let the scene he's set for us deter me from the conversation we need to have.

"Is this your plan?" I ask letting go of his hand. "You think you can arrange for me to enjoy a day of pampering and arrange for a romantic evening in hopes that I'll forget you have my cousin strung up in the basement?"

"I arranged this evening before last night."

"After last night you should have cancelled."

"I took a gamble."

"Well it's not going to pay off. Why the hell is Marcus strung up in your basement?"

"I'm sorry you had to see that."

That's all he can say?! Sorry you had to see that? I need to tweak Georgina's description of Prescott. She needs to add ruthless to her list. I'm scared to ask but I have to know...

"Is he still alive?"

"For now."

Prescott's stoic expression scares me a little. He speaks with such finality.

"You can't do this," I whisper. "I know you think what you're doing is right but this is not how the justice system works."

"Says who? He was going to kill you! Don't you get that? When you sent out your text to your girls Pamela was the first to arrive. She knocked and knocked and got worried when you didn't answer. Thankfully she contacted Ralph at the front desk who was kind enough to give her your key. When she left to get the key Marcus used that opportunity to slip out unnoticed. If he had more time he would have beaten you to death! As far as I'm concerned this is justice!"

"How long are you going to keep this up?"

"Until that son of a bitch takes his last fucking breath."

I motion to speak but he stops me.

"What I plan to do with Marcus is not debatable. He sealed his fate the moment he laid a hand on you."

Prescott's jaw tightens. The shadows beneath his eyes are prominent. It's clear this entire situation has had a huge impact on him. He's always such a pillar of strength. I never stopped to think about how almost losing me has affected him. All of this is new to me. I've never had anyone willing to go through such lengths for me. To see what he's capable of still unnerves me yet I also feel loved. He's never actually spoken the words yet I know. Through his actions he's shown me just how much he loves me.

"Are you ready to eat?" he asks taking my hand in his.

"Yes."

He's moved on and so should I.

We take our seats at the beautifully set table for two. Prescott sends out a text and Adele returns. I can't believe he arranged for our own private concert. The wait staff wastes no time in bringing out our meals. We sit and dine while Adele sings to us. I could not have imagined a more perfect setting.

I do feel silly sitting across from Prescott in a t-shirt and sweats. Men don't usually take my breath away but to see him in his tux with his beautiful blue eyes and slightly wind-blown hair takes my breath away.

After our private concert and dessert Prescott and I lie out on one of the chaise lounges by the pool. I lean back against his chest and I feel him harden. We haven't had sex since our return from New York. I'm still sore yet the feel of his massive strength pressed up against me leaves me in a state of arousal. Old urges start stirring between my legs. I feel his rock hard erection on my ass.

My face is still a wreck and my body still feels beaten but that doesn't stop me from wanting him. I need him. I need his closeness now more than ever. Sex can't fix everything that lies between us but it has always helped us connect. I don't know how he will respond to me wanting him. I understand if he's still repulsed by my face. As if reading my mind with great care and tenderness he turns my head towards him and kisses my swollen lips.

"I know what you need," he whispers in my ear.

Gently he slides my sweats off exposing me to the elements. His fingers gently coax my folds open and like a flower I blossom for him. His head dips between my thighs. With the first swipe of his tongue my body comes alive. With care and tenderness he kisses my sex back to life.

"I need you now," I whisper. Although my body is still tender and sore I still want him. I want to feel him bury himself inside of me. Usually I'm patient but not tonight. Tonight I want to feel whole. I want him to cleanse me from the inside out with his seed.

"Tell me if it hurts," he says undressing himself.

I already know it's going to hurt but it's a pain I'm willing to endure. I lay comfortably on my side while he lifts one of my legs. He teases my entrance with the hardness of his muscle. My breath quickens in anticipation. I stretch as much as I can to accommodate him. Slowly he inches his way inside me until he's fully sheathed. My body is deliciously shocked by the large intrusion. Slowly our bodies rock back and forth together. The feel of Prescott inside of me brings me great peace. I feel like I've found the missing piece to a puzzle. He picks up the pace but only a little. I feel every inch of him. With each stroke my body grows stronger and greedier for him. He places soft kisses on my shoulder while holding my leg steady.

"Faster," I whisper.

With a grunt he slightly picks up the pace stroking my insides, working to get me the release I need. I squeeze him tightly and hear a low moan escape his lips.

"I can't hold on much longer" he whispers in my ear.

Neither can I. With great triumph I let go of everything I was feeling and enjoy the sensations as a soothing orgasm courses through my body. Who would have ever thought an orgasm could bring peace to a troubled soul? Prescott also comes undone squeezing me tighter. I feel drenched from his seed spilling inside me.

"I love you," he says moving my hair to the side to place soft kisses on my neck.

I smile at his admission. "I love you too," I say snuggling closer to him.

I feel Prescott's body relax against mine. We lay still until his body stirs then a red box is placed in front of me. My heart immediately starts to race.

"What's that?" I ask nervously.

"You're the first woman to ever see me cry," he whispers, holding me tighter.

I hear the hope in his voice.

"I don't know if this a good idea right now. We still have too many secrets between us."

"Starting tomorrow I'll tell you everything you need to know," he says kissing me gently. "For now I just want to enjoy this moment."

He pulls me in closer and I smile just knowing Prescott and I have a tomorrow together.

THE END